CUT
THE BLUE
SAPPHIRE

By profession, **S.V. Divvaakar** is an independent evaluator and advisor to the United Nations agencies and governments, helping build a better world, a better tomorrow, for all. He is dedicated to the achievement of the Sustainable Development Goals, which countries have espoused with a commitment to eradicate poverty and hunger, reduce inequalities and improve the quality of the environment.

He writes under his nom de plume, Avik Davar, which is an anagram of his real name. His stories draw from his extensive travel (he has been to over a hundred countries) and his first-hand experience of the rich diversity of the world and its people, besides a collection of real life incidents that are stranger than fiction.

CURSE OF THE BLUE SAPPHIRE

AVIK DAVAR

RUPA

Published by
Rupa Publications India Pvt. Ltd 2020
7/16, Ansari Road, Daryaganj
New Delhi 110002

Sales Centres:
Allahabad Bengaluru Chennai
Hyderabad Jaipur Kathmandu
Kolkata Mumbai

ISBN: 978-93-5333-811-4

First impression 2020

10 9 8 7 6 5 4 3 2 1

The moral right of the author has been asserted

Printed by HT Media Ltd, Gr. Noida

*For Dad, Shreys and
Maharaja Duleep Singh most of all*

1

Tasukete!'

The scream tore through the humid night air, cut off by a brief shattering of glass. The language was foreign, but the horror, familiar. Not unlike the helpless shriek of an impaled bird attacked by a feline that has broken into its cage.

'*Tasukete!*'

There was a sharp sting on her cheek. Ouch!

Her eyes struggled to open. Her head was woolly and distant; her back was stiff as lead and her body hurt as though she had been run over. She saw her wrists wrapped thick in gauze crusted with dried blood. With a mountain of will, she rolled to her right and held the metal bedpost. She struggled to heave herself up, but there was no force in her hands. A fresh warm redness formed on the bandage and her grip loosened; her hands went limp and the world slipped into the dark hollows behind her eyes.

Tap! Tap! Tap!

She awoke to the loud thuds coming from the left. Above her, a fan, its blades covered in clumps of dirt, hung perilously from the cracked ceiling whose plaster had fallen off at many places. A spider dangled from a broken cobweb and clawed its way up the strands. Beneath, the floor was ice-cold and reeked of blood and phenyl.

Tap! Tap! Tap!

It was a stick, pounding the floor inches away from her, in the foot-wide space between a pair of dirty boots, one of which had caked animal dung on its sole. Her eyes stared listlessly at the grease-spotted khakis that hung from a worn-out brown belt. A rubber-coated baton dangled on the side, its loop closed around the belt. Further above, a stained shirt battled against a bulging bustline.

Two hands heaved her up and she saw a pair of shining eyes appraising her. A smile formed on her lips and froze just as quickly at the sight of a huge scar that ran from the edge of the right eye, all the way down the cheek. The skin had been stitched crudely and tiny shards hung off the seam. A gasp escaped her mouth as she cringed and turned away from the ghastly sight.

A stern voice reclaimed her attention.

'Now, that should have woken you up! What's your name?'

Words struggled to come out of her parched throat. 'Gurleen.'

'Gurleen what?' Fingers pinched at the loose skin of the scar.

Gurleen hesitated. 'Rambal. Gurleen Rambal.' Her eyes strained to read the name 'Chameli Singh' off the plastic badge dangling from the uniform.

'And you are—'

'Delhi Police. Station house officer, Naba Karim Police Station. Women's Cell.'

'Police? Where am I?'

'Lady Hardinge Hospital.' Her tone, even though a bit softer, betrayed her irritation.

'What happened?'

'You don't know what happened last night?' the inspector asked incredulously.

Gurleen felt the intense distrust singe her like heat off a blowtorch flaring inches away. Slowly, memories of the dreadful night returned, and with them the shrieks from the hollows.

2

housands of monsoon insects were attacking the sodium lights above the signpost that blinked 'New Delhi Railway Station'. The air had a putrid stench from brushing over the sewage from the overflowing drains alongside the rail tracks.

She shuddered at the thought of the insects brushing past her and rushed to roll up the window. The ratchet jammed midway and came off, leaving the window half-open. The air, thick with faecal stench, almost made her puke.

Unperturbed by the horrid smell, the station's loudspeaker sputtered and seemed to mock her to work out the train and platform numbers it was announcing. There was no other sound except the drizzle drumming gently on the tin roof above the taxi stand. It was unusually quiet for a place through which over six hundred thousand people commuted every day.

Getting used to being a woman taxi driver doing night shifts in the notorious city of Delhi wasn't proving easy. The rickety black and yellow Ambassador, with its askew non-powered steering wheel, was a crude downgrade from the spotless, fragrant Toyota Altis she had driven just two months ago. Not to mention the Mercedes, Bugatti and the Rolls Royce that chauffeured her until… Hell, was that just a year ago?

She was parked near the Paharganj gate of the station, tired from the diabetes—she hadn't been regular with her Galvus 50 pills—and bored from waiting for the super speed 'Shatabdi' trains from Agra, Jaipur or Dehradun that would arrive soon. The driveway was deserted, and the traffic policemen were huddled with autorickshaw drivers, playing cards, sipping tea and puffing away at beedis, with no intention of getting wet in the rain that gave no signs of letting up. She distracted herself by tugging gently at her locket, her witness and companion for more than twenty years on the roller coaster called Life. Then the glare of headlights from another taxi fell on the rear-view mirror. She looked up and took in the unkempt hair, puffy dry eyes, droopy shoulders and furrowed neck folds—signs of cracks in the resolve to stand up and begin all over. *Leena, you've given up, haven't you,* she mocked and turned away.

The quiet was punctured by the blare of a diesel engine. Soon, there was an exodus at the gate, rather like the wildebeest migrations she'd seen in the Masai Mara plains of Kenya. Only, this was the Dehradun Shatabdi Express, extruding over two thousand people through the gates in some fifteen minutes.

Her favourite passengers were the bare-bones budget foreigners, looking for cheap hotels in Paharganj, the most popular hub for backpackers. She charged foreigners four dollars, sometimes more, for the barely one kilometre-long ride from the station. Most passengers would walk it if they knew how close it was to the station, and increasingly were beginning to figure out with Google Maps.

She was lucky that night, all set for a fourth trip, as she saw two young girls stepping out of the platform. They seemed to hesitate under the shade, waiting for the downpour to subside. She switched on the ignition, turned the headlights on and issued a short honk to grab their attention. Taking the cue, they waved her over. She pulled over at the kerb with the rear door open to prevent them from getting drenched.

'Namaste, welcome to Incredible India,' she offered the national introduction.

'Shanti Om Hotel, Paharganj, *s'il vous plait*?' The one in the yellow top said.

'Yes, madam-ossel. I can take you there. *Quatter euro, ca va*?' The atrocious smattering of French was the result of a crash course sponsored by Delhi Tourism.

'*Oui, quatrre euro, c'est bon,*' Yellow Top said to her partner in a sleeveless white T-shirt and shorts, who had begun brushing the raindrops off her hair.

The Ambassador's engine died down and coughed back into life only on the fifth try.

Shanti Om Hotel was a shady little joint in an interior lane of Paharganj. Gurleen suspected it to be a den for drug trafficking, as she had come across many unusual Russians and Africans asking for the place. Unusual, because they had constantly clutched their abdomens through the short bumpy ride, discomfited by the plastic bags retained in their gut. Yes, she had learnt about that from taking two emergency cases to the nearby Lady Hardinge hospital instead of the hotel. This French duo seemed genuine tourists, though.

She dropped them off and pocketed a five-euro note; the one-euro tip was for feigning that she didn't have change. She had earned enough for the night and was ready for a spicy tandoori chicken and naan at the nearby Kake Da Dhaba before heading home. She had just about turned into an empty street when she heard a scream in a strange language.

'*Tasukete! Tasukete!*'

There was no one about and all she saw was a Suzuki van parked some fifteen feet ahead of her. She slowed down and could see it shudder and move. Oh no! She'd been long enough on Delhi's roads at nights to not be surprised by movements inside stationary cars. Her headlights shone over the van and she could see a man in the rear seat.

And then the scream tore through the humid night air.

'*Tasukete!*'

Gurleen grappled with her decision. *Do I need to get involved? It's been a long night. And after everything I've been through lately, I don't need any more trouble.*

'*Tasukete!*

Should I? Unsure, she wavered over the gas pedal, when she heard the shattering of glass. A pair of heels shot out of the van's window, and bloodied legs flailed in the air. Thick blood dripped from the jagged window glass. Then she heard a coarse voice hurling abuses '*Haraamzaadi… Saali… Teri maa ki*' and the crack of repeated slaps and punches.

Gurleen remained frozen in shock and fear. Then the screaming stopped, and the legs went limp.

At length, she steadied herself and pushed the pedal, when a metal-knuckled hand broke through the glass window of her taxi and grabbed her throat. The vice-like grip choked her and soon everything around her was spinning. She struggled feebly to release the grip with her right hand and dug her fingernails into the man's flesh and stretched her left hand as far as she could, groping for the glove compartment.

The grip tightened, and another hand grabbed her right wrist and tugged it through the broken window. Blood gushed as the glass tore into her wrist and ripped through her forearm. She kept stretching to the left, using her last ounce of strength to reach inside the glove compartment. Her right hand was being pulled so hard that she thought her shoulder joint would be yanked off. The deadlock remained, and time froze, until she relented. She had found her weapon.

She turned to the window, aided by the force pulling at her right, and heaved the heavy pipe wrench clutched in her left hand at the aggressor. The metal head slammed into his jaw. She heard the teeth crack and the jaw snap like a dry twig. The giant's grip loosened. It was her only chance to break free. She swung the wrench at his knuckles and pushed the door open. It threw him off balance and he fell on the road, screaming and jerking his palm. Gurleen stumbled out and clutched the edge of the car door, which creaked under her weight.

She breathed in deep to summon all her strength. Now steady, she cried out 'Waheguru di fateh' and swung the wrench a second time at his mouth. Blood splattered and he coughed out fragments of broken teeth. She was still in a daze as she took a huge swing, this time connecting with the temple. And then another walloping blow to the centre of his skull. She could hear the bone crack as the giant form went limp, the wrench still lodged in his skull, a small spout spewing from it.

Blood flowed from the gashes on her wrist and arm. The gashes opened further as she struggled to get a hold of the taxi's open door. Disoriented and directionless, she staggered and tripped over the fallen body. Her legs buckled and she fell headlong, her face touching the overflowing drain at the edge of the street. Raindrops hurtled down one by one, crystal marbles hitting her face and exploding into the warm red puddle forming around her. The smell of alcohol, reeking from the still, giant form lying next to her, brought back memories of an old neighbour.

3

*W*here is the girl, the foreigner?' Gurleen's voice was feeble and sounded distant.

'What foreigner? No one was around when we picked you up.' Chameli Singh's look said, '*Every suspect denies the act initially.*'

Gurleen cried out. 'She was being raped! I was too scared to save her!'

'Listen, woman, all we found was the van's driver. His brains were splashed out, and your wrench was planted inside his skull when we arrived. He is still critical. I'll be taking you into custody soon as you are discharged.'

'Waheguru, I can't believe I could have done something so gruesome!'

Chameli Singh inferred from the phrase that the woman was Sikh.

'That's what they all say when caught in shady places in Paharganj.' Chameli Singh's cold, steel tone betrayed utter disbelief and disgust. '*Hai Ram!* She's passed out again,' Chameli groaned and slapped Gurleen's face lightly to stir her back into consciousness but to no avail.

Aimlessly tapping her caked soles with the baton, Chameli Singh looked at her detainee once more. Her attention went to a shining object that had slipped out of the open blood-doused linen shirt, whose top three buttons were missing and the eyelets ripped open.

It was a locket, its gold dull with age, unlike the large blue stone in its centre, which dazzled as the room's light bounced off its countless edges. Surrounded by a curve of small glinting diamonds below, it looked like a smiley. Above the stones, the number 1837 was countersunk into the gold surface. *Is that the year? Could it be that ancient?* Chameli wondered as she lifted it off Gurleen's chest and took it in her hands to examine it closely. Feeling the weight, she deduced it was made from a single slab of gold. Impulsively, she turned it over to inspect the reverse side. There was an inscription she assumed to be in Gurumukhi. She released it softly, still looking at it with a mix of disbelief and disapproval. It looked like an heirloom. *How the hell does a taxi driver have something that looks so precious? Is it stolen?*

The woman stirred back into consciousness and her hand went as if by reflex to clutch the locket. She saw the inspector's gaze still fixed on it and tucked it inside.

'Does it belong to you?' Chameli asked.

'Yes. It's been with me for years.'

'You look like a well-off woman. Why do you drive a taxi?'

There was no reaction.

Chameli Singh plonked into the visitors' chair and took out the discharge papers. 'I'm taking you into custody. I forgot, what did you say your name was?' she mumbled as she dug her teeth into a cheap ballpen, whose cap had been chewed off to almost half its size.

'Gurleen. Gurleen Rambal.'

Chameli Singh looked up in surprise and eyed the locket again. A crease formed on her brow as she mangled the pen cap, trying to recall where she'd heard the name as she scribbled it on the discharge slip and took her into custody.

Gurleen was still drowsy when they arrived at Naba Karim, the only women's police station in central Delhi. Her back was stiff and her head still woolly. A wave of revulsion swept over her as she watched Chameli Singh chewing at the ballpen cap. The driver and the station guard helped her out of the jeep.

Two empty lock-ups, a worn-out desk, three creaky chairs, a rusty rifle on the wall, a dust-covered computer terminal and a small TV reflected the state of law and order in India's crime capital.

However, there were no cobwebs on the ceiling, no greasy fluff over the fan blades and no dust layers on the officer's desk. The floor was mopped clean, and a half-burnt incense stick protruded from a small hole in the wall, below was a calendar with a picture of Lord Ram, his consort Sita, brother Lakshman and the devout monkey-god Hanuman.

The guard, the sole male member of the station, locked her in a cell that had a mattress riddled with lumps, a soiled bedsheet, a mud pot with water and an aluminium tumbler, and handed the keys to Chameli Singh. Tossing the keys aside, she spat out the last remnants of the cap—its blue had by now discoloured to white from the chewing—and collapsed into her chair shouting, 'Balram Singh, FIR file *le ao zara.*'

The guard got up from his stool and browsed through a dilapidated wooden shelf in the far corner. Of the fifteen-or-so files piled in messy disorder, he took out the dirtiest one; the First Information Register 'FIR 2011–12' and handed it over to the inspector.

Chameli Singh thumbed through to the last filled-in page and turned it over to begin a fresh entry with the current date. She put the ballpen down without writing anything and let her gaze adrift. It stopped at the far corner of the room, where the station's sole computer terminal lay draped in a dust-laden plastic cover. She had been trained to use it, but seldom found the time or need. After Balram Singh had dusted the cover outside and wiped the screen with a wet cloth, she switched the modem and desktop on.

The screen came to life. Chameli entered 'Rambal' in the Google search box and turned up 2.1 million search results. The top result was a photo of the woman and a handsome young man standing next to the famous cricketer Kaviraj Singh. They were holding the Players International League trophy, a crowd cheering behind them. Chameli spent the next two hours clicking on links that unveiled glimpses of the lavish lifestyle of the enigmatic woman sleeping in the lock-up.

~

The first was an old magazine post about the family's patriarch, Rai Bahadur Lala Vijendra Singh Rambal. Chameli Singh read:

> Lala Vijendra Singh Rambal's family had served the British for three generations, and it was just a matter of time before his service was recognized and duly rewarded. In the 1930s, he was conferred the title of Rai Bahadur, the equivalent of an OBE. The honour was followed by other material rewards in the form of exclusive licenses and concessions.
>
> By the late 1940s, Lala owned several Burmah Shell petrol stations in New Delhi's finest locations, besides some prime land parcels of commercial and residential real estate. The crown jewel among these was 'Rambal Acres', a two-acre estate with a bungalow in Nizamuddin West, in the heart of Delhi. The Earl's cousin had occupied it before gifting it to Lala for his loyal service to the Crown.
>
> Almost adjoining the historic Humayun's tomb, Rambal Acres was among the most beautiful—and coveted—locations in all of New Delhi. It had been featured in every high life magazine of international standing as one of Delhi's most exquisite residences. Its media coverage was matched only by the tales of its flamboyant owner, who was known all over town as a Casanova. Lala was rumoured to have sown his wild seeds in many of Delhi's homes, until tamed in 1950 by a buxom village girl Lajwanti Devi. Unfortunately, despite various treatments, amulets and penances, Lala's wife could not bear him children. Deep inside, Lala felt ashamed that he was an empty pod, a caricature of the Rambal dynasty whose

men had been known for their prolific libido.

Lala died in 1954, succumbing to liver cancer, without seeing his progeny. However, the entire gathering in mourning cheered as the family priest announced that Lala ji would not be missed for too long, for he would soon return to the world; his devoted wife Lajwanti Devi had been blessed with long-awaited motherhood.

Lala stirred a controversy even after his death, with his last wish that his widow marry her childhood fiancé Jivan Singh. Some say it was an act of atonement, for rumours had it that Lala had settled off Jivan with a parcel of fertile land in Punjab to clear the decks for himself to marry Lajwanti, who had repeatedly turned down his overtures.

Chameli Singh paused at another item, a *Nation Today* sports feature: 'India revives pyjama cricket: Business bets big on PIL'

The Players International League, with its short twenty-over format, is perfect for an impatient generation that could not wait five days for a result. But it's not just about more adrenaline for cricket fans; the PIL is turning out to be a money-spinner for India's business houses too.

Speaking to *PNN*, Razia Haroon, PR advisor to the Rambal Group, said 'The PIL marks the Rambal Group's entry into the sports entertainment business.' The Rambals bought over the Ludhiana Lions, bidding a whopping twenty crore rupees for the team's new captain, Kaviraj Singh, the dashing all-rounder and leg-spinner. A friend of the Rambals shared that Ludhiana Lions was a birthday gift to Aryan, the only son of Vikrant and Gurleen Rambal. In a country where millions of people get excited with passes to a cricket match, Aryan gets gifted a cricket team on his eighteenth birthday. Whatever, the Ludhiana Lions are ready to roar!

Chameli was about to log off, when a salacious caption 'Rumbles in Rambal House?' above a video clip caught her attention. Shot on a cell phone camera, the video was shaky but the sound crisp and clear and the visual, self-explanatory. It showed a heated argument in a lawn. A man, drunk and with an unsteady gait, was shouting foul abuses at the Rambal lady. The others there watched from a safe distance.

'To hell with you, bitch! If you can't put up with it, buzz off. But you can't, now that you've had a free ride for twenty years on my wealth.'

She was giving it back to him. 'Vikki, you married me because you were afraid you'd lose half this estate if I married your cousin Vish. You were jealous of him. Always. Because we both know he was the better ma—'

He slapped her and spat on her face as the public stood still, stunned.

~

The monitor went blank from a power cut, a regular irritant in energy hungry Delhi. *Some family, these Rambals!* Chameli thought as she returned to her desk. The blank page on the First Information Report began filling up as she wrote while mangling a new pen stub. After she had written in her report, she tossed the pen away and looked into the cell and saw Gurleen was awake.

'Madam, read the FIR.'

Gurleen stepped out and sat on a metal chair and read through with ease; the words were beautiful pearl strings formed out of gel ink. The text, however, was bare cold facts. Screams, broken glass, one female unconscious, one male dead.

Chameli Singh ordered, 'Sign here.'

Gurleen hesitated to accept the drool-dripping pen. 'What are my chances, inspector?'

'Bad. Your luck ran out an hour ago.'

Gurleen gaped at the inspector in shock. 'What are you saying?'

'The van driver died. It was expected, you know, street dogs were eating his brains when we arrived.'

Gurleen's hands trembled, her lips quivered and she exploded. 'He would have killed me, even raped me, like he was raping her!'

'Calm down. Water?' Chameli Singh lobbed a half-filled bottle of water at her. When Gurleen had gulped a mouthful, she seemed no more composed to deal with the questions and Chameli Singh rubbed in her authority.

'This is a police station, not your palace. Now, this girl, who was she?'

'How do I know, inspector? I just heard her scream and saw her legs shoot out through the glass. They were gashed and bleeding.' Gurleen's chest heaved.

'But you said she was a foreigner?'

'I presumed. She was screaming in a strange, squeaky language.'

'If she was bleeding, where did she disappear?'

'How do I know? Maybe there were others in the van, maybe they took her away. I have no idea. It all happened so fast. Please believe me.'

'Under the circumstances, you're being booked for manslaughter.' Chameli broke the news rather nonchalantly and lowered her gaze to stare at the FIR register.

Gurleen rose to walk to her cell in a stupor. Her legs caved in and she slumped to the floor, sobbing and whispering, 'Aryan!'

4

She woke up with no idea what time it was. The cell was blind with darkness. Her hands were numb with the free sugar in her blood; she had not taken her diabetes tablets for days.

Thoughts hovered in her mind like bats on a dark night. How much life had changed in one year! She had lost her home, lost her taxi, and now, even her freedom. And Aryan, did he even care to know where she was? Did he hate her so much, just because she wanted to retain her dignity? Alone in the cell, all she could do to fight the rising panic that slammed at her gut was close her eyes and pretend that it was bright and sunny outside.

Her heart pounded against its cage when the station door creaked open. *Hai Rabba, it must be the bloody guard. Is there more trouble now?* A key fumbled to find the cell door's latch. She wanted to scream, but the words stopped inside her throat, and a little trickle ran down her panties.

She had nothing in the cell to defend herself with, except a dented metal tumbler. *Waheguru, I'm going to maul his lousy face.* She picked it up and moved to where the sound came from and hit out at the grill with the tumbler, its edge facing down.

Someone yelped. Gurleen felt she had hit the fingers clutching the prison bar. She hit repeatedly and screamed, until another scream drowned hers.

'Stop it! It's me!'

The lights came back on right then. Chameli Singh was nursing the back of her palm; it had a nasty long cut from the tumbler's edge. Gurleen burst into tears. *She's going to kill me.*

Chameli Singh stepped inside. 'There's been a long power cut. I just thought of checking up on you….'

'I'm sorry, inspector. I almost died. I was so scared. I thought that guard…'

'He's fine. He's a eunuch, by the way. You must be hungry. I've brought you something to eat.'

'Why aren't you home?' Gurleen asked.

'Home? That little ten-by-ten shack I've got from the department?' Chameli Singh grimaced.

'What about family?'

'I had family, until I ran away with someone who later did this to me,' Chameli Singh said, rubbing her cheek. 'Even I am terrified of the dark. I was asleep when he did it.'

Gurleen looked at the scar and fought the urge to turn away. 'How do you deal with it?'

'With Ram and rum.'

'Ram and rum?' Gurleen was intrigued.

'That's Ram,' Chameli pointed to the calendar on the wall, 'and this is rum,' she took out a bottle of Bacardi Reserva.

The guard wiped two ceramic teacups and saucers and set them on the floor, and fetched a bottle of Coca Cola and some kathi rolls. The rolls went onto the saucers and the Bacardi Reserva into the cups, followed by Coke.

'Ram knocks sense into my meaningless life each day and rum knocks me senseless each night. Cheers!' Chameli Singh polished her drink in one gulp, refilled her cup to the brim and gulped that down too. Gurleen hesitated and then felt she ought to follow. And she had never had rum in a teacup.

Soon she had downed two cups, musing that her Page 3 folks would die to get a glimpse of her having cheap rum in a chipped teacup.

'Why hasn't anyone visited you yet? Don't you have family, Madam Rambal?' Chameli asked.

'Madam Rambal. That sounds so strange to my ears. The man

whom I called my husband died some months ago. And my boy, he's somewhere in fucking America. That's all there is to my "so-called" fucking family.' *Bloody hell! The rum's loosened my tongue! I've never used that word in public before! No wonder men talk so loosely when drunk.*

'Brothers, sisters, relatives…?'

'Inspector, I grew up in an orphanage.'

~

1965. Akhnoor, Punjab.

The sounds of Pakistani gunfire drowned her faint birth cries, and the heavy shelling orphaned her the day she was born. She remained without a name until the head of the Sat Bhravan orphanage in Amritsar named her Gurleen—the one lost in the Guru's devotion.

Gurleen, or Leena, as she was affectionately called, looked forward to school and was fascinated by English; it had such a strange yet friendly feel to it, and she thought it was dignified, unlike others around her who felt it was the 'foreigner's imposition' on a great civilization. She learnt it with a hunger and imitated her teacher as she pronounced words like school, station and spherical as *sa-kool*, *sa-ta-son*, and *sa-ferical*.

Much as she loved being amidst people, Leena could also spend hours without any conversation. She was petrified by any loud noise; it awakened a deep, inexplicable fear in her. And she could not tolerate any conflict: she hated action films, especially the sounds of gunfire. She even avoided aggressive sport. She loved visiting the Golden Temple during weekends and found peace in arranging the visitors' footwear, helping out with the langar seva, or cleaning the marble floor of the sanctum, her mind lost to the soothing strains of raagis' hymns, a deep gentle peace erasing the deep fears lurking in her subconscious.

Gurleen blossomed into an unconventionally good-looking, intelligent, deeply religious and principled teenager—a role model at Sat Bhravan Ashram. The new patron, Mrs Lajwanti Devi Rambal, a rich widow from a well-known family from Delhi, took a liking to her and spent considerable time with Gurleen during her quarterly visits and even took her a few times with her to Delhi during the holidays.

Under Lajwanti's mentorship, Gurleen gradually overcame her timidity and began asserting herself, although never enough to deter others from cajoling her for assistance. She also overcame most of her rural manners and became fluent in English, although the *sa-pe-shall* and *sa-mall* remained stubborn and occasionally escaped her vigil.

She completed her BSc in Home Science, learning the basics of interior décor, housekeeping and cookery/nutrition, but lacked the sophistication and quick wit of the urban socialite that were essential to land cushy jobs at hotels, clinics and architecture/interior décor firms. However, Gurleen was content playing homemaker. It suited Lajwanti.

Gurleen was brought to the Rambals' opulent home in Delhi to tend to Lajwanti, who was suffering from arthritis and who constantly worried about her son, the flamboyant Vikrant Rambal. Vikrant had embarrassed everyone with his sexual fling with a teacher, which had led to his expulsion from college.

Convinced that the grounded Gurleen could anchor Vikrant, Lajwanti announced on his twenty-third birthday that Gurleen would be her daughter-in-law. Knowing Vikki would resist, she made it a condition to his inheriting the Rambal estate. The announcement shocked Gurleen and Vikrant both, for Vikrant hardly ever spoke to her; for him she didn't even exist.

Their wedding celebrations were ostentatious and the who's who of Delhi was in attendance. But Gurleen soon realized that the marriage was a huge compromise. Vikrant had been honest enough to admit that Leena just wasn't his kind of woman and she shouldn't be surprised or offended by his attention to others of his ilk. Unfortunately, his honesty had poured out only after the estate titles had been registered in his name.

To his credit, Vikrant never ill-treated Leena, except when he was overcome with anger. She was no better than the furniture of his well-appointed house. Dignified, elegant, good to display, comfortable to recline in and always available for instant use. But she wasn't good enough to parade in the presence of his high-flying circles. Gurleen tried her best to fit into the mould by attending a three-month 'finishing' programme in England and appointing a socialite widow to initiate her into Lutyen's Delhi's Page 3 habits.

With Lajwanti Devi's death a few years later, Gurleen Rambal's life became one of regal dignity spent in solitude except while playing hostess to Vikrant's heady social events, besides looking after their son Aryan, who had begun following his father's ways.

~

Gurleen woke up to the sound of a bell tinkling. It was morning already. Her head was throbbing with a hangover. She had never drunk more than a glass of wine or an exotic cocktail. Black rum, never, unless one counted the Jamaican sugar cocktails in the Bahamas. Yuck!

She stirred out of the unlocked cell. Chameli was in a fresh uniform and was now in her Ram mode. She was shaking a small bell and reciting Mahatma Gandhi's favourite hymn.

'Raghupati Raghava Raja Ram
Pateeta Paavan Sita Ram!'

A fresh aroma of jasmine wafted from the incense sticks stuck into the wall. When she had finished, Chameli Singh handed everyone in the station a piece of the prasad and asked, 'Gurleen, don't you want to get ready?'

Gurleen heard it as: 'Don't you want to get Reddy?'

5

2004. New Delhi.

The election results had come in. Once again, the fragmented Indian electorate had ensured that no single party got a majority. In the week of horse-trading and inducements that followed, small political parties bargained for their pounds of flesh. The biggest Shylock among them was Poorna Chandra Reddy, popularly known as P.C.R. or Reddy. His Hyderabad-based Telengana Party held the 12 (of 548) crucial seats in the Lower House that would return the Socialist Party to power. Reddy had extracted three plum ministries as his tonne of flesh.

Seated in the VIP rows at the Durbar Hall of the Presidential House, Vikrant Rambal waited, like the hundreds gathered, for the president to arrive. Peeping out of his weightless Armani bespoke navy-blue jacket sleeve, his Rolex Oyster Chronograph Champagne told him the president was twenty minutes late. His eyes swept the hall and he saw P.C. Reddy and two other family members in the special enclosure cordoned off from the audience. The rumbling in his queasy gut told him that the times had changed.

The Reddy family owned businesses in construction and minerals in south India, but found it almost impossible to break into the central government tenders over which Delhi's business families led by the Rambals had a stranglehold. Vikrant, with no interest in the south, had constantly rebuffed the Reddys' overtures for partnership. A miffed Reddy ceased all communication, and even avoided eye contact when they came across each other in public, which was rather often.

That evening, as the president swore-in Reddy and his relatives and gave them charge of petroleum, sports and urban development,

Vikrant knew it was too much of a coincidence. These were the three ministries that governed the three Rambal business lines.

~

The first blow came just a few days later.

The new petroleum minister signed off a new policy that allowed the state-owned National Oil Company to compete with private companies. NOC gas stations were given prime land free, and were allowed to host ATMs, restaurants and twenty-four-hour shopping facilities. Within a month, National Oil inaugurated the first of its swanky stations in a vacant parking lot in the heart of Delhi, less than two hundred metres from Rambal Gas's biggest, and most profitable, gas station.

Business plummeted overnight as all government offices, the crème de la crème of Rambal Gas's clients, switched loyalties to National Oil, lured by credit as much as a government whip. Vikrant waited three months to get an appointment with the new minister. When it took place, the meeting lasted all of three minutes. The minister had his decision ready even before Vikrant could plead his case.

He had said without demur, 'Sell your stations to the Reddy Group, Mr Rambal.'

Caught by surprise, Vikrant had blurted out in rage, 'Tell Reddy to fuck himself!'

~

'In tender businesses, one's gain is another's loss.' Reddy's wife placated her husband, unmindful of his scowl as she placed the steaming rice before him.

The family was huddled at the dining table, laid out with a typical Andhra fare: chintakaya podi, kodi vepudu, ulli rasam and heaps of steaming Krishna rice marinated in fragrant ghee, amidst vibrations of a train passing by. They were ruminating the loss of a big tender.

As he bit into the spicy red leg piece, the patriarch fumed at his son and nephew for losing the prestigious hotel tender to the Rambals. '*Vray vedhavaa*, how did we lose even after agreeing to a ten per cent kickback? I thought the minister was in favour of our offer!' He lavished abuse at his *pedda koduku*, the eldest son.

The son repeated all the details to assure his disbelieving father. '*Naana*, I did exactly as you told me. We offered the Delhi government a five per cent royalty for ten years. The tourism director was sure we would get it.'

'*Lanja kudaka*, what went wrong then?' Reddy blasted out, unmindful that his wife winced at his invectives that blasphemed her as much as her first-born.

'I don't know, *Naana*. Everything was settled—'

'—What did Rambal offer?'

'He offered a signing bonus of ten crore rupees, besides matching our royalty,' said the nephew.

'Bastard! It's all those free American dollars coming from his foreign investors. We should never have supported foreign investment in Indian real estate.'

'Couldn't we have bid more? We have lots of money too.' It was the son.

'You fool, foreigners can invest white money. Our wealth is mostly black, undeclared. Questions will be raised if we start showing off.'

'In that case, we need businessmen to front us in such deals, *Naana*.'

'That's why I have been trying to cultivate Rambal. But he thinks we're too small for him. I'll finish him one day.'

The son reasoned. 'We need to get used to this new environment.'

Reddy paused his mastication midway and repeated,

'Environment, environment.' The pulp was still in his mouth as his frown gave way to a smirk and then a full-blown smile. 'Well, if I don't get something, I'll make sure others don't get it as well.'

Four days later, the principal secretary at the Ministry of Environment sat with two officers, staring at a fifteen-year-old notification that had yellowed with age and had dead silver fish skeletal imprints stuck on it. After scrutinizing it for the third time, the secretary concluded, 'Looks like this should help our minister.'

An hour later, they were sitting before P.C. Reddy, Minister of Environment, with an amendment to a long-forgotten and unused provision under the Environment Act. It was titled 'Heritage Sites (Protection) Order'.

As the minister went through each line carefully—he had a degree in law—for the third time, a sly smile formed on his rotund face, and he hummed a popular Bollywood song. The secretary didn't have the balls to tell him the rendition was completely off-key.

~

A week later, the Reddy family were in celebration over how easily Reddy had clipped Vikrant Rambal's wings.

'How did it happen, *pedda naana*?' the nephew asked in awe.

Reddy looked pleased with himself. It showed in his rare smile. 'The world knows Rambal's planning to build a seven-star hotel at his estate adjacent to Humayun's Tomb. I signed an order banning all new commercial activity near any national heritage monument. Rambal can't move a single brick into his estate.'

'That would seal the fate of his Ronald Grump venture. They've advanced him millions of dollars against it.'

'Yes. Go get my briefcase.' Reddy chuckled and drummed his fingers on the dining table as he waited to read out his order:

Under the powers given to it under the Environment Act

1965, the Government of India hereby notifies an immediate ban on all new commercial activity within five hundred metres of any national heritage monument under the List of Historic Sites, as amended from time to time.

Issued by and on behalf of the President of India

By the Ministry of Environment Protection
P.C. Reddy

At the end of the hearty meal, Reddy asked his son to dial a Dubai number. It was a conversation he had been looking forward to, ever since they had lost the hotel tender to the Rambals.

~

Around midnight, there was a call on Vikrant's mobile. It was the big man Grump. Vikrant cleared his throat and spoke, smiling. 'Hi Ronald, back from your Dubai res—'

The smile disappeared as he was cut off mid-sentence. He turned red and his head shook violently as he tried to butt into the monologue from the other end.

'Ron—listen, let me exp—let me explain. It isn't like what you say—but no—it's not—OK, you go first.' Vikrant gave up and listened, shaking his head in disagreement and silently mouthing Punjabi expletives. *Pancho... Maayyaava... Maa da...* When he put his Vertu down, it was wet with the sweat from his ears, despite the chill of the air-conditioner in the den.

~

Days after the Grump pullout, one morning Vikrant was surfing business channels on the wall-mounted LED screen. Hitting the Times Business Channel, his eyes fell on the text scrolling across the screen. He skipped channels and winced. It was the main business news that day splashed all across.

'Grump sues Rambal for 100 million recovery.'

The anchor spoke about the reasons.

'The Rambals were responsible for getting all approvals for a seven-star hotel. The new environment order has stalled the project indefinitely, forcing the Grumps to cancel the venture and recover their investment.'

With Reddy's order, Vikrant's money was stuck in many heritage sites. The most grandiose of them was Mughal View, adjacent to India's most visited monument, the Taj Mahal. Unable to repay Grump, Vikrant tried to raise money against his petrol pumps, but there were few takers—on paper, the petrol pump sites still belonged to the government; they had only been leased out to the Rambals.

Following advice from his accountants and friends in politics, Vikrant settled with Grump by transferring his hotel licenses and petrol pumps to a shell entity, PCR Holdings.

Fortunately, he had put together a brand-new money-spinning business—Ludhiana Lions.

6

2006. New Delhi

The Reddy family announced their first project in the capital, partnering with the Grumps. However, they were unprepared for the media digs about their rustic origins.

The son was upset over a social media comment that had gone viral. '*Naana*, do you know, they say we're the "political crass", they call us the "lungi brigade"?'

PCR tugged at his son's blue and green checked lungi, almost yanking its knot open.

'Rascal, don't underestimate the power of this lungi. It is our identity. And these highflying Punju folks, they might wear designer jeans, but I won't be surprised if many of them don't wear underwear. When I take their pants off one day, there will be nothing to hide!'

Irked by his son's remark, Reddy left his half-eaten curd rice, rose from the table and went to the living room. To divert himself, he mindlessly flicked the TV remote and stopped at SET MAX, which was beaming a cricket match live. Reddy had no interest in cricket, but his attention was drawn to the VIP box, where the camera had zoomed in. He saw Vikrant Rambal dressed in a blue Nehru jacket clinking glasses with a lady industrialist. Their teams were playing against each other.

Reminded of the 'lungi' remark, Reddy cursed and switched the TV off. Soon, he was smiling, as the germ of a plan formed in his wily mind. The sports ministry was under the Reddys.

~

The second Players International League series was around the corner. Marketing agencies were on overdrive, bagging last-minute sponsorships, spot advertising rights and special endorsements. Everyone was cashing in on the insatiable Indian appetite for the quick-gun version of 'the gentleman's game'. With the play-off schedules already announced, it was the worst time for a controversy.

Two weeks before the inaugural event, the *Hindu Times* headline screamed: 'Cricket Board to ban Ludhiana Lions?'

Jimmy Peters, captain of Ludhiana Lions, had complained to the India Cricket Board, the game's regulator, about non-payment of match fees and bonuses by the team owner, Vikrant Rambal. On hearing the news, many advertisers had called the board, worried over adverse implications for their brands that rode on the Ludhiana Lions jerseys. It wasn't good for the players either; bad press would affect morale and performance.

The Ludhiana Lions board convened at once to discuss the crisis. The Cricket Board had checked out that Peters's claim was correct. No fees had been paid to three cricketers for the previous season. Fearing revenue loss from the bad publicity, the board asked the Ludhiana Lions for a hundred crore rupee bank guarantee. Failure to issue the guarantee would result in the team's disqualification and cancellation of the Ludhiana Lions' license.

Vikrant was upset over having to explain things to the board, which had representatives of the main sponsors. He was enraged by the accusation. 'Gentlemen, do you believe I'm stealing my players' money? Me? Vikrant Rambal?'

'Just tell us, have you paid Peters and his mates or not, Mr Rambal?' It was the marketing head of a large British corporation, the principal sponsor, whose logos were printed prominently on Ludhiana Lions' safety gear—helmet, gloves and pads.

'Bob, we're the highest paymasters in the PIL. You know that, of course.'

'Here's what. Peters saw me a week ago. He said that you paid them pittance for the last season. That's many months overdue.'

'*Ghanta*! Peters and his boys didn't want money; instead, they wanted apartments in our new luxury project and adjusted match fee and salaries against the booking amount.'

'Can you prove it? Do they have an allotment letter or something from your company?'

'No one has been allotted apartments yet. It's a verbal understanding. Usual in the business.'

'But Peters has denied it.'

'Don't know why. He'd been hounding me for the apartment.'

'No one will believe you, Vikrant. Not just because of Peters.'

'Why?'

'Because everyone—especially a developer like you—knows foreigners can't buy property in India.'

'Yes, but Peters planned to cash out on the secondary market. We launch projects at X price and the prices touch 4X by the time the building is ready for occupancy. Peters would make 3X. All in cash.'

'Why should he complain if they stood to gain so much?'

'Look, Bob, do you think I'm stupid to risk the PIL over a few apartments? Here's what, I'll pay Peters and his men right now. And I'll issue the bank guarantee too. But the Cricket Board has to make a press statement clearing the misunderstanding.'

'Where is the guarantee money coming from?' Bob was concerned because he knew that the company was tight on cash.

'From your sponsorship, of course. The money hit the bank yesterday.'

'I was afraid you'd say that. Sorry, Vikrant, but we are cancelling our sponsorship.'

'You can't do that, Bob. The tourney's just days away!'

'That's your problem. You may not know this, but Peters is refusing to wear our logo. He's English, which makes it real messy for a British brand like us. We're pulling out. That's final.'

'You can't do that. Relax. All this will be forgotten soon, it's just a small hiccup! And everyone here has big money riding on the PIL.' Turning to the others, he asked, 'Don't we, gentlemen?'

The others were too scared to rock the boat and sided with Vikrant.

The Brit saved face by announcing, 'I am resigning from this board with immediate effect. And we'll go into arbitration over this oppression.'

When the minutes had been signed, Vikrant called the chairman of the Cricket Board to assure him that the guarantee money would be on his table before the deadline. The chairman, whom everyone heard on the speakerphone, sounded relieved.

'Thanks for sorting it out, Mr Rambal. Let's meet at the inauguration party and celebrate the return of the Ludhiana Lions.'

The crisis defused, the Rambal PR machinery under Vikrant's trusted advisor Razia Haroon immediately went into overdrive to quash the 'fictitious' news article and got the *Hindu Times* to agree to an editor's errata, sweetening the deal with a huge advertisement for the Ludhiana Lions.

The next day, the headlines cried out: 'Ludhiana Lions ready to roar at PIL 4!'

~

Inside the first-class cabin aboard Emirates' new Airbus 380, Jimmy Peters bit his fingernails as he read through the article vindicating the Ludhiana Lions. Things hadn't turned out as planned, and now the embarrassment was entirely his. He had no problems with the Rambals; they were as friendly and fair as owners went. He'd never wanted to rat out on Vikrant.

He had been forced, all because of his sexual kinks. He should never have had sex with that ten-year-old girl aboard the yacht off Mumbai's Apollo Creek. She had died midway, succumbing as much to weight as to thrust. Fortunately, the sea had saved him; her body had sunk without a trace. All was normal until one day Peters received damning photographs and a video, which showed him in the act all the way until the body had been tossed overboard.

As EK 503 touched the tarmac at Sheikh Rashid International Airport, Peters cursed himself for befriending Leilah, the Lebanese model who did bit roles in Bollywood and picked out celebrities for extortion by the insane don, Toufeeq Ali, a.k.a. Chota Bhai, of Dubai. He would be waiting at his Jumeirah villa for Peters.

~

Toufeeq, five feet eight inches tall, of medium-build, a flowing beard and a deep scar above his lip; paced outside the swimming pool. Dressed in a robe to conceal his paunch that hung over his swimming trunks, he wondered how he could deal with the *gora*.

The don ran a roaring 'celebrity management' business, using a widespread network of baiters like Leilah who infiltrated the Page 3 circuits and attended every event in town. At these events, these well-endowed girls stalked celebrities, like lions stalking weak prey, to spot the odd ones with unspoken needs, problems, or, as in Peters's case, perversions. Once they were in his grip, Toufeeq 'managed' his celebrities with indulgence, followed by extortion and later the raw fear of death. He even kept a catalogue of the last moments of all those who had dared to stop 'being managed'.

Yes, a catalogue show would settle Peters, he concluded, just as the *bhosdi ka* got out of the car and began walking towards the poolside.

'Peters, come here, *gaandu.*'

'Bhaai, I did my job. You can ask your friends back home in India.'

'Don't play *shaana* with me. You want me to release your film? It will be a super hit!'

'Bhaai, I told you I did exactly as you wanted.' Peters spoke with an anger he hadn't wanted to display.

Toufeeq looked at his cronies and spoke in Hindi. '*Saale ke taav dekho. Lagta hai iske tatte ukhaadne padenge!*' Not a word made sense to Peters, who remained silent as the others guffawed. Then Toufeeq's phone rang and he motioned everyone to silence. He remained silent throughout and hung up saying, 'Done, Reddy Sir. Good night.'

Turning to Peters, he said, 'Now, you play a new role.'

'What role?'

'Stripper!' Toufeeq laughed aloud, and the others joined the chorus. Peters had no clue what Chota Bhai meant by that.

~

With the Peters nightmare behind them, a relieved Vikrant uncorked an exquisite bottle of Dom Perignon, over dinner. For a change, it was just Leena and the solitude of their home. It had been her wish, and he had relented, for once.

'Leena, this could have been immensely humiliating, especially with this entire new retail venture I'm planning for Aryan.'

'*Waheguru da shukar*, it's behind us now. It's the gossip club I worry about; they're going to pester me for passes.'

Over the years, she had overcome her teenage timidity and compulsion to please others, but the true-bred urbanites of Delhi still gave her a huge complex. She never understood what they actually *meant* whenever they said anything; it was always camouflaged, misleading, devious. 'I am too *sa-traight* for them,' she often lamented her naivete.

With seventy-six matches to be played in eight cities, her socialites had calculated that Gurleen had 228 complimentary passes to be doled out. For months, the Page 3 bees had been hovering over the nectar. Conversations with Gurleen increasingly veered to cricket, without ever mentioning the word PIL. She dealt with them as best as she could, making the odd concession after consulting the pecking order given by her husband. A couple of inadvertent mistakes had led to a dreaded yelling at home.

'I hope you haven't promised anyone passes for the inauguration.'

'Vikki, I only do what you tell me to do.'

'You make it seem like such a big sacrifice. Don't you enjoy this heady life, this grandeur?'

'Am I complaining?' She defused the situation instantly, not wanting to ruin the peaceful dinner that she enjoyed more than the outrageously gaudy parties they hosted at Rambal Acres.

'Good. We'll need every pass. When Prince Hassan is here, I want him to see as many celebrities in the stands as on the field. Imagine, the heads of the world's top luxury brands sitting in our pavilion, the media drooling over us! Prince Hassan will see the Rambal magic at work. Who else can give them this kind of hype and visibility?'

'And it's a great launching pad for Aryan.'

The PIL was the perfect opportunity for Vikrant to ink his deal with Prince Hassan's Samara Holdings, which owned twelve of the world's best-known fashion brands. Prince Hassan intended to set up ultra-premium, exclusive outlets in Rambalux Arcade, an uber-luxe shopping arcade. The slew of VIPs and CIPs (commercially important persons) that Prince Hassan's team would meet at the PIL inaugural would leave them in no doubt as to the Rambal connection with bling.

'Lucky bastard, he gets everything on a platinum platter.'

She winced at the way he referred to Aryan.

A day before the inauguration, the bees buzzed even more, for a last attempt to get passes. They were delicately and deftly shooed away by Razia's team. Only direct calls from ministers to Vikrant elicited last minute passes, the casualties being people who were at the bottom of the Rambal list and thus ripe for expunction.

For the inaugural event, Vikrant had chartered a twelve-seater Falcon 900 to shuttle his VIPs to Mumbai. A bevy of Bentleys hired from Delhi's Inter-Continental Hotel took the guests to the airport, where Vikrant and Gurleen would meet them at the private departure enclave at the Indira Gandhi International Airport, Terminal 1.

An hour before they were due to leave, Vikrant felt an excruciating pain in his abdomen. It was so severe they had to stop by at Max Hospital en route to the airport. 'Give me a strong painkiller, Doc. I need to be active for five hours,' Vikrant had pleaded. But when the pain hadn't subsided even after a second injection, the specialist advised his new VIP patient against travel and put him under observation.

Reconciling with the unavoidable, Vikrant asked Gurleen, who was nervous already, to stand in for him.

'Leena, you just need to be around, that's all. You don't need to talk to the media. Razia will handle any tricky questions. If they insist on a bite from you, just tell them, "All that is behind us. The truth is there for everyone to see!" Ah! This damn pain is unbearable!'

Gurleen was palpitating, but made a mountain of an effort to disguise it in the presence of her usually vain, but now helpless, husband. Finally, she resolved herself with a giant breath and said, 'I'll do it, Vikki. Let's hope your VIP guests don't think I'm rude or boring if I remain silent during the flight.'

'They'll be too busy,' he winked. 'I've got three beauties on board as stewardesses to keep them occupied. You just take the front seat and let them have their privacy behind you.'

'What should I tell the board folks about your absence?'

'Tell them my pain was so bad I had to disembark from the plane, but it's under control now.'

Even though she put up a brave front, it was the first time Gurleen was attending such a high profile event by herself. Vikrant, always unsure of her social skills, had never let her be in charge. As a result, she had a deep-seated complex when it came to doing things for her husband.

~

The Falcon touched down at Chattrapati Shivaji International Airport. It was rush hour and even the best of Mumbai's drivers wouldn't wager making it to the downtown venue in anything less than two hours. Gurleen's helicopter made it in eleven minutes from the airport to the Scintilla, Mumbai's only seven-star hotel and one with a rooftop helipad. An exclusive photo-op with the media had been arranged on the rooftop, and every alighting celebrity had a two-minute interview about their interest in the PIL.

The press meet ended with a pre-arranged question: 'Any comment on the team controversy?' Gurleen had her rejoinder ready, rehearsed many times in Vikrant's presence. 'All that is behind us. The truth is there for everyone to see.'

Only, the truth turned out to be something different.

Gurleen sensed something was amiss when they arrived at the foyer of the stadium. She waved at Prabhu Chinappa, the affable chairman of the Cricket Board, who had met her at many social events. To her surprise, he turned abruptly and walked away. The intentional avoidance was not lost on her companions, even though she brushed it off saying, 'Maybe he didn't recognize me with all the dazzle around!' She knew that the laughter that followed was as specious as the explanation. Swallowing her pride a second time, Gurleen composed herself and waited at the VIP entrance for someone to escort them. No one came up to them for minutes, even as many other celebrities were being received.

Finally, she spotted the manager and lashed out. 'How can you keep team owners waiting like this?'

'Sorry, Madam, but teams have their own exclusive entrance. Far down, at the Platinum Lounge. Which is yours?

'Ludhiana Lions, of course.'

'Madam... uh... please follow me.' The hesitation in his voice unsettled Leena. *It seems as if they weren't expecting us at all,* she thought.

They stood before eight decorated gates each with strobe lights flashing the name of a PIL team. At the far end was a ninth door. The signage over it read 'Ludhiana Lions' but the lights were off.

Stepping inside, Gurleen found the Ludhiana Lions box empty. All the other boxes were brimming with cricket crazy youngsters blowing horns, whistles and shouting team slogans. Her guests kept a stoic silence inside the empty box. *Something is wrong! Where is the team? Where are the fans?* She tried Vikrant's phone several times. It was switched off.

The ceremony began with the winners of the previous PIL series marching onto the stage led by Bollywood's King Khan holding the trophy. The crowds went mad, cheering their favourite star. A similar fervour greeted the teams that followed. The Ludhiana Lions were last. Gurleen wondered whether she should go to the stage, for no one had told her what to do. She was still looking out for anyone she could recognize, when there was an announcement.

'Ladies and Gentlemen, we regret to announce the last minute cancellation of the Ludhiana Lions participation this season. We'll miss Jimmy Peters and his boys! Let's give them a big hand as they come on stage now!'

Murmurs filled the auditorium as the Ludhiana Lions came dressed in their uniforms and bowed before the audience. Then Jimmy Peters stripped off his uniform slowly and threw it into the audience. As everyone watched he jerked his pelvis and walked away from the stage in his underwear. Then the booing started. Within minutes, the stage was littered with missiles of all kinds amidst shouts, 'Rambal down, down!'

Suddenly, someone from the media spotted Gurleen, and the cameras were all over her. She swooned in full view of the shutterbugs.

A dazed Gurleen was whisked off by the security—her embarrassed guests in tow—and led to the terrace to the waiting helicopter. But not before the media had had a blast with the coverage. The most played television clip was Gurleen's cocky, prepared reply, 'The truth will be there for everyone to see.'

~

Vikrant was devastated. The Ludhiana Lions was finished. Whatever had happened? And what had Razia done for damage control? She hadn't even called after the fiasco. In anger, Vikrant terminated her contract with a curt SMS, and prepared to leave for Mumbai right away, after instructing his accountant to get all the facts.

By noon, his accountant had everything ready, and had reached Max as instructed.

'Sir, our bank PNB issued the guarantee the same day, and had it couriered to Andhra Bank, Mumbai. That's where the board has its account.'

'How do you know the board received it?'

'The dispatch register confirmed the DHL docket number.'

'Then where the hell did it disappear?'

'I even confirmed that the packet was received by the chief manager's office boy.'

'Did he hand it over to the chief manager?'

'That's where we stumbled into a wall. The boy didn't turn up for duty the next day.'

'What?'

'He was a temp staff, a replacement for the regular office boy who had been hospitalized for malaria.'

'Did you check with the staffing company?'

Avik Davar

'It's odd, he didn't report back there, either.'

Vikrant's 180/110 blood pressure had the doctor worried enough to disapprove travel. However, seeing the futility of an argument when the stakes were so high, he reluctantly allowed Vikrant to leave for Mumbai, after giving him a tranquilizer. It had helped.

Well-rested from sleep aboard his part-owned jet, Vikrant charged into the PIL management office.

'Hello, Rambal Sir, how are you today?' asked the young receptionist who recognized the visitor but had no clue about his mood.

'Stuff your Hello! Where the fuck is your director, that pimp Tiwari?' he lashed out. Her face reddened with humiliation, and she held the intercom receiver to her ears to steady her shaking hands.

Dressed in a grey bespoke Armani that now hung an inch loose around his paunch, Vikrant paced the lobby until the lift doors opened. At the seventh floor, he charged out and headed straight to the corner room at the far end of the cluttered office. He pushed the door so hard that it slammed against the sidewall and startled the director, who was on the phone.

'—Baby, don't worry; I'll get you three nights at the Sahara. All free, all on us. See you s—' He was distracted by the crash of the wood against concrete. '—Hey, who's that?' Shock appeared on his face as he slammed the phone down. 'Vik—Vikrant ji, I, I—didn't… please take a seat, Sir. When did you come to Mumbai?' He rose, a half-smile formed on his lips and he extended his hand, which was not taken.

'*Randi ki aulad!*' Vikrant yelled so loud that everyone in the office could hear him. Couldn't you call me just once to check if I had sent the payment? Instead, you kept your puny black ass stuck to your seat, and enjoyed my humiliation in front of TV cameras?'

'Vikrant ji! Please control yourself. Please understand! Please listen to me.'

After Vikrant had calmed down, the director explained, 'It was the chairman's decision. I couldn't do anything about it. I didn't even know about it until last evening. Why don't you see him?'

'I'll see that pimp right away.'

The chairman's office was in the adjacent building. Vikrant could make it in ten minutes, door to door. He dialled the Cricket Board chairman's direct line, and was placed on hold for over ten minutes, after which the phone disconnected. He re-tried, twice. Same result. Finally, he dialled the switchboard.

'Mr Chinappa's office, please!'

'Sorry, Sir, Mr Chinappa is no longer here.'

'Come on, I just called his direct line. It's busy.'

'That is our new chairman; he took charge yesterday.'

'New chairman? Who the fuck is that?'

Vikrant's blood froze on hearing the name.

'Dr J.C. Reddy, the sports minister.'

~

On the return flight, Vikrant was able to think without the distraction of rage. Andhra Bank. Reddy! From the sat-phone on the plane, he dialled Bruce Glotter, the country head at Group 4 Securitas. They handled the Ludhiana Lions security.

'Bruce, I've got an urgent job for you.'

Five days later, Group 4 had all the evidence.

The CCTV footage had shown the temp at his desk at 2:42 p.m., when his mobile rang. His side of the entire conversation had been captured.

'No Saar...the courier has not come yet... I know, Saar. I will take it to the general manager... Oh...Okay Saar, I won't hand it here. I will bring it to Delhi. Today itself, Saar.'

The next footage was from the despatch desk. At 4:10 p.m., the man got a call on his phone and said, 'The DHL package has arrived.'

The clinching footage showed him leaving the front glass door, with the DHL package in his right hand. The time: 4:30 p.m., one hour before the end of his shift duty.

In a few days, Bruce's team had found out that the man had been sent for a 'one-day' duty by the contractor Krishna Godavari Manpowers, owned by a Telengana businessman related to the Reddys.

The board reinstated the Ludhiana Lions into the PIL with full honour. Vikrant Rambal was also inducted to the PIL governing committee. But the damage was done; the team was demoralized from the scandal that never was. Under the new captain Sanjiv Sharma—Jimmy Peters was sacked in absentia, he never returned after the inaugural event—the Lions did their best but finished at the bottom of the heap at the play-offs. The good news was that they were still in the PIL and were determined to put up a much better show in the next season.

7

With cricket-crazy India bombarded by the World Cup, the Tests against Australia, England and the T20 in South Africa, all in quick succession, the PIL Ludhiana Lions' scandal was soon forgotten, erased from the short-lived public memory. After a one-year gap, everyone, including the Rambals, waited for the new PIL series.

The new captain, Sanjiv Sharma, had proven to be an excellent find. Under him, the team had bonded well and were motivated to prove themselves. It showed when they made it to the semi-finals, at spot No. 4 in the ratings. It was good news for Chota Bhai. And time to call in the dancer.

Leilah met her quarry at the lavish party thrown for the semi-finalists. She was one of the special performers and her graceful yet utterly erotic belly dance had left the audience spellbound. Dressed in a turquoise harem dress with a gossamer veil, she was easily the most attractive and inviting lady around. She knew he was drawn to her from the way he eyed her body and complimented her dance. Over a drink, he asked her to sit beside him as his team's lucky mascot for the semi-final.

Her charm worked, for next day, Sharma's blitzkrieg eighty-four runs off forty-two balls against Chennai Cholas took the Ludhiana Lions into the final, pitting them against the mighty Royal Rowdies of Mysore. It would be a vindication for the Rambals if Ludhiana Lions won the PIL this time. He insisted she ask for a gift. After great reluctance, she asked for a phone like the one he had.

He bought her a Vertu Platinum that night and asked her to rub her luck in until the final. She spent three nights with him, pampered by the exquisite hospitality of the restored and renovated old wing at the Taj Mahal Hotel, Mumbai. Things were working out as planned.

He had fallen for her innocent line, 'Get me a phone like yours!'

The final was just hours away, when a player got a call from his controller. He had better not fail, or Chota Bhai would gouge out his eyes and stuff his testicles into his eye-sockets. He had seen gruesome photos of the 'disappeared' Jimmy Peters hanging by his testicles in a dungeon cellar, his face a pulpy mess, without a nose, earlobes and eyeballs. No, there was no going back. He knew his controller would be watching him at every ball from the President's Box.

The final between Ludhiana Lions and Royal Rowdies turned out to be a cliff-hanger. Chasing 241, the Lions had lost nine wickets and were at 221 after the nineteenth over.

Batting at the crease, Sanjiv Sharma let the first two balls go without scoring. Fortunately, the second was a no-ball, adding a precious one to the board.

Five balls, nineteen runs, and one wicket.

The batsman at the other end was a spin bowler. The pressure on Sharma, The pressure on Sharma was telling, who wanted to avoid a single at any cost, and keep the strike to himself. With a score of eighty-one, he was in top form. If he could pull it off, it would be a double whammy—the PIL trophy and his maiden PIL century.

The bowler pitched the next ball a foot short and was punished by a hook shot over the deep third man boundary for a six. The yellow flags came up along and someone played the PIL's trademark trumpet sound.

Ta-ta-taa–ta-ta-ta-ta-taa-ta!

The crowds cheered.

The fourth ball came a tad slow and Sharma took it on the front foot, converting it into a full toss and slammed it beyond long on, for another six. The mnemonic played again.

Ta-ta-taa–ta-ta-ta-ta-taa-ta! The crowd was ecstatic.

The score: 233 for 9. Eight runs off three deliveries. They could still make it.

The bowlers huddled to consider field placement changes. Sharma surveyed all possible loose spots for his last chance. He had to get another six before running any singles.

It was this ball or nothing!

The bowler began his long run up amidst the cheers, which reached a crescendo as the ball hit the ground. There was a deathly silence in the stands as the off stump jumped out. The red flags waved and red T-shirts stood up as Sharma looked behind, crushed. He had just turned to walk back to the pavilion when the Yellow T-shirts cried out again. The Kiwi umpire had called it a no ball! The replay on the giant screen showed the bowler's right foot stepping on the crease while pitching. It seemed the gods were siding with Ludhiana Lions. Another ball, and another run, with Sharma still at the batting crease.

Seven runs off three deliveries.

The next ball was an out swinger that narrowly missed the bat and landed into the wicket keeper's hands. The crowd sighed.

Seven runs to go from two balls.

The bowler returned to his run-up after a long consultation with his captain. Three fielders ran to the boundary line, at cover, long on and deep square leg. Sharma pounded his bat nonstop at the crease as the bowler approached the wicket, his eyes looking out for the instant the hand overshot its highest point in the swing action. Once the hand came down to toss the ball, it would be too late for the bowler to change his action.

As the bowler's hand crossed its highest point, Sharma took three paces forward and connected the ball ten feet before the crease and lobbed it above the bowler's head into the box for a huge six! The Yellows went mad!

Ta-ta-taa–ta-ta-ta-ta-taa-ta!

The PIL's recognizable mnemonic was followed by a sound quite like a furious ocean's waves crashing against giant rocks.

The scores were level at 241. One run to win, and one ball to be bowled. Sharma was still at the striker's end. As the bowlers huddled again, he ambled around the crease, looking all around the stadium.

The bowler shortened his run-up. He only had to bowl an out swinger, pitching at the off stump to avoid the bat. The Rowdies would win even with the scores tied, as the Duckworth-Lewis rule would apply which would decide the winner based on the total runs scored by each team in the tournament. All the Rowdies had to ensure was that the last ball did not touch the bat.

At the batsman's crease, Sharma's plan was clear. He had instructed his partner to start running as soon as the ball left the bowler's hand. Sharma had to simply touch the ball lightly and run across to the bowler end. With the runner already having a huge head start, they could complete the run easily. The giant board flashed statistics that in cricketing history the batting side had won every last-ball victory.

Sharma looked at the VIP gallery straight ahead of him at the deep third man boundary line. He saw a huge placard with the number '400' stencilled in red. Phew!

There was drop-dead silence as the bowler's raised his arm to release the ball.

The runner leapt across from the bowler's end and ran wildly to the batsman's end.

The ball pitched three feet before the crease in line with the off stump.

Sharma lifted the bat high and brought it full face to the ball. It would be a huge hit into the stands!

A spectator in a yellow T-shirt had already run into the field in anticipation of a win.

The bat's face was level with the ball.

The crowd roared, and then groaned.

Sharma's front knee buckled and he tripped, falling to the right. The ball ripped past in the wide space that had formed between bat and batsman, and uprooted the off-stump.

The yellow T-shirts were shocked, and the red T-shirts cheered to the trumpet.

Ta-ta-taa–ta-ta-ta-ta-taa-ta!

Sharma lay lifeless on the ground, as the Royal Rowdies jumped all around him.

As the red T-shirts streamed into the field, he got up listlessly and rambled to the dressing room, avoiding eye contact with everyone. He had done his best to rescue the side, and they were looking at a win, until the last ball. He had played a captain's knock of 99 runs and was the highest scorer in the match. No one could blame him. He had nothing to worry about. However, when he got the 'Man of the Series' award, despite being on the losing team, he felt a twinge of humiliation, not over losing the trophy, but over the way he had thrown it away.

He would have to bid goodbye to cricket for a while. People would forget the event soon and forgive him for giving away the title. But they would publicly lynch him if they ever found out that it had all happened for a spot-fixing deal with four hundred million dollars riding on it.

The placard at the third man boundary had told him that the stakes over the last ball had crossed four hundred million dollars. His cut at 2.5 per cent was ten million dollars. He could never hope to make that much money from match fees, not in ten years.

He hoped cricket fans would never get to know. If a scam ever broke out, it would taint many others and they would all fall like dominoes.

Damn Chota Bhai.

~

Some days after the spectacular final, five men were closeted in a projection room, viewing the last of the seventy-six master tapes that contained the ball-to-ball footage of the final match.

After countless re-runs of the suspicious last over's footage, there was unanimous agreement that something was just not right with the way the Ludhiana Lions' captain had played the crucial last ball.

The men were the Cricket Board's internal vigilance team and were acting on a tip-off that the last ball result was a result of the new betting racket called 'spot-fixing', which was cricket's equivalent of 'insider trading' on the stock markets.

'Gentlemen, I think we have him,' announced the head, a former Indian captain known for his uprightness both on and off field.

Within days, the news hit the roof.

'Betting scandal tarnishes PIL!'

'Ludhiana Lions under a cloud again!'

The Central Bureau of Investigation (CBI) swung into action right away and rummaged through the lives of Sanjiv Sharma and Robin Andrews, the two batsmen at the crease in the final over. Sanjiv Sharma had received several calls from three cell phones, all registered in the Bahamas. The tapes constantly referred to terms '*malai*', '*kabaab*' and '*kasai*', which pertained to the butchery trade.

Following the trail, the CBI intercepted an email message from a bank in Monte Carlo. It had nothing other than a string of numbers. A gentle diplomatic push had brought the news that the string was an encrypted code for Sharma's numbered account, into which ten million dollars had been received after the final match.

When presented with the evidence and the threat of a seven-year jail term, Sharma sang.

After six days of investigation, Vittal Mani, the head of the CBI team, reported his first breakthrough on the Rambals. Speaking to the media outside the swanky new CBI headquarters, he shared: 'There is solid evidence of spot-fixing. Sharma got all his information from the deep third man boundary, where his accomplices held out white placards with code numbers. Sharma saw the number '400' before the last ball. It meant that four hundred million dollars were at stake over his action.'

The next day, the Cricket Board convened an emergency meeting. The chairman, P.C. Reddy was fuming when Vikrant arrived, twenty minutes late, looking pale.

'All well, Rambalji?' The minister asked without looking at Vikrant.

'Sir, I underwent a check-up. I rushed here from the clinic.'

'Anyway, you'll have plenty of rest now. We want you out of the governing committee.'

'What? Why?'

'The owner of a tainted team cannot be on the governing committee, that's why.'

'Mr Reddy, I haven't indulged in betting.'

'What about your son? Weren't the last calls to Sharma made from his number?'

'That is still being investigated by the CBI. I will prove his innocence.'

'We can't risk the board's reputation, Mr Rambal. Please resign.'

'Sir, I can't risk my reputation either. I shall not resign.'

'Sorry, we have to keep the board clean, and it's cricket's reputation at stake!'

The board voted 11:1 against Vikrant. When the news of Vikrant's expulsion came in, the media celebrated its victory as the keeper of India's conscience. Public anger mounted against the Rambals. An hour after the channels announced Vikrant's resignation, an angry mob of cricket fans had landed up at Rambal Acres and pelted stones, until a police van had rounded up the vandals and stationed a patrol jeep outside the gates.

~

The Rambals took a forced holiday at Macau to avoid the public gaze until the evanescent social interest ebbed out. When they returned in the wee hours one morning, Gurleen spotted a police van outside Rambal Acres. They were waiting to take Aryan into custody for interrogation.

Working on Sharma's leads and running special decryption software, the sleuths had quickly pieced together that 'Malai' was Leilali Danish, a Lebanese dancer; 'Kabaab' was Sanjiv Sharma himself. The unidirectional conversations between 'Kasai' and the other numbers, and more leads from Sharma unravelled that the king pin was Toufeeq Ali, a.k.a. Chota Bhai.

However, the most shocking find was that the last two calls to Sharma had been made from an Indian number 98107*7**7. It was registered to Aryan Rambal.

Vikrant looked at Aryan with rage smouldering in his eyes and thundered, 'What the hell have you been up to, bastard?'

'I swear I have no idea. Swear, dad.' Aryan sounded genuine.

'Then how were the calls made from your bloody phone?'

'I have no clue, dad. I think...I've been trapped.'

'Know this, *haraam ke*, if you go to jail, your whole life's finished. So much for your dalliance with that belly dancer.'

Vikrant pulled all his political strings to prevent an arrest warrant against Aryan. The investigation dragged on and Aryan was asked not to leave the country until the CBI had filed its report. Meanwhile, rumours floated that the Reddys were building bridges with the sponsors to pull the plug on the Ludhiana Lions. Soon, someone approached Vikrant for a sell-out. In his usual Punjabi bravado, he ticked off the messenger and readied to brace himself for another battle. Only, this time Gurleen showed a rare aggression.

'It's your son in the crossfire, Vikki! Please, for Aryan's sake, buy peace with the Reddys.'

Vikrant was taken aback; she had never spoken that firmly to him. 'You want that Reddy to walk over me, you bitch! And your bastard Aryan, why does he have to fill every hole that comes in his sight?'

She was adamant. 'Get Aryan out of this mess. Even if you have to sell everything to that vulture.'

Vikrant finally sent out a truce emissary to P.C. Reddy. It was nearly two weeks before he heard back.

When Vikrant arrived at Reddy's office, he was frisked for weapons, gadgets and bugs, and even made to remove his clothes and footwear before being sent inside the minister's chambers.

Dressed in an ill-fitting white gown, swept clean for bugs and electronic devices a second time, he stood before P.C. Reddy for the entire duration of his three-minute meeting.

'Arre, Rambal Saar, what brings you to this crude south Indian farmer?'

'Sir, please don't wreck my son's life. He is innocent.'

'I know he is innocent.' Reddy plucked a hair off his nostril.

'Please tell me what I need to do to get him out of this mess.'

Reddy spoke slowly, his gaze burning into Vikrant's flesh. 'Transfer your PIL business to my son. And I will spare your son. Okay?'

Worse news awaited Vikrant at home. Even before he could brief Gurleen, she pointed him to a bunch of legal notices from the sponsors. Even Samara Holdings, the Saudi monarch's fund, had pulled out of Rambal Ultra Luxe. It was a deathblow to the luxury malls Vikrant was rushing to complete. He had leveraged the PIL sponsorship to fund the malls.

By evening, when the financial controller had summed up the claims, the Rambals were staring at bankruptcy.

~

Vittal eyed the Platinum Vertu he had confiscated from Aryan. The SIM card was still in place. He switched the phone on and soon calls started coming in. They remained unanswered, but the caller IDs were noted for investigation. It seemed rather unusual to Vittal that before the last match, there had been not even one call from Aryan's phone to Sharma, or to any cricketers or known bookies for that matter, and definitely not to the cell phones listed in the Bahamas. For someone being accused of actively conspiring in a spot-fixing racket, Vittal found it very odd that the sole evidence against Aryan came from the two calls made during the interval of the final match. What intrigued Vittal more was: Why would Aryan Rambal set himself up by calling from his own phone? He wondered if there was an unseen angle to it all.

His curiosity heightened when he got a call from the mighty Reddy himself. A powerful man with increasing political muscle and one who could boost Vittal's career in exchange for personal loyalty.

'Why hasn't Aryan Rambal been convicted?'

'Unfortunately, sir, we don't have conclusive evidence of his involvement, yet...'

'Why? You said the calls were from his number.'

'Yes, but they were all made by a woman. That's a big gap in the investigation. We'll have to let him go.'

The politician from his state gave him instructions couched as advice. 'Don't rush it. Investigate at least a week or two before you close it.'

~

Vittal was wrapping up the investigation inconclusively, when his patron called a second time that week.

'Vittal, let that Rambal boy go.'

Why was the minister softening his stand over Rambal? Vittal kept wondering. Until he heard that afternoon from his network that

Vikrant Rambal had transferred Rambal Entertainment and Rambal Ultra Luxe to Telengana Investments for a token price of one rupee.

Vittal smiled to himself. The hidden angle had revealed itself. It seemed consistent with all their earlier moves against the Rambals.

Later that day, his team reported a strange development. 'Sir, Dubai has reported three calls from Aryan Rambal's phone today.'

Vittal was annoyed. 'Are you crazy? I have his phone here, right in front of me! And the boy is in Delhi, we all know that!'

'We have confirmed it is from the same number 98107*7**7*. But the cell location is Dubai. International roaming.'

'Double check and report back.' Vittal scowled.

Two hours later, Vittal was reassured by Etisalat Telecom Dubai that the calls had indeed been from Dubai, put through from the Etisalat switch. Damn!

The forensic team concluded that the only way it could have happened was by cloning Aryan's SIM card.

Digging further, the calls were geo-tagged to a villa in Jumeirah Beach, Dubai—the residence of Chota Bhai. Once again, the calls had been made by a woman. A voice sampler software confirmed that it was the same voice that had called during the PIL final.

The media went overboard and drummed up a new beat.

'Aryan Rambal absolved!

'Fugitive Dubai based don behind betting!'

Vittal continued to dig like a rat that had smelt the cheese. He had to get to the bottom of the case.

Vittal spotted his cheese when he learnt that Leilah had spent three days with Aryan at the Taj Mahal Hotel. Aryan then told him of the new phone he had gifted her after the semi-finals. It was identical to his Platinum Vertu, as she had wanted. The final breakthrough came when Dubai Telecom, now armed with a name, matched the voice on the phone calls with Leilah's.

Vittal asked Nokia for the IMEI—the unique number given

to every mobile phone device—of the Vertu phone sold at the Taj Mahal Hotel. The IMEI was sent to Dubai Telecom to match against any active SIMs and then GPS track the device. Within the hour, they were able to track the device.

However, the trail went cold, once again, with the discovery of the phone close to Leilah's mutilated body in the Al Ain desert dunes.

~

Chota Bhai watched the news of Leilah's death on Dubai 33, his brow creased in worry. He had no clue that phone devices could be traced even after changing SIM cards. He would have to go underground again, for everyone in Dubai knew that Leilah worked for him.

'*Ma da lauda* Reddy. I should never have agreed to work with that *haraamzadaa*,' he swore aloud as he turned off the screen. Chota Bhai had no interest in the Rambals. He had been forced to do the job for the mighty P.C. Reddy. The wily politician had arranged for Chota Bhai's brother-in-law to be 'caught' by Naxal insurgents in Telengana and had forced the don's hand.

Vittal closed the file with a reconstruction of the most plausible story line.

Leilah had intentionally asked for a Platinum Vertu, to switch the phones. With Aryan taking the wrong phone, she had a five-hour window to get Aryan's SIM card cloned. She had used the cloned SIM card to place the betting calls. The inquiry had traced the calls to Aryan Rambal's phone number. Aryan was implicated due to the number trace and freed by the caller voice trace.

Motive unknown, suspected business rivalry.

Case closed. Unsolved.

~

Within just three years of Reddy's arrival in Delhi, he had managed to wrest Rambal's crown jewels, using the deadly mix of politics and crime. Somehow, Gurleen's intuition told her this was beyond business rivalry. Vikki never gave an inkling, though.

One day, she broached the topic and was surprised by Vikki's outburst.

'Don't ever mention that bastard's name in this house!'

'Vikki, it seems too personal. Are you sure it has nothing to do with that young south Indian teacher who was at Aryan's school?'

'Shut up, you dirty bitch!' Vikrant hurled the fine Wedgewood tea set on the Italian marble floor.

8

2003. New Delhi.

Official records showed the name as Sangeetha R. An ambitious young girl from humble nondescript origins, right since her school days Sangeetha had her eyes set on being amidst the rich and the famous. It seemed the best way to erase the 'bastard' tag that tormented her.

Breaking free of her past, she had left Guntur, a small town in Andhra Pradesh, and had landed in Delhi in search of a new identity. Landing a receptionist's job at a private hospital to support herself, she studied BEd. at an evening college, hoping to become a teacher at one of Delhi's upper-crust schools. She loved children and dreamt of having her own school one day.

Per chance, a patient had struck up a casual conversation with her and learnt that she had topped her BEd. He happened to own a new school, Whiz Kidz, and while talking to her found her smart enough to offer her a job, not in teaching but in business development.

In less than a year, Sangeetha had shown her knack for 'sniffing the money' by homing in on the nouveau riche. Whiz Kidz became the favourite among Delhi's rich traders and industrialists, because of its fancy trappings. Its swanky premises and the canary yellow, imported, air-conditioned buses soon became the talk of town, and nearly everyone with money wanted to get their kids admitted to Delhi's first 'Five Star School'. Including the Rambals.

After some years, one afternoon, she ran into Vikrant in the coffee lounge at the Taj Man Singh Hotel. She recognized him at once, but he was struck by her transformation. The skinny, mid-twenties girl had blossomed into a luscious, full-bodied, infinitely more charming woman.

'How nice to see you again, Vikrant ji!'

'Oh, Sangeetha! You've changed and how! How's life treating this beautiful lady?'

She blushed at the unexpected compliment. 'For starters, I'm no longer a teacher; I am trying to branch out on my own.'

Over coffee, she told him of her plans. 'Kinder Care Education has a licence from an international chain of preschools. All our teachers will have a degree recognized internationally. We also have a tie up for all our preschoolers to be picked up by Modern School. I'm looking for investors to set up two schools in Delhi to start with. Today seems a "no show". I've been waiting more than an hour now.'

The coffee made way for a Margarita, with Vikrant's casual discovery that she was single and uncommitted. After her third refill, he laid the bait. 'Maybe I can help there. There must be someone on the list who can step in.'

'What list?'

'The Rambal list. Delhi's movers and shakers, invited by rotation to our parties.'

'Those famous Page 3 parties?'

'How about getting you invited this Friday? I'll try and seat you with some investors. How does that sound?'

'You're a dream!' She couldn't hold back squeezing his hand in excitement and gratitude. Another Margarita later, she was struggling to steady herself, and leaned on his shoulder until her valet-parked car pulled in at the porch.

That night, Vikrant lost sleep as he relived the afternoon's conversation that had ended with a firm kiss on his cheek. Heck! That had rekindled old passions. The same heavenly body scent. The same glowing, flawless skin. *This is going to be painful, she reminds me so much of Sh—Oh God!*

~

On Friday, Sangeetha came in two hours early, as it would have been impossible for her to go home—in Noida, the eastern suburb of Delhi—and return to the city in the evening.

She sat in the living room, overawed by the 'Ranthambore Kill', a rich painting of two men holding a tiger carcass. She was savouring exquisite Columbian coffee as Vikrant entered.

'Hi, Vikrant ji!'

'Sorry you had to wait. Gurleen must be busy with last minute things, else she would've taken care of you.'

Vikrant had been gracious enough to arrange for her to shower and change for the party. But there was a small problem.

'What?' Sangeetha asked.

'We have more guests than I expected. I'm going to put you in our bedroom suite. The bathroom connects both the bedroom and the study on the other side. Hope it's not a problem if I take a shower when you've finished. I'll enter from the study door.'

'You're asking me? And please, you can shower first.'

'No, no. You get ready first. Be sure to lock both doors when you're inside. Come, let me show you.'

After he had left, Sangeetha checked the bathroom once again. It was as big as her one-room flat. The all-mirrored glass doors made the bathroom appear twice its size.

Half an hour later, when she was in the shower, the intercom rang. She draped a towel and stepped out.

'How are you doing?' It was Vikrant.

'Oh, just about to get ready.'

She locked the bathroom door from outside and let the towel fall, appreciating her shapely figure in the huge mirrored wall. She liked what she saw.

Vikrant entered the bathroom from the other side, with a lighter-sized console in his palm. He looked into the huge mirror and pressed the OUT button. Soon, the reflective grains disappeared from the mirror's surface, and provided an unhindered view of the bedroom. He liked what he saw.

Sangeetha waited for her waist-length hair to dry before putting on her dress. She reached for her body lotion and applied it leisurely, first on her arms, then her feet, and then worked it up her thighs. The cold touch and the velvety viscous lotion brought goose pimples on her flesh. Her heart fluttered as she thought of the meeting with the banker.

As the VIPs trickled in and the decibel level rose at the Rambal lawns, she stood somewhat alone and uncomfortable, overwhelmed and out of place. Until Vikrant brought a portly, paan-chewing man and introduced him to her.

'Meet Vinod Kejriwal, a billionaire on the Bombay Stock Exchange. He's also on the trustees board of India's fastest-growing private university. He now wants to set up a kindergarten chain. He's your man!' Turning to the man, he ventured, 'Sangeetha built up Whiz Kidz. Look no further, Keji.'

'I'm impressed by your talent-spotting flair, Vikki,' said Keji, wiping the red paan trickle off the edge of his lips.

An hour later, Vinod and Sangeetha were still engrossed in conversation. As Vikrant's secretary passed them, Vinod stood up and clutched his arm.

'Look son, I can't stand the din here, can you get us some quiet and privacy inside? We've got business to wrap up.'

'Sure, sir. Why don't you go upstairs to the family wing? You can even use the projection screen if you want.'

'Perfect,' said Vinod even as the secretary was already summoning a valet to set up drinks upstairs.

'I know it is Scotch for you, sir. What shall it be for ma'am?' asked the valet.

'Chablis,' answered Vinod, before Sangeetha could voice her preference.

By eleven, the crowd had started thinning down. Sangeetha and

Vinod were nowhere to be seen. Vikrant surmised that either they were still in conversation, or she had left the party without telling anyone. Curious, he climbed the winding marble stairs, and upped his pace as he neared his suite.

There was no one in the lobby. One whisky glass, one wine glass, a couple of used napkins with lipstick smudges and the remains of chicken bones told Vikrant that they had sat there. At a distance, he saw lights on in the bedroom and walked towards it. The door was unlocked. He stepped inside.

Sangeetha had a glass filled to the brim and was toasting herself. 'Here's to me!' she squealed like the wards she had taught at Whiz Kidz. A bottle of champagne peeped out of an ice bucket atop a trolley.

Vikrant moved behind her, his reflection forming behind hers. First startled, then relieved, she turned, pressed the glass to his lips and said, 'To the most powerful man in the city.' As he steadied her, she clung to him even more.

'Vikrant ji, you can't believe it! Keji's investing ten crores in my venture. I think I am drunk, I can't believe things happened so fast.'

'I'm very happy for you. Shall I have you dropped home? Or you could sleep over.'

There was no answer. Instead, the glass slipped from her hand and fell on the plush Belgian carpet, spilling the exquisite champagne all over. By the time he had picked it up and placed it on the sideboard, she had already collapsed on the bed.

She woke up in darkness with a throbbing headache. It took her several minutes to reorient herself. Her recollection came back, in stages.

She had had a great meeting. She had had too much to drink. She had stayed back. She was still at the Rambal house.

Her clothes were spread on the floor, next to a man's clothes.

He had removed her sandals. And she had told him how grateful she was.

She had woken up to the sound of running water. From the bed, she had seen him in the shower. He had left through the connecting door into the study.

She wanted to scream, but held back, telling herself it was a bad dream. Except the part about meeting Keji.

Vikrant arrived at the lawn and stopped by 'Keji', who was pouring a Blue Label.

'Thanks, Vikrant Sahib. I enjoyed myself,' said Rakesh Shukla, the alcoholic and bankrupt ex-banker who now made his living by brokering small loans. It was his first visit to the Rambal estate, and he had had a thorough briefing.

'You did a great job, Shukla. You were totally immersed in "Vinod Kejriwal's" character.'

Holding up his glass to the host, Shukla said, 'The first "Blue Label" of my life.'

Mimicking his sloshed guest, Vikrant aped, 'The first "Teacher" of my life!'

They laughed aloud at each other's pun, the noise reverberating in the long, empty corridor.

Sangeetha never heard back from Vinod Kejriwal. Her Google search showed over fifty results, but none were relevant. No one seemed to know any Vinod Kejriwal connected with the stock market. However, all of Delhi came to know about Sangeetha when her suicide note was published in a tabloid. She had named Vikrant Rambal and Vinod Kejriwal both.

The far-reaching Rambal influence had the case quashed. It was made easier as there was no Vinod Kejriwal. However, Delhi's gossip mills missed the report in a less-read tabloid in Hyderabad, which claimed that Sangeetha R., alias Sangeetha Reddy, was the illegitimate daughter of an upcoming politician fighting for a new state, Telengana. The name: P.C. Reddy.

BOOK II

9

$\mathcal{E}$ven though the Reddys had bought over the business, the income tax department made a huge tax claim on Vikrant and froze his bank accounts. At the same time, the customs department slapped an import duty evasion charge and impounded his entire fleet of imported cars—a Bugatti, a Bentley and a Rolls Royce Silver Ghost. Including interest and penalties, the demands added up to more than four hundred crore rupees. Vikrant made it to the top of the tax defaulters' list that year.

Attaching and auctioning Rambal Acres, which had a market value of more than five hundred crores, could easily settle off the tax demands. However, the government could not attach it, for it was not Vikrant's earned wealth. It was an inheritance in which his wife, son and 'missing' cousin brother had inalienable rights too. As a weak alternative, the income tax department served a public notice prohibiting the purchase/sale of Rambal Acres without getting tax clearance.

Immediately, the phones stopped ringing at Rambal Acres and the invitations thinned down to a sliver. Soon, an entire month had passed without the Rambals stepping out of Rambal Acres. At the end of three months, Gurleen had gained enough practice to turn straight to Page 5 after reading the front-page news.

She worried increasingly about Vikki. Shattered by the debacles that had come in rapid succession, he had stopped going to the office and had sacked all his staff. It wasn't that they couldn't afford them; Gurleen thought it was to save face. With nothing to do, he had started drinking heavily, and his mood swings were getting to everyone. Most to Gurleen, who herself was coming to terms with life's rapid shifts. It pained her that Vikki, instead of being grateful for her stoic acceptance of their downfall, had begun hurling the foulest abuses at her. She withered in humiliation and anger whenever he called her 'slut!' or 'whore!'

There were also strange physical changes in him. He was constantly tired, and out of breath doing even the simplest of chores like tying his shoelaces. His body odour and breath were foul despite good personal hygiene—he still did four rinses with Plaque Mint and spent liberal splashes of Fahrenheit talc after showering twice daily. Gurleen also noted several purple patches on his body. Yet, he never gave in to her pleas to visit a doctor.

~

Amidst it all, Gurdwara Bangla Sahib became her refuge for sanity and succour. She found solace in voluntary service at the kitchen, entrance gates, or at other assigned places, and lost herself in the mellifluous hymns of the raagis.

One day, while doing langar seva at the gurdwara, she bumped into Dr Inder Singh Koeli, a reputed physician and old friend of the Rambals.

'Inder, you've forgotten us!'

The surprised Sikh struggled to place her. 'Leena, is that you? My, of course! Sorry, I couldn't place you right away.' He gave her a tight Punjabi jhappi and patted her shoulder. 'Good to see you, after all these years!'

'Don't lie, you never tried to keep in touch, Inder!' she said without malice.

Vikki and Inder had both gone to the same school. But academically, they were two ends of a pole. While Vikrant could barely get a BCom seat at a third-grade evening college, Inder had made it to Delhi's prestigious Maulana Azad Medical College, popularly known as MAMC. After a few years of general practice, he got a half-scholarship to go to England for his doctorate;

Rambal Trust had covered the rest of his costs. Gurleen had even made all arrangements at a Chandigarh hospital for Inder's wife's delivery. Inder could not be there, as his final exams were under way on the due date.

Months later, Gurleen had come to know that Inder had come to India to take his family to England and had left without getting in touch. Somehow, Vikrant had remained reticent and Gurleen knew better than to push him beyond a point.

Inder had now returned to India to set up a small hospital but had still remained out of touch. Whatever had gone sour between the two friends, it was so long back, she thought it couldn't possibly matter any longer. She hoped he would accept her request and drop by one day.

Over the next hour, while collecting shoes and issuing tokens to visitors entering the shrine, she brought Inder up to speed with life's highlights in the years gone, right down to the recent rumblings in Rambal Acres.

'When are you going to visit us, Inder?' she asked, when he was about to leave. 'It might do Vikki some good, who knows?'

Inder merely nodded his head and left, without any commitment. Continuing her kar seva for the rest of the evening, her thoughts kept returning to Inder and Vikrant.

Since that chance encounter, Leena met Inder often at the gurdwara. Each time, Inder asked after Vikki and she told him of his resistance to see a doctor. Eventually, Inder agreed to visit them. 'Leena, I'll come by one of these days, for old times' sake. But he must also see a psychologist. I think he has some deep-seated guilt.'

Back home, her mention of Inder's suggestion about consulting a psychologist blew Vikrant's fuse. 'I'm not seeing any psycho. You want to prove I have gone mad, now that I am no longer rich or powerful?'

Gurleen reasoned patiently. 'Vikki, do you want to suffer, or do you want to be treated? See Inder just once. He is still a well-wisher, even though I'll never know what went wrong between you both.'

One Sunday, Vikrant was shocked to see Inder driving through the gate. They shook hands, but it wasn't the exuberant Punjabi body-lifting hug of old times.

Inder sounded restrained as he asked, '*Aur lale di jaan*, what's been happening with the health?'

Vikki remained silent.

Gurleen broke the ice by repeating everything she had told Inder earlier.

'His appetite has gone, and the fever remains mild but doesn't go away. And these hundreds of purple *sa-pots* on his skin, they weren't there before. Of late, he's also been finding it hard to breathe.'

When she had left them alone, Inder examined his old friend, and made intermittent observations into his Dictaphone. 'Flaky skin… rashes…swollen lymph glands…fever…shivering…' Later, over a helping of samosas and tea, Inder advised a special blood test and a biopsy of the skin tissue. He left soon after but not before telling Gurleen, out of Vikrant's earshot, 'Let's hope it's not what I think it is.'

A couple of days later, Gurleen came home to find Inder looming over Vikki, with a magazine in his hand. He was threatening Vikki.

'—If anything happens between them, I'll kill you. Know that, Vikrant.'

Seeing Gurleen walk into the room, Inder calmed down and forced a smile. But his face was grim again as he broke the news. 'Leena, Vikrant has Kaposi sarcoma and lymphoma.'

'What's that, for heaven's sake?'

'A cancer of the skin, that's spread to the lymph nodes. That's how he has these new eruptions, besides the frequent fever and loss of energy. Has his breath become foul of late?'

'Abominable. But I can't tell him, because he feels I'm humiliating him.'

'Well, that's what it is.'

'How did it happen all of a sudden, Inder?'

'Kaposi sarcoma can remain latent in the body for years. It gets triggered when the body loses its immunity.'

'Vikki's never fallen ill. He's always taken good care of himself.'

'Well, probably not enough.'

'Those horrible cigars of his. Is it that? I kept telling him not to smoke so much.'

'I don't think his cigars have caused the sarcoma.'

'Then what has, Inder?'

'His libido. Leena, your husband has AIDS.'

Her head reeled. She caught the arm of the sofa and steadied herself. Inder helped her sit and handed her a glass of water.

Gurleen locked her eyes with Vikrant's. There was a smouldering rage in her words. 'Why do I feel I was going to hear something like this someday, Vikrant Rambal?'

It was the first time Vikrant couldn't look straight into his wife's eyes.

'I wonder how I will ever be able to deal with your... It's disgusting! I can never be with you again.' She stormed out of the room, leaving the two men alone.

After a long silence, Vikrant mumbled. 'Justice has been served. Right, Inder?'

Inder avoided looking at his one-time friend. 'Who am I to judge you, Vikki?'

'You can forgive me, at least.'

'I have forgiven you; else I wouldn't be here.'

Vikrant was unconvinced. 'No, you do that for your profession, not for me.'

'Okay, let me lay it straight, then. Do you think you should be forgiven? Do you think you deserve it? For what you did?'

Vikrant remained silent. Inder continued. 'You have to bear your own cross. But if it gives you any peace, then, yes, I forgive you.'

'Inder, if you want me to have peace, just do me one last favour. You know what it is.'

'No, I will never let your dirty sight fall on my daughter. Never.' Inder stood up and picked up the magazine. Tapping at the photo again, he spoke slowly yet firmly. 'Vikrant, our past, however disgusting, is buried. Now, you just make sure your bloody son stays miles away from her. If anything happens between them, I'll kill you both. Remember that, Vikrant.' He threw the magazine on the bed and stormed out.

After Inder had gone, Vikrant picked the magazine up. The open page showed a girl dancing with Aryan. The caption below read 'Aryan Rambal's new flame!' He rubbed his finger over the girl's face. She had blue eyes with a grey ring around the pupils, just like Aryan. And the same cleft in the chin and prominent jaw line. Unmistakably Vikrant.

The tell-tale clues to Inder's estrangement.

It never shamed Vikrant to hear about his son's liaisons. Rather, he felt proud. After all, the boy was merely playing true to his genes. The insatiable libido was a definitive family trait and the Rambal men were notorious for their wild promiscuity. However, there was a greater reason for Vikrant's acceptance of Aryan's exploits.

Aryan's wild ways were Vikrant's biggest reassurance of his fatherhood because Aryan did not share Vikrant's physical features. Rather, it was Vikrant who had not been born with the Rambal trademarks. Vikrant's father Lala Vijendra Rambal and his uncle Chattar Singh both had aquiline noses, mahogany hair and blue eyes with a light grey ring around the pupils—a rare trait among Indians. Although rumours went around about English influence making it into the Rambal bloodline, no one dared talk about the 'blue-eyed' Lala Vijendra Rambal, for he was truly a blue-eyed boy of the empire.

Gossip had fanned in the Rambal estate when people noted that Vikrant had none of his father's distinctive features, unlike his cousin Visham, Chattar Singh's son. Even though genetic theory could explain it, the stigma remained. Thus, it was an undisputable vindication for Vikrant when the Rambal marks returned a generation later, in his son. Aryan's eyes, nose and hair were incontrovertible proof of Vikrant's own legitimacy.

Assured of his heritage, Vikrant went after people who he felt suspected it. His punishment was poetic; he sought out and seeded the women of those who had dared to scorn him. He chose them well and nurtured relationships that thrived on the edge of risk, and unprotected sex. Vikrant not only considered it an insult to create a barrier to natural passion, but also despised the womanly caution of contraception, which he saw as a sign of non-surrender. To him, their ultimate surrender was to bear and guard his progeny, in secret.

He left behind many footprints: beginning with his driver's wife when Vikrant was fourteen, and progressing in their complexity to more delicious victories – teachers, friends, advisors and, ultimately, relatives. The only times he ever experienced a fleeting twinge of conscience were while filling up forms that asked for a count of his children. Although the official answer was always 'one', the biological truth was closer to 'twenty'.

As the fast-spreading sarcoma sapped his energy altogether and confined him to bed, Vikrant often rationalized that his sins had come to haunt him, that the silent curses of embittered men and remorseful wives had begun their manifestation.

10

How devoted can you be to a person who doesn't love you or even trust you one bit? Gurleen often asked herself when she thought about Vikki's condition and his behaviour.

For long, she had heard rumours of his steamy liaisons with several women, but her dignity and faith had overpowered her suspicion and quelled her urge to confront him. She accepted it all because he had been forced to marry her. She was never his choice. However, she was devastated by the news of Vikki's shameful disease. The mention of 'AIDS' had sent a pulse of revulsion inside her. That day, she moved out of their bedroom and never touched him again. She could sense that it only hardened Vikki; he hated her even more. Soon, she stopped talking to him, except when they fought, which was—every day.

Of late, Vikki had begun calling her 'slut!' and increasingly linked her with his cousin Visham. She felt dirty, impure, at the thought that he could even think that way. Yes, Leena had been very fond of Vish, who was soft-spoken, polished and dignified, unlike Vikki, who was crass with women. But that wasn't a sin, was it? Liking Vish was like appreciating the mesmerising spectacle of a quiet lakeside sunset. It was beyond the carnal, beyond possession; one just savoured its grandeur fleetingly, and moved on. Was that cheating? And Vish, poor fellow, he had vanished, somewhere in England almost twenty years ago.

Vikrant's health deteriorated rapidly. He became so weak he needed help even turning from side to side or getting out of bed. His breath had become so foul people shuddered to enter his room. Purple spots had erupted all over his body and brought a stench of their own. All this made him even more irritable, and he insulted everyone, even the attendants.

One morning, Gurleen heard him shout from his room.

'Leena, come here, you bitch!'

Waheguru, there he starts off again! She winced, as she stepped inside.

'Where is that bloody nurse? She's supposed to sponge me.'

'She just phoned to say she quit.'

'Get the fucking agency to send a replacement.'

Gurleen hesitated before answering. 'She was the fourth one to quit. They all find you too abusive, and your spots scare them. They worry if they'll catch…'

'Bitches! Double their wage and the whores will even suck me off with all this!'

'Vikki, we'll find someone. Be patient.'

'Why can't you sponge me today? Do I repel you too?'

'AIDS isn't an inspiring word, Vikki.'

'I'm still your husband, you whore!'

Not bothering to answer, she turned to leave.

With a sudden burst of strength, Vikrant heaved at her arm and pulled her on top of him and began licking her neck and earlobes. Gurleen choked over the foul stench. Seeing the viscous saliva drool at the edge of his mouth, she couldn't hold her puke, which fell all over his chest. He let go, panting from the exhaustion of his rabid attempt.

After she had cleaned up the muck, she stormed out, cursing, 'Damn you, Vikki, I'll have peace when you're gone!'

Seething in rage, Vikrant shouted after she had stormed out.

'Bitch! I'm going to punish you like hell. You just watch out.' In minutes, he heard the car start and saw Leena leave through the gate. Rage mounting inside, he took out his cell phone and looked up 'Lawyer Raina'.

~

Rattan Lal Raina was a small-time lawyer. Short, overweight and dressed in ill-fitting clothes, his appearance gave the impression he was more a fixer than a lawyer, which wasn't false. Using his network of moles in the government, Raina ferreted out sensitive information to help Vikrant win government projects and minor legal disputes. The Rambal account added to his prestige as much as his wallet, for which Raina was grateful. Therefore, it was natural that he came within an hour of being summoned by Vikrant. Moreover, Raina was eager to share his latest trysts with astrology and numerology.

As Raina entered and shook hands, Vikrant looked at the crude silver rings that adorned Raina's thumbs and laughed uncontrollably. 'Raina, why do you have rings on your thumbs?

'Sir, my astrologer said that Saturn entered Venus last Monday. I must wear a sapphire so that my opponents always remain under my thumb. But he didn't say which thumb, so I have taken the precaution of wearing rings on both thumbs.'

Vikrant looked at his hands that looked ridiculous and laughed once again, as Raina continued.

'Sir, I am also officially changing my first name, based on his expert advice. He said ROTTEN would be much better than RATTAN, numerologically.'

'Rotten Raina, how appropriate!' Vikrant couldn't hold back his chuckle.

After answering the mundane and specious queries about his health, Vikrant came to the point. 'Raina, I want to change my will.'

'Yes sir, definitely. Is it registered?'

Vikrant pointed to the cupboards flushed to the long wall. 'No. It's in one of the lockers in there. Can you check? As you can see, I'm in no position to get up.'

'No problem, sir. Just tell me where I should look for it.'

'Open the last cupboard on the left. It has two steel lockers.

The brown one is mine. The white one is Leena's. The will must be in either.'

Raina tried the brown locker first; it had a four-lever tumbler lock.

'S-H-I-V.' Vikrant spelt the code. Raina turned the levers and reached inside, grabbing a set of property documents and share certificates. There was no will in there.

'No. Check the other one,' Vikrant rasped as Raina stood before the white locker.

'What's the code, sir?'

'L-O-V-E.'

It opened just as easily as the first one. 'What should I be looking for?' Raina said.

'A transparent plastic cover. You can see the first page of the will, with my photo.'

Raina muddled through the contents and gave up. 'There's nothing like that in here.'

'Are you sure, Raina?'

Raina looked once more to double-check. 'Yes, sir. Do you want me to look inside the small blue box too?'

'What blue box?'

Raina took out a small blue box from inside the safe and held it up to Vikrant's view.

'Is it locked?'

'Yes, sir. It has a four-lever lock. The code reads L-I-V-E.'

'Try V-I-K-I.'

Raina rolled the tumbler rings. Negative.

'Try L-E-E-N.'

Some more turns. 'Nope.'

'A-R-Y-A.'

It went on for ten minutes. After a long pondering silence, Vikrant said, 'Try V-I-S-H.'

'Bingo. That worked.'

'Bitch. What's inside?'

'There's a big manila envelope; and a plastic folder inside. Ah, yes, I can see your will now.'

'Good. Bring it to me.'

Raina took the will out and flipped through it. Then he looked inside the manila envelope. 'Sir, there's another envelope, from England.'

'England? I'll check it, while you go over the will.'

Raina pulled out a sky-blue envelope. Vikrant recognized the logo of the Norwich Hospital, Norfolk, England, where Aryan was born. In a wave of nostalgia, he opened the envelope. He recognized the *laissez-passer*—the infant travel document given by the Indian embassy—and put away the various other reports, which he knew or cared nothing about.

As he put them back, he noticed a rusted gem clip on the edge. He turned it over to see a note. He recognized the handwriting from over twenty years ago.

Forgive me for being a coward.

Do what you consider right: bring him up or give him away. I will understand your decision as I hope you will mine.

Don't forget your promise. Whatever happens, it must never come out, or it will shame the whole family.

God take care of you both.

Vish

Vikrant's eyes reddened. *Gurleen, you whore. And Vish, you ungrateful swine. No wonder Aryan doesn't look like me. I wasn't wrong!*

Raina had finished reading the old will and interrupted Vikrant's thoughts.

'Sir, what would you like me to do?'

'Put all these papers back. Except the will.'

Avik Davar

Raina put the envelope back inside the blue box and placed the will on the bed. 'You have willed everything to your wife. What would you like to change?'

Vikrant dismissed him saying, 'Everything, Raina, everything.'

Vikrant's doubts multiplied since the chance discovery. He was constantly reminded of a stray remark Gurleen had made some months earlier. 'Doesn't Aryan look exactly like Vish?'

That remark had remained buried deep inside his subconscious, until the sighting of Vish's note. Vikrant now became painfully aware of what everyone else had always noted but had never dared mention. That Aryan was a spitting image of Vish.

To confirm his fears, Vikrant burrowed into the old family albums. The first random photo that he turned to blew his breath away. He found himself staring at a photo of Aryan with his arm over a young Vikrant's shoulder. Except it wasn't Aryan, it was Visham.

At nineteen, Aryan was seven inches taller than Vikrant and the same height as Vish. Nothing unusual about that. But there were other signs that couldn't be brushed aside. Vikrant was tone deaf; Aryan, like Vish, had a pitch-perfect, baritone voice. Vikrant had no sense of rhythm; Aryan, like Vish, was a graceful dancer and never missed a step. But even these distinctions were not recognizable unless Aryan sang or danced.

The immediate and unmistakable difference was that both Aryan and Vish had shining deep blue eyes with a grey ring around the pupils—the undeniable Rambal family trademark that Lala and Chattar Singh had, but somehow had not found its way into Vikrant's features. Vikrant had dull-brown eyes. Most people didn't know of the amazing similarities, as they had not seen Vish. But Gurleen had to have known it all. It could mean only one thing. *Bitch!*

~

One day, Vikrant spoke of his torment to Gurleen. 'Leena, I want

Aryan to take a DNA test.'

She was defiant. 'To prove my loyalty?'

'Why not?'

'Vikki, you're the one that has cheated time and again and even have AIDS to show for it. Now, hear this loud and clear, I'm not going to let you humiliate Aryan.'

He was furious. 'I can cut you off from my will, you whore!'

'Don't threaten me. I grew up in an orphanage, and I can fend for myself.'

'Then I'll have Aryan tested, you bitch!'

'He will walk out of the house if you even hint about it.'

Her persistent refusal convinced Vikrant he was right. But he was powerless. Had he been in good health, he would have forcibly taken Aryan's samples. Even bloody Inder had refused to help him, saying it was unethical. But Vikrant felt Inder was only settling an old score.

For the first time in his life, Vikrant missed Visham. Had he been around, Vikrant would have confronted him. Unfortunately, no one had a clue where he was or whether he was even alive. Vish had simply disappeared in England, days after Aryan was born.

Unable to find a settling answer, Vikrant often mumbled in his sleep. *I have beeι paid back in my own coin. It is poetic justice that I suffer just as the nen in those twenty homes raising my wild seeds.*

~

One afternoon, Aryan was surprised to find a 'confidential' note. He was taken aback by its frankness.

Aryan
You must be surprised to get this note even though we share the same roof.

It is unfortunate that I constantly think I may not be your father. That doubt tormented me since you were a toddler; you would push me away unless I brought you a chocolate. Since then, I have bribed you with gifts and rewards and deluded myself of your love.

I believe now that I am not your father, even though Gurleen insists as convincingly as ever that you are my child. I believe that your mother brought you from the seed of someone befitting your beauty—my cousin Visham—who disappeared from our lives some days after your birth. See the photo and you will know why.

I would like to be proved wrong, and you alone can set my doubt at rest. In the name of everything I have given you in life, I ask you this— please agree to a DNA test that Inder will organize.

It is unfortunate that I ask you this shameful task, but I think you will understand. And being the man I expect you to be, I trust you to not talk about this to Gurleen.

Vikrant

Aryan was shell-shocked. However, as he looked at the photograph attached to the note, he saw why Vikrant felt that way. The man in the photo was, every follicle, every cell, Aryan. But the real reason why Aryan believed Vikrant was Razia Haroon, the Rambals' long-serving public relations advisor.

Razia was a rising star in India's public relations business. Rambal was a big account for her fast-growing career. She was married to a UN official who had international postings in strange places she had no desire to go to. They had no children, which made it easier for her to indulge in her own pursuits that were usually male, young, rich and powerful. Aryan ticked all the boxes and had been on her radar ever since she first met him.

One afternoon, during the heady high-adrenaline days of the PIL season, Razia had dropped in. Aryan was alone in his room, nursing a headache. She had stayed over to comfort him and had ended up staying a lot longer. After that, they met often, and spent days and even slept together during outstation trips. It was convenient that

Razia's husband was posted somewhere in the Pacific Ocean, with a thirteen-hour time difference and lousy Internet.

One afternoon, Aryan had dropped in and found her crying. Her husband had called from Brisbane airport. There had been a military coup in the Solomon Islands, and he was coming back. He would arrive in Delhi the next morning.

'You should be happy,' Aryan said.

'You won't understand, Aryan.'

'I would if you told me.'

'He's getting posted to New York. I'll have to go with him this time.'

'Got to go means got to go.' He held her close and comforted her stroking her hair and face.

'I've gotten used to you. So much that...'

'That...?'

'I can't bear the thought of...you've been with me all this while. I wonder how I will...when he...'

'Oh, that way?'

'You men, you just cannot understand.'

Aryan remained silent, not wanting to concede anything. As they were in her most voracious episode, she got frenetic and pleaded. 'I want to have your baby.'

'What? Are you sure? Honestly, I don't know what to say.'

'I promise you'll have no responsibility.'

Aryan gave in to everything she asked that day. Later, resting his head on her belly, Aryan felt possessive enough to ask, 'What if...? How will you know whose...?'

She smiled for the first time that day. 'Jealous? Relax, my little koel.'

'Koel? What did I miss?'

'The beautiful koel always lays her egg in the ugly crow's nest. She doesn't take on the pain of hatching and feeding and focuses on singing beautiful songs instead. When the eggs hatch and the young koel comes out, the poor crow dotes more on the beautiful one that isn't her own. Eventually, when it is strong enough to fly, the koel leaves the crow and joins its real mother.'

And then, the Peters controversy had erupted, and Vikrant had sacked her. She never contacted him again and Aryan often wondered whether Razia became pregnant and whether she gave birth to his child or not.

All that replayed before Aryan as he read the letter. As he folded it, Aryan's only thought was: *How many times I must have asked people in sheer arrogance: Know who my father is? And now this.*

~

Arvind Nigam had been Vikrant's banker for over twenty years. Whenever Arvind moved, the Rambal account moved with him faithfully, from a small private bank to a nationalized bank and then to one of the largest foreign banks in India.

At Global Bank, Rambal's Platinum Account had come in for a review and serious downgrade. Arvind noted with regret that the enormous tax claims and penalties had decimated the Rambal net worth, from over one thousand crore rupees to less than twenty crores. The sale of the PIL franchise and the petrol pumps had dried up all cash flows.

Based on current earning capacity, the best Arvind had managed was an overdraft limit of one million dollars against the security of Rambal Acres. It was paltry by the Rambal standards. And one-third of it was set aside for a stem cell regeneration experiment at John Hopkins Hospital, Maryland in the US.

Soon, they had readied the paperwork. Vikrant went over the details one last time.

'Arvind, I hope you've shown this to my lawyer Raina.'

'Yes, indeed. He's cleared it. Let's go over any specific points you may want to confirm.'

Vikrant began listing his points. 'One, Gurleen and Aryan are both eligible to use the overdraft.'

'Yes. Mrs Rambal will be the primary recipient; your son will be a co-recipient.'

'Two, they can withdraw up to a total of ₹3.5 crore, any time during the next six months.'

'Right. They can draw the entire limit in one go, or as and when they want. They will have to pay interest monthly.'

'Three, she can't sell the estate before repaying the loan in full.'

'Surely not. The estate will be pledged to the bank. No one can sell or buy it without our release letter.'

Vikrant then laid down the key question. 'What if she were unable to repay?'

Arvind was pat with the reply. 'Then the bank would have the right to cancel the loan and take over the premises.'

'How would you do that?'

'We'll get a court order, then seal the premises.'

It was time for the next big question. 'What if I die and the property must pass on to her or to Aryan?'

'As inheritors, they must undertake to honour your commitments. If they don't, we shall proceed for recovery.'

It was now time for the most important one. 'What if there is ever a dispute on their ownership?'

The banker smiled. 'Sir, you're brooding too much.'

Vikrant remained nonchalant. 'Just in case.'

'If the bank sees any uncertainty, we shall ask for additional security. If it is not issued, we will revoke the loan immediately and demand full repayment.'

'Arvind, suppose she leaves town?'

'We take two signed blank cheques upfront. They are reserved for extreme circumstances like the one you mention.'

Avik Davar

'But if she doesn't have money, the cheques will bounce!'

'Yes, that will invoke a jail sentence. Section 138.'

'Are you sure?'

'One hundred per cent. We slammed two people last week. One is a film star. The other, a former cricketer.'

Vikrant licked his lips and rubbed his ears. 'May that day… never…come.'

'So, is it all clear now, sir?'

'Where do I sign?'

After the papers were safely in the banker's hands, he said, 'You don't worry, sir. Madam won't have any problem. I am always at your service.'

'Thanks.'

'Sir, when can I collect my two per cent service fee?'

When Arvind had left, Vikrant thought over everything once again. It was perfect. *Gurleen, you bitch, I have you in a vice-like grip now. Whore!*

~

Dr Inder Koeli was leaving India for good. He had got permanent residency in Australia and had begun visiting his patients to refer them to other doctors or to simply bid goodbye. Each time he had visited the Rambal house, Vikrant had made a single request, and each time Inder had turned it down, until only a fortnight remained before Inder's departure. This time Inder was reluctant, as though he was battling something within. Eventually, he relented.

'Vikki, let me make this clear. I will never test Gurleen, because I have immense respect for her. But as a parting gesture, I can test Aryan's DNA samples against yours. On one condition.'

'What is that?'

'I will show you the result but I shall keep the test report with myself.'

'Why, Inder?'

'So that you know the truth but can never prove it. That's your punishment for all the hurt you caused me.'

Vikrant remained silent for a while and then yielded.

'Fine. Can you certify that my mental health is sound? I need it for my will.'

Inder patted his old friend on the shoulder and left, leaving Vikrant to deal with a new challenge.

Vikrant was upset with Inder's condition. He had to have the test result in his possession. As he mulled over it, an idea began to form in his mind. Yes, it could work.

That evening, he summoned Raina for a new task. Heeding his master's voice, Raina arrived with a technician dressed in overalls with a blue 'PTI' logo stamped across. As the technician drew samples, Vikrant repeated his instructions. 'Raina, you'll need this to execute the will, but keep the results with you.'

Raina nodded, as he toyed with the printed envelope, which had the same blue logo as the technician's overalls. PTI. Below it was the expanded form: Paternity Testing Institute.

Aryan spent some time with his non-father each day, tolerating the repulsive odour without much fuss. Sitting at the foot of the bed, he even read out aloud news highlights and stock prices of few shares and commodities that still interested Vikrant.

One day, Aryan was basking in the benign winter sun in the lawns, when he saw Inder saunter across.

'Hello, young man!' Inder wore latex gloves and took out a stick out of a sterile pouch and handed it to Aryan. 'I need your buccal sample.'

'What?'

'Put this spatula inside your mouth and scrape the inner cheek skin gently a few times. That is the buccal sample.'

It was all over in fifteen seconds. Inder put the stick back into the sterile pouch and sealed it.

Some days later, Aryan stirred out of bed hearing a wail and rushed downstairs. Vikrant was crying uncontrollably.

From the window, he saw Inder driving out through the gate. 'What happened? Why was Inder uncle here?'

Vikrant made a feeble effort to pull him close to his chest and continued wailing. Soon, his breath became long and arrested, and ceased, his hand still clutching Aryan's shirt.

Midway to his clinic, Inder heard the news and rushed back. After checking the pulse, he pronounced Vikrant dead. He held Aryan's hand and said, 'Try to forgive him, my boy! He can be at peace only if forgiven.'

Aryan wiped a tear. 'Yes. I forgive him. I understand what he must have gone through.'

11

On the thirty-first day after Vikrant's death, they were assembled at the office of Crawshaw-Baxterley, solicitors, where Raina had been entrusted the task of disclosing the Will's contents before the inheritors. It was the strangest will anyone had known of.

The Last and Final Will of Vikrant Singh Rambal

I am preparing this final and irrevocable Will in full senses and in sound mental condition, as attested by my physician Dr Inder Koeli.

Upon my demise, I will that all my assets shall go to the safe custody of our family lawyer Rattan Lal Raina, for a period of six months. During this custodial period, Aryan and Gurleen shall prove beyond any doubt that Aryan is our legitimate child.

If it turns out that Aryan is my legitimate child, all my assets shall pass on to Gurleen. If during this period, Gurleen or my cousin Visham Singh Rambal acknowledges that Aryan is their illegitimate child, one-fourth of my assets shall go to Aryan; the lawyer shall dispose the remainder, and Gurleen shall inherit nothing. If the custodial period expires without either of the above actions taken, neither Aryan nor Gurleen shall be entitled to my assets. In such an event, all my estate shall remain under the custody of the lawyer, to be dealt as deemed fit, after releasing it from any charge or hypothecation or securitization with the Global Bank already signed by me.

During the custodial period, Gurleen and Aryan shall be entitled to a cumulative overdraft limit of ₹3.5 crore created with Global Bank, securitized against Rambal Acres. The liability of repayment shall be solely Gurleen's. In case of default in payment, the bank and the lawyer are hereby fully empowered to initiate proceedings to recover the dues, including by auctioning the property on the market. Any surplus after settling bank dues shall be retained by the lawyer and disposed as deemed fit.

This is my final and irrevocable Will.
Vikrant Singh Rambal.
Witnessed by
Rattan Lal Raina (Advocate)

After reading the contents, the reader handed the original and three copies of the will to the custodian, Rattan Lal Raina, along with an invoice. The feelings and reactions varied across the room.

Aryan was fuming.

Thanks, Mr Rambal. The stink that's left your cancerous body is now reeking in my life. I didn't know you were planning revenge while I foolishly thought we had made peace. You want me to bring out the truth. But you've put your trust in that slime, that sleaze Raina, of all people. He isn't going to give us even a rupee, even if Imma accepts I am illegitimate. So thanks for screwing up my future just because you and Imma couldn't hold back sleeping with everyone in town! We're one hell of a horny little family! But I give it to you; in your place I would have done the same, so RIP.

Gurleen was relieved.

Vikki, I'm happy that you came out in the open about Vish and me. In case you're wondering whether I'm sad, the truth is, I'm feeling nothing, as usual. Because, nothing is what our life together was all these years. And now that you've challenged me to prove my loyalty, let me give it back to you. I don't want even an asshole's hair from your estate. And I know Aryan will want it that way too. You slimy suspicious creep!

Raina was overwhelmed.

Sir, it is once in a lifetime that such an opportunity comes to a lawyer. And I shall make the best of it, Sir. It is my supreme duty to protect your estate as long as possible. For Aryan to stake a claim to your estate, there must be a record of your DNA test. But you have not disclosed in the Will that I have your test result with me. I interpret that to be your intention not to disclose its existence to anyone. I promise to guard and deal with your estate as my own as long as I live, as ordered by you. Have a great time in hell, which I suppose is your current abode, sir!

~

The Reddy vendetta continued even after Vikrant's death. With the tax claims and cases against Vikrant Rambal now un-actionable, all the tax authorities had were a few incomplete malls, offices and a fleet of old cars to auction. It wasn't enough to meet the arrears. Rambal Acres couldn't be attached, as it pre-existed Vikrant and others had rights to it too.

Desperate, the income tax department conducted a fresh round of raids on the Rambals and confiscated Gurleen's personal jewellery, not finding enough evidence of their purchase. The list had eighty-seven items. Gurleen trembled with rage when she saw the estimated value: ₹7.7 crores. *Bastards, it should be close to ₹30 crores. Rot in hell!* She cursed silently. Her heart wrung as they hauled all her favourite possessions away. All they had left behind, as per law, were the articles on her body—two solitaire earrings, the wedding ring, six gold bangles and an old locket.

As rumours spread that even friends of the Rambals could be raided, visitors, mail and even phone calls to Rambal Acres stopped altogether.

~

The tumultuous and humiliating events made Aryan desperate for a change, away from Delhi, away from the public eye. After toying with a few ideas, he settled on a meditation centre. Not just any centre, but the Osho Bhagwan Rajneesh Ashram in the city of Pune.

Upon arrival, a Norwegian volunteer checked him in and handed him his robes, maroon for the day and white for the evening meditation. It was a sharp contrast to his Vanderbilt jeans and Lindeberg nappa leather jacket.

'Mr Rambal, you've chosen the special twenty-one-day Osho Mystic Rose course. Here is the full introduction kit. Before we formally admit you, there is a small procedure left.'

Aryan, bored with the tacky welcome rituals at hotels, declined mechanically. 'Oh, I don't need a garland and welcome drink.'

'It is a blood test.' She pointed to another girl who was ready with a small sharp incisor and a swab of cotton smelling of spirit.

'I am O+,' Aryan said.

'We test only for HIV+.' The attendant blushed.

The colour drained from Aryan's face. *Damn, they're going to test me for AIDS,* he thought. He remained edgy and nearly swooned when the assistant came back saying, 'Need another sample.'

He panicked. 'I've got nothing. Let me go.'

'Don't worry, sir. I had placed the slide wrong side up. It might have become contaminated.'

It was an endless wait before she came back and announced, 'You made it, Mr Rambal. Welcome to Osho Meditation Centre.'

Aryan protested. 'No one tests guests for HIV, for god's sake!'

'The Master did not restrain us from physical pleasures. But we need to make sure ashram inmates do not get exposed to infectious diseases, for physical suffering will only impede their spiritual progress.'

A relieved Aryan was escorted to his large, luxurious two-room pad that could match any hotel suite. After unpacking, he sat down to consider how he was going to fare in this five-star hermitage for an entire month.

The Osho Auditorium housed in a black pyramid was a fascinating structure. Rumoured to be the world's biggest meditation hall, it could seat twenty thousand people. Inmates had to cross a small walkway over water to reach the auditorium. They had to be in white robes and white socks, which were compulsory for the evening meditation.

Aryan was inside the huge, air-conditioned hall fitted with modern psychedelic lighting. At the stroke of six, the speakers came to life with the Master's voice. 'That which cannot be said has to be experienced. This is a great experience of getting into the inner space…'

The first part was a high-energy dance celebration, ten minutes of wanton, selfless dancing, compulsory for everyone. It was a free-for-all, anything-goes kind of ritual, called 'A Dance with Totality'. Most were dancing alone, but there were also many couples clinging to each other, some swaying out of rhythm, oblivious to the tempo of the music. Several had their eyes closed, and a few had their hands raised above their heads, moving from side to side.

The bizarre ten-minute ordeal ended with three shouts 'Osho! Osho! Osho!' followed by ten minutes of sitting with their eyes closed, listening to the waft of soft music. The silence ended with three loud drumbeats, followed by the Master's address. It was a soft hypnotic voice, with a prolonged emphasis on the cadence of words ending with the 's', sounding like a snake's hiss. Blissss…missss… and so on.

'—Don't listen to me as you listen to a philosopher; listen to me as you listen to the birds. Listen to me as you listen to a waterfall. Listen to me as you listen to the winds blowing through the pines. Listen to me not through the discursive mind, but through the participant heart…

'—Put the mind aside. While listening to me, don't try to understand, just listen and be silent. Don't figure out whether what I am saying is true or not true. Don't be bothered with its truth or untruth… Listen to me as you listen to the birds singing or the wind passing through the pine trees or the sound of running water…'

When it was over, Aryan headed across to dinner at Zorba the

Buddha, the huge outdoor restaurant where inmates flocked after the evening meditation. He saw over three hundred people chatting away and thought it not much different from the Page 3 soirees in Delhi, minus the alcohol and the bling. As he settled down to his pasta, someone tapped him softly on his shoulder. He turned to see a blonde, green-eyed girl smiling at him.

'Hi, this is Inés.'

The next day, Aryan spotted Inés seated alone and joined her at lunch. 'How do you find the ashram, Aryan?'

'A bit bizarre. I wanted to experience being an ascetic. But this turned out to be as opulent as it could get.'

'I feel the same way. I wanted to experience a simple Indian life. Now, I'm not sure.'

By the time they finished lunch, he had already told her about the Rambal family's history, right up to the isolation he was grappling with. 'What about you?' he probed, after a minute's reflective silence. Before she could answer, she was called back to her 'volunteer' duty at the kitchen, in the dishwashing section.

Inés' stint at the dishwasher gave her enough time to think of the incredibly handsome Indian. His family history had been rather intriguing. But having known many men who exaggerated their wealth and performance, she also discounted their claims. After the last of the dishes had been dried, she changed into her robes and went to the Plaza Café. Picking up a tall coffee, she headed to the communications centre equipped with high speed Internet. Typing in the keyword 'Rambal' in the search box, Inés found out all that she needed to know.

A few days later, they were together at the tranquil Osho Teerth, a beautiful park built on the city's dump, which was all of twelve acres. She looked ravishing in her cream blouse and brown dungarees, her fingers brushing away her blonde hair that the gentle breeze kept blowing away over her face. Aryan took in her smooth skin, her perfect manicured fingers, and the side view of her left breast exposed through the sleeveless blouse as she swept away a strand of her hair that had remained stubbornly stuck on her lip.

She caressed his flawless face and touched his lips, stopping his speech midway. His heady aftershave made her linger. He instinctively felt her breasts. It seemed the best therapy to shake him out of his gloom.

'You need to make a clean break, Aryan. You'll never be your own man as long as you live surrounded by your father's glorious past and unfortunate end.'

'That's why I came to this place, to forget the past. I just want to get out of this country!'

'Why don't you go study somewhere?'

'Heck, no. That's not my deal. Business is what runs through my veins.'

'What kind of business?'

'Any kind that takes me out of here.'

Aryan watched her with curiosity as she took his iPad and typed in something into the Safari browser and handed it back. The screen showed 'Canadian Fit', Canada's fourth-largest fitness chain.

'What's that?'

'Our family business. We have been struggling with these outlets in Toronto, where there are more Indians than any other natives put together. Problem is, we just can't get the Indians interested enough in fitness. My mother wants to sell it or take in a partner.'

'Why not hand the franchises over to an Indian settled there?'

'It is a mindset problem. Most Indians there are into small-time businesses, barely pulling through. A lot of them aren't conversant in English. We need a solid, upper-class partner.'

'So what do you plan?'

'I'm looking for a business investor for the operations in Toronto. We can arrange a residence visa, which will be converted into citizenship in one or two years.'

'Hmmm…Have you been in touch with anyone yet?'

'I was hoping I would meet some people during this trip. Do you know someone who might be interested?'

'How much would one need to invest?'

'Less than a million dollars, I am sure.'

'That's about five crore something in Indian rupees. I could do it.'

'It's too small for you, Aryan!'

'Trust me, we aren't big anymore; all our money is stuck in disputes and tax claims. I want to get out of this country. If I do manage the million dollars, you think it can be worked out?'

'I think so.'

'It's a deal, then. I'll start working on it.'

Four hours later, she dropped him at the Lohegaon airport to catch a flight to Delhi. On returning to the Osho Resort, she sent an SMS to an international number.

Caught Big Fish.

The reply was instant.

I'll start the fire.

12

*g*urleen was shattered. *He wants to go. He is all I have in my lonely world. When I need him the most, he's thinking of going far away. Does he feel my pain?*

But then, Gurleen also understood why Aryan wanted to go away. She worried how he would cope with these tough times. He had grown up in luxury; he had never known what it meant to be deprived of the basic things of life. Would he adjust and survive the tough times ahead? He had never had to work hard or compete for anything. He had been born with the proverbial silver spoon. She knew she was responsible in a way, making things too easy for him, telling him that he deserved only the best in life.

He had already filled out the application form for an investor visa. But they had to deposit six hundred thousand dollars in a Canadian bank. *That's over three crores!* Some months before, it would have been a split second decision. But now it frightened her. Aryan told her it would remain safe and would be returned once he got his citizenship. Even so! The price was too steep—she was being forced to accept Vikrant's vindictive conditions and confess to an unfelt guilt.

'Imma, how are you ever going to prove that my DNA matches with dad—sorry—Vikrant Rambal's?'

'Look, I have known it since the time you were born.' *Why am I even tolerating this?*

Aryan pushed. 'But you've got no proof. What do we do when the deadline expires?'

She wanted him to face reality. 'We've got to start living life differently, that's all. You should be working harder for your own good.'

'But how are we going to raise money to send me to the US or Canada?'

'You could study further, maybe get a sa-cholarship, work hard and save up. That's how most Indians succeed abroad.'

'All my life, Da…sorry…Vikrant Rambal told me studies were only for ordinary folks. He always said we could hire the best brains. I'd like to go as an investor.'

'Where am I going to get that kind of money, Aryan?'

Aryan shifted his eyes away. 'The will…the will…does have an option to confess…'

She was aghast. *Is that what Aryan wants me to do?* She couldn't believe it. 'Aryan! Don't you have an ounce of self-respect?'

His face filled with hatred. 'Don't you have any? If you had, you would have done the test and thrust the results in his face when he was alive. Didn't you want to prove him wrong? Or wasn't he?'

Why haven't I scratched his face for saying that? 'You won't understand.'

'Let's face it. Even if I were his son, we can never prove it any more. There's no way I can get his DNA report from hell. Take the practical option. At least, I'll get my freedom from this rotten country!'

Whack! The sound reverberated through the drawing room. She had never slapped him before.

'Do you want me to stoop that low to gather Vikki's crumbs? Instead of fighting for my honour, you want to abandon me and find your own easy life?' She hated herself as much as her dead husband.

'Then go gift it all to that slimeball lawyer! Be practical, Imma. I will at least get a part of what ought to be mine, unless you have something to…'

'Do you mean "hide"? You ungrateful….' She stopped, disgusted.

He pushed again. 'Why else would you be so stubborn? Well, I don't care. At least take the loan, Imma.'

He has hurt me so much he should have killed me instead. She gave up, her loss much more than the money he was asking her. 'So you want me to borrow from the bank?'

'That would be the fair thing to do. After all, I am in this mess because of you and dad—why do I keep saying dad!—Mr Vikrant Rambal.'

'I still can't believe you said that. I wish you weren't…'

'Weren't your son! Come on! Say it! Just like he disowned me conveniently.'

'You have really hurt me today.'

'That's life. You hurt him, he hurt me and now I hurt you,' Aryan stormed out without looking back to see how crushed his mother was.

The life drained out of Gurleen. She couldn't bear it any more. *Aryan believes that I… Hai Rabba!*

Was he the little bundle of happiness she had held in her arms in England?

I can feel that first tender little tug at my finger, the lips curving, the silent crying and then, eventual relief on being put to my breast. It's always had a hypnotic effect on me and made me so powerless I could never challenge him. He could never hurt me and he can never be wrong, even when he called my name for the first time. Imma. Not Amma, not Mama, not Mummy, but Imma.

Collecting herself, Gurleen reconciled with the reality. She wouldn't let him carry this feeling about her. Also, she wouldn't let him down. It wasn't his fault.

She went to his room. He was still seething.

'Aryan, it's not your fault. Why should you suffer for whatever went wrong between your father and me? Come, let's work things out.'

'Are you going to do it, Imma?'

'Yes, baby. But not by confessing to anything. I'm going to use the overdraft facility.'

He gave her a hug that almost wasn't one. It was restrained, and she felt it. Though she smiled, she felt something die in her!

~

The bank had completed all the intimidating paperwork. Gurleen visited the bank and was given the same welcome as in their Platinum Days. It was the special express elevator, and a valet waiting to take her to the VIP lounge where Arvind was waiting with his team. Over excellent Assam Royal Flush tea—her favourite, Arvind explained it all in very simple terms.

'We've given you a loan of three and a half crores. After deducting the processing fee, you'll net ₹3.45 crores. We use three crores for the Canada deposit. The remaining forty-five lakhs will be enough to take care of thirteen months of interest payments. Your son should have got his immigration by then. Then, we break the deposit and retire the loan. Simple.'

'Is that all, Arvind?'

'Yes, Mrs Rambal, that is all.'

'I worried about it no end. And what if his visa gets delayed?'

'We can find you a suitable tenant for the first floor of the house. Maybe a foreign company. That will fetch you enough rent to pay the monthly interest. Simple.'

It did sound rather simple and easy. *I guess I will trust him, as long as I get to see the money.* But there was something else that nagged Gurleen. The tax department.

'Arvind, will the taxmen get to know of the rent? Will they take it all away?'

He thought for a while and then answered with finality. 'Well, they can't do anything if the bank gets money directly from someone else into the loan account.'

Fully assured, Gurleen signed a mound of papers without understanding the jargon. She also signed two undated blank cheques that every borrower had to sign when taking out any kind of loan.

Returning home, she felt happy and proud that she had lived up to Aryan's expectations without compromising on her honour and without bowing to Vikki's perverted conditions. She had taken upon herself the entire liability of repaying the loan. It bothered her though that the bank had made Aryan a co-applicant in the loan. *Why? In case I die before paying up? I won't.*

~

It was time to say goodbye. Aryan's bags were on the trolley. The traffic police was pushing them to hurry and move away. She couldn't even hug him one last time, or pat his cheek or wipe away a streaking tear from her eyes and tell him, 'Don't leave me, I don't know what to do.' Instead, all she said was, 'Don't worry about me. I'm going to take good care of myself. You just focus on your job, settle down quick, and don't bother about money…Listen, eat on time. And, lazy boy, wash your clothes regularly. You won't be having servants or me around to *sa-niff* them out from your cupboard.'

Soon, he was gone, without once turning back to look at her from the departure gate. She pressed her cheeks against the glass and strained to catch a glimpse of Aryan at the check-in section in the hope he would turn and wave one last time and leave behind another lifelong memory.

She saw him smile at the officer, collect his boarding pass and head straight on, beyond the Longchamps kiosk. He was then past the Rolex window, and the big info screen cut his head off from her view. He didn't turn to look at her even once. She wanted to scream his name out loud! His cellphone! She speed-dialled 1 and got a 'busy' tone. Minutes later, she was still trying impatiently to reach him till she heard the operator's message: 'The Vodafone number you're trying is beyond network area. Please try later.' She dialled again. And again. And again. Desperate and furious, she texted 'Pl cl bk.'

She gave up around midnight, by when she imagined him already aboard, staring at a pretty Air Canada stewardess demonstrating the safety procedures before take-off. *Couldn't he have called me just once? Does he even care how I feel? All alone in the world, with nothing to look forward to, no one to look up to, no one to wait upon, no one to share my affection with!*

She woke up to find the lights still on. The wall clock showed 2.40 a.m. She could catch him in transit at Frankfurt in a few hours and planned to give him a real dressing down. She double-locked the front door and got ready to change and settle into bed. She usually fell asleep within minutes of lying down, but tonight sleep eluded her. She saw dark shadows everywhere, heard Vikki's ranting, his swearing and even smelt his foul smell. Then, she shifted into Aryan's bedroom. It felt a lot better, she sensed his smell, his clutter; it helped. She left the lights on, and knew she would leave them on all night, every night until Aryan returned home.

13

*A*ryan arrived in Toronto and met the immigration advisor to complete the formalities. Chase Manhattan Bank had confirmed the deposit and issued a 'Proof of Funds' certificate, the most important document for the investor visa. The deposit would remain locked-in for a minimum of one year after the visa had been granted. Of course, it could be withdrawn prematurely, with the simultaneous cancellation of the visa application.

After completing the paperwork over the next two days, Aryan took off for Denver, Colorado, USA, armed with an L1—a short term US business visa, sponsored by Denver Fitness Centre, an arm of the Canadian Fit Company, all because of a last-minute change of plans.

A few days before Aryan's departure, Inés had called with rather disturbing news. 'I'm afraid there's been a change of plans, a small detour, Aryan. The Toronto gym has been sold off,' Inés had said.

Aryan was fidgety. 'That's bad news. What do we do? I'm almost ready to leave.'

Inés had set him at ease. 'Relax. We have other centres. We could show you as an overseas employee of Canadian Fit, stationed in the US for the time being. Is that okay with you?'

'How long before I can return to Canada?'

'One year at the most. You'll like it in Colorado.'

'Colorado, USA?'

'Yes. My stepsister, Veronique, will take good care of you in Denver.'

'I don't get it. What's she got to do with it?'

'She runs our Denver Fitness Centre. You could even stay with her, Aryan.'

Desperate to move out of India and unwilling to return the bank deposit, Aryan had agreed, and had hidden the news from Gurleen. One year would pass soon, with Inés's sister, Veronique. The name reminded him of the black-haired, tight-assed, rich girl in Archie comics.

~

An hour after getting out of Denver International Airport, Aryan pressed the doorbell outside Suite 100X, City Highs on Champa Street, Denver. The excitement of spending a year with Veronique escalated when he heard the sweet voice on the door phone.

'Step right in, baby.'

Veronique sounded very promising, if the voice was anything to go by. Archie comics' best images flicked past Aryan's mind as the electric door lock clicked. The door opened a crack and he heard the beautiful voice again.

'Hiya, you've got to be my Indian candy!'

Aryan stepped inside and reeled in horror and revulsion. Six-feet three inches tall and weighing over one hundred and fifty kilos, Inés's half-sister Veronique Veques was a black human mountain.

~

'We have good news, Mrs Rambal. Your problem is solved.' Arvind was his usual chirpy self. Only, he had brought the slimy Raina along. That one, Gurleen had never felt good about. She shook hands with him and felt as though a slimy leech was wriggling in her palm. Maybe she was wrong, or paranoid because of the crude rings on his fingers, the red paste on his forehead and those beads on his wrist—wondering what tantric hocus-pocus he was into. She didn't understand what Vikki had liked about him; to her, he was plain sinister.

'Good news, Arvind?' she asked, warily.

'Raina's got a nice offer for the first floor.'

Her stomach churned.

Raina filled in the details. 'A three-year lease, a monthly rent of three and a half lakh rupees and fifteen lakhs as upfront deposit. You can easily service the loan!'

'That *is* good news.' She felt a tinge of shame about the impression she harboured of the man. Then her brow creased. 'No problem with the taxmen?'

Arvind shook his head repeatedly. 'The payments will come straight to the bank; it won't go through your account.'

Gurleen then remembered the unspent loan money lying in the bank. 'What about the forty-five lakhs we set aside for interest payments? Isn't that still in the bank account?'

Raina butted in. 'Madam, it is best that you withdraw it soon, in cash.'

'And where would I keep the money, Mr Raina?'

'In a bank locker, somewhere else.'

She could use their old locker at the Christian Bank, which she hardly used.

Arvind chipped in. 'There's one thing, though. The tenants want to renovate the place.'

Gurleen was defensive. 'Why, it is quite nice and beautiful as it is. I don't want anyone making any alterations in my house.'

'Mrs Rambal, foreigners have their own taste.'

'Arvind, it will be a mess with all the dust and noise. And it's not going to be cheap.'

Raina spoke again. 'I've told them you shouldn't be bothered with these problems. They have agreed to bear all the renovation costs.'

Something felt wrong but she couldn't put her finger on it. But then, Raina had brought this timely tenant. *Raina doesn't seem to be too much of a rogue, after all.* 'Hmm, how thoughtful of you!'

'In fact, Mrs Rambal,' Raina went on, 'I've bargained with them to pay for a return ticket to the US, so you can spend three months with your son while they renovate here!'

Her eyes widened and her heart beat loudly. She wanted to jump and scream in joy! Then, she felt that uneasy squirming in her gut again.

Raina continued ranting. 'I am only worried about the lease period. I don't think you should accept a term of more than eleven months. Renew the lease, if required.'

Gurleen agreed. 'I would like to cancel the lease the day I've repaid the loan. Can you put that in a clause?'

'No problem at all. We'll put in a two-month notice period.'

'Oh, I never asked, who is the tenant?'

Raina brushed it off. 'An NRI lawyer. Close family. Consider it as though I were your tenant.'

'That's fine; I won't have a problem with you, Mr Raina.' *Do I mean it, or am I just being polite?* She wasn't sure.

He swept away her doubt. 'Unfortunately, Mrs Rambal, I can never be your tenant; it would be a conflict of interest, for I am the custodian of Mr Rambal's... Sorry to remind...'

She smiled. 'No, Mr Raina, you've been very considerate.'

'Madam, I served your husband loyally. And I will serve you even more loyally.'

Gurleen was overcome with sentiment. 'Both of you are God-sent today.'

Raina wrapped it all up. 'I shall draw the papers and complete everything except the lease period, which I will renegotiate with the tenant. We can sign it the day you board the flight. I'll also arrange for your tickets.'

'I haven't travelled since Vikki's illness. And I think my passport's expired.'

'Don't worry, Mrs Rambal. I'll get a new passport made in a

week. What about your visa?'

'I think my US visa might still be valid. Thank you, Raina, for all that good news.'

She couldn't believe she was going to America to be with Aryan for three months! *Wait until I tell him! Let me call him right away!*

~

Aryan woke up with a jolt. His phone was ringing. *God, Imma, she's crazy, calling me at this hour,* he cursed and turned on the bedlight switch. The light fell on Veronique's face. Shifting her nude mass away, she kicked Aryan off the bed and covered her face with a sheet.

'Fuckin' Indians! Pu'them bloody lights out and getoutahere. When you done talking to that broad, don't ya come back in here, sleep on the fuckin' couch.'

Aryan was sore with Inés for moving him out of Canada. She hardly spoke to him now and was always travelling. However, his biggest problem was being with Veronique, who not only disgusted him but also scared him.

It had been an endless humiliation for Aryan since arriving in Denver. Fully aware of the power she held over him as his sponsor, Veronique used the foulest language, made him do all the chores and often kicked him without a warning. Worse, she forced him to make love to her stinking, hairy body and taunted his manhood by calling him a 'Chillie Willie'. The fact was, nothing seemed to get Veronique going. It made him try harder, only to be mocked later. And she blamed it all on him and men in general.

He had the strength to hit back but knew that would be the end of his dream. He had no option but to stay put in Denver and put up with this Amazon.

Amidst all this, there was the irritation of Imma's untimely phone calls. What could he tell her? She was already upset about not being told about Denver.

Cursing his fate as he adjusted his shorts, he stumbled out into the living room and whispered softly, 'Imma, it's three in the night here. What's so important that you couldn't wait?'

He heard her almost shout. 'Aryan, you won't believe it. I'm coming to see you. I've got a new passport.'

'What? How come? When?' Clouds formed in his head.

He heard her say, 'I land at 4 p.m. tomorrow. Aren't you happy?'

He put the phone on his lap without disconnecting. He heard her shout 'Hello! Hello!' for long until the call disconnected. He kept looking at the huge sleeping form that would raise a storm over the news of a visitor. *Damn all the women in my life,* he cursed as he readied for the nightmare that awaited him the next day.

~

They were at the airport. Kartaar Singh, the familiar taxi driver from the stand a kilometre away from Rambal Acres had removed her check-in bags and had gone to grab a trolley. Gurleen had taken out five hundred rupees to pay him.

A burgundy Mercedes van behind them started to honk like mad and inched forward, almost knocking over her bags.

'Hey, wait! My bags!' she screamed and dashed over just in time to save them from getting crushed by the imposing beast. Meanwhile, Kartaar had brought a rickety trolley whose front wheel was stuck. The trolley kept veering to the left, and he had trouble wedging it between his taxi and the Mercedes. The trolley veered again and nicked the Mercedes's front fender.

A tall, burly driver charged out of the Mercedes hurling a volley of curse words and hit Kartaar on his nose. His nose bleeding, Kartaar hit the other chap on the jaw and kicked hard at his ankle. A crowd gathered to witness a free round of gruesome entertainment. Even the rotund security guard at the entrance gate left his seat to catch the goings-on.

Gurleen was too scared to call out to Kartaar; he was busy winning back his Sikh honour. She quietly pulled her bags out of the war zone, put the bags on a trolley and hobbled across. The guard, back at his post after passenger protests, looked at her two passports and e-ticket and allowed her inside the terminal.

Inside, a sweet young porter offered to take her trolley.

'Air India 127?' He brought her to rows H–K and the Economy line. *What?* It hadn't occurred to her to check the ticket. But then, they had always flown First or Business Class. There was a serpentine queue of trolleys ahead of her. Eventually, a plump woman in a sari checked her passport and the US visa on the older passport once more and handed her an immigration form.

Gurleen got her boarding pass, she had been allotted seat 48F, and headed to immigration, where she was beckoned by a lady who ignored Gurleen's beaming smile and appeared more interested in her diamond ring.

'Is it real?'

Gurleen became defensive. 'Why do you ask?'

'If it's expensive, better to declare it at customs,' the woman clarified.

'Oh no, it's just twenty thousand,' Gurleen tried to lie as professionally as she could.

The woman took her passport and boarding pass and disappeared inside the room behind, and soon returned with a man who appeared to be her senior.

'Have you travelled abroad before?'

Gurleen nodded with pride. 'Of course. To many countries.'

'You don't have the ECNR stamp.'

She had no clue what he was talking about. She tried to be as calm as she could, but her throat was dry and her voice quivered. 'Sorry, what ECNR?'

'It means "Emigration Clearance Not Required". Without an

ECNR stamp on your passport, you must take permission every time you leave the country.'

'But no one's ever asked me that before. This is a new passport; my old one expired. This was done by an agent, officer. Maybe he made a mistake.'

'Agents don't bother to check these things.'

'What do I do now, sir?' She was shivering even though sweat formed over her brow and her heart banged against her rib-cage.

'Sorry, you can't travel today, Madam. Unless you convince the boss inside.'

Can't travel today, Madam. Dizziness took over and she could feel her body fall across the counter.

Gurleen awoke and looked around. She was past the immigration rows, inside the chief officer's cabin. Two immigration officers in grey uniforms stood next to a woman who towered over them. Her paunch could pass off for a full blown, any-moment-delivery condition. It was 12.48 a.m., thirteen minutes past boarding time. Gurleen had no idea how long she would take to reach Gate 15A. But that was only if she got out of here.

The officer explained it in a way she understood. Her passport had an 'Emigration Clearance Required' stamp. It meant that she had to get an ECRS—Emigration Clearance Requirement Suspension—each time she left the country. The clearance, given by the passport office, took two days and usually a thousand rupees to grease palms.

'Please let me go, I am visiting my son in America. My flight is boarding!' She begged the officer, pulling at his shirt.

There was a silence, after which the hippo spoke. 'Come with me.'

Gurleen was taken inside the empty cubicle next door. The lady locked the door and said, 'Twenty thousand, and you can go!'

Her sobs had no impact on the hardened professional who reeked of alcohol as she came closer and repeated, 'Twenty thousand.' This was all business.

Gurleen couldn't bear it any longer. 'How can you do this to another woman?'

Gurleen emptied her bag and handed over the ten thousand rupees cash in there. Disappointed, the blimp walked away to consult with her conspirators.

You aren't going to find it, Fatso! I've put seven hundred US dollars and fifty thousand rupees cash inside my check-in baggage.

Meanwhile, Gurleen saw a stewardess walk past, shouting 'Last and final call for AI-127. Passengers please head now to gate 15 A.' She dashed out to meet the stewardess, but froze, remembering that her boarding pass and passport were still with Fatso, who had followed her.

Fatso looked Gurleen in the eye and then at her fingers, twice, as if to give a hint. Her eyes darted again to the solitaire on Gurleen's ring finger.

It was an instant decision. Gurleen took the five-carat ring off and thrust it in Fatso's thick palm and yanked her passports and boarding pass. Aryan was worth more than all the solitaires in the world. *And so much for lying, Leena, serves you right.*

They were paging her already. 'Gurleen Rambal, passenger on AI-127, please report at Gate 15A, or your bags will be offloaded.'

'Here, here!' Gurleen shouted and waved.

The stewardess saw Gurleen and came running towards them. *Whew!* Gurleen turned back one last time and spat at Fatso's face with force.

Fatso didn't react. She wiped the spittle, twirled the ring that was now on her little finger, and smiled. 'Happy journey!'

The stewardess shouted at Gurleen, 'Come on, quick!'

Gurleen hobbled like a bird flapping on one wing and kept talking to the stewardess all the way to the gate. 'I'm going to get back in shape and fighting fit. After all, my son's becoming a fitness entrepreneur.'

She squeezed into 48F, between a young Marwari man and a Tamilian lady, and checked her passport one last time before putting it into her handbag.

She tucked her handbag in the overhead compartment and sank into her seat. The video screens in front came alive. Soon, her Marwari neighbour got engrossed in a Bollywood movie that had Amitabh Bachchan gyrating with a bottle of whiskey and mocking Rekha. On the other side, the Tamilian was laughing away as Rajnikant struggled with a cobra running down his neck.

Then she remembered that Raina had called her at the airport. She had already signed the lease deed and initialled next to the blank space for the lease period. Raina was to negotiate and insert, 'eleven months, renewable twice'. He had called when she was checking in; to say that it would take another week as the tenant was travelling. Gurleen still had a copy of the lease agreement in her bag, with the lease term left blank.

When the air hostess came and refilled Gurleen's drink, the screen in front showed the plane's icon blinking above Afghanistan.

14

$\mathcal{T}$wenty-four hours later, she stood tired and excited outside Concourse A at Denver International Airport, dying to meet Aryan. She would wipe out the past, all the old memories, and old hurts. *Why isn't he here?* She had been waiting close to an hour and was getting nervous. Her cellphone still showed no signal. She ambled into the deserted parking lot when an Indian/Pakistani accosted her.

'Assalaam walekum. Madam is from India or Pakistan?'

'India.'

'I see you been waiting long. My name is Aftab. Licensed taxi driver.'

'Aftab ji, I have been waiting for my son. I don't know if he is on his way here. I am unable to call him. My cellphone doesn't work here.'

'No problem, give me his number; I dial from my phone.'

After a few tries, he gave up. 'Switched off. Do you have address?'

She took out a sticky note. 'Here. City Highs. 17442, Champa Street, Suite 100X, Denver, CO 80202.'

'I drop you. Forty-five dollars. No extra. OK?'

'You seem like a good man. Will you see me safe into my son's apartment? It is my first time, you know.'

'Mata ji, I will take you right to the door.'

'Thanks. God bless you.'

During the ride, she kept trying Aryan's number from Aftab's phone, and found it switched off each time.

They arrived at Champa Street in less than an hour. Gurleen could see the City Highs neon sign atop a high rise. Aftab parked the taxi in the basement and convinced the Bangladeshi security guard to let them into the lift.

Minutes later, they stood outside Suite 100X. Aftab rang the bell. She could hear loud noises from inside. A major argument was on. Aftab pressed the doorbell a second time.

The door was opened by a huge woman to whom Aftab said, 'Hello, looking for Aryan Rambal from India, please!'

She turned and went back inside shouting, 'Willie, your Indian baggage has arrived.' Soon, Aryan appeared at the door.

'Aryan!' Gurleen screamed with joy.

There was no excitement on his face. It was as if he didn't believe she was there.

She thanked Aftab and gave him a fifty-dollar note. He put her bags near the door and left. 'Khuda Hafiz.'

'Khuda Hafiz, Aftab Bhai.' She sent him off, eager to go inside. But there was an unsettling feeling of alienation. She didn't even know who the woman was. But it wasn't the best time to ask, not yet.

~

Gurleen sat in the living room while the argument continued inside the bedroom. At length, Aryan stepped out. His ears were red. The bedroom door slammed shut again. Soon, loud snoring could be heard from the bedroom.

Assured by the rumble, Gurleen asked Aryan in the safety of Hindi. '*Kaali koun hai* (Who is the black one)?'

He told her everything.

She was devastated. 'You never told me any of this, Aryan!' she lashed out.

'I was supposed to be in Canada, not here. And now you've piled on. She's wild, naturally.'

'Is this how they treat investors?'

'Let's drop it now, Imma!'

'And our money? Is it safe?'

Aryan looked away. Gurleen pulled his shirt to get his attention. 'What?'

'It's temporarily being loaned for the gym business. Veronique's making me partner.'

She couldn't believe he was putting in his money with this amazon. It was her money, not his! She battled against herself to stay calm. *Leena, let's deal with it later. The boy's been under pressure, alone. We'll handle it somehow, together. But you need to settle in first.*

'Where do I put the bags, beta?' she asked, eyeing the two open doorways. One opened into a small bedroom with a nice view to the skyline. The other opened into a small store with a cot and a foot's width of space all around. Aryan put her bags in the bigger room. As Gurleen began unpacking, there was a loud rap on the door. It was Veronique.

'Hiya, nobody ain't sleepin' in ma Momma's bed, you kin park yer ass in the goddamn store. Gethat!'

Gurleen froze in shock. *Did she say what I think she said?*

Her eyes glowed even as her lips remained silent and she even forced a faint smile to hide the embarrassment. Aryan had crept up behind but hadn't spoken a word.

'Well, move it!' Veronique bellowed, her giant breasts heaved behind her cheap faux silk shirt and roadside shiny orange skirt.

Gurleen's clothes were on the bed. She began to put them back into the suitcase. Then she lost it. 'Listen lady, it may be your mother's room, but it's my son I've come to. He decides where I sleep.'

'Oh, yeah!' Veronique's face muscles twitched, and she turned to Aryan. 'Willie baby, whatcha gotcha saytya Momma here?'

Aryan remained as silent as a rabbit trapped between two lunging lionesses. Finally, he squeaked.

'Veron, please, let Mom be here, it's just a few weeks.'

'Tellyawhat, dickhead. Take em bags and take yer bags too and getha fuckoutahere the both of you!'

Aryan resigned to the reality. 'Imma, can we adjust a little?'

Gurleen was aghast. *Is this Aryan? How could he treat me this way?* Standing at the doorway of the store room, Gurleen figured out that the only way to get inside was to step right on the cot and crawl on her elbows like a combat soldier. *How could Aryan even accept this? And me, always the idiot, signing all kinds of personal liabilities to borrow three crores for him?*

'Of course. I don't want to cause you any trouble. Please let my bags remain here, there's no space inside the *sa-tore*.' Minutes after shutting herself in the windowless box she howled away into the thin pillow and hoped they wouldn't hear her. *Rabba, please hold these tears back.*

It was past midnight, but she was wide awake. Her body clock was still set to India. There was nothing to do. Her eyes spotted a pale novel lying on top of old newspapers. It was *Master of the Game* by Sidney Sheldon. Very soon, she was hooked to Kate Blackwell.

By morning, Kate Blackwell had taken over. Gurleen was all business at the breakfast table, ready with a coffee and toast, as Aryan and the amazon walked in from their room, eyes half-closed.

'Aryan, do you mind telling me what you've done with the deposit?' She loved being Kate.

'Imma, I've just woken up. Let's do this later.'

'Well, then. Let's discuss in an hour.' *Thank you, Kate Blackwell.*

Veronique looked at Gurleen with a new hatred. 'Hey, Mammy, what's botherinya? It's his money, ain't it? Whatch ya gottado with it?'

'Well Vero—whatever your name is, I'm speaking to my son. Keep out of it.'

Veronique was mad. 'It's ma damn gym he's puttin all that fuckin money inta, ye get that?' Then she looked at Aryan and shouted, 'Dickhead, have ye gone mute since the bitch walked in yestday?'

Aryan cooled her down and hissed at Gurleen. 'Imma, the money is going to be invested into their gym. And I'll get the investor visa against it.'

'That isn't what we'd agreed on. You were to keep it safe in a deposit and use the interest to repay our bank in India every month. This is not right, Aryan. Had I known, I'd never have let myself get tricked into this.'

'What shitya talkin woman? Who's trickin'ya? I gotchim a nice job downtown. Like he's gettin paid and he's gettin laid too!'

Gurleen turned her ire at Aryan. 'At least stop her from talking like this to me!'

Veronique worked up a fake laugh. 'He he he! Him stoppin' me! He dun have big enuf balls below that Indian dick to stop me! And he aint gonna be listenin tya anymore, because I been takin good care of him down there, like ya never did!'

Gurleen's blood boiled. She had never heard any woman speak like that, not even in the movies! And Aryan, he simply stood there like a zombie, powerless and incapacitated.

She tried to drill sense into his head. 'Can't you see, the money's going to disappear? You think she's doing all this out of love?'

Veronique teased her even more. 'Yeah Mammy, I love my Chilli Willie!' She kissed him and grabbed his c… Oh no! Aryan was squirming as Veronique lifted him and carried him inside the bedroom, and slammed the door shut.

As she sat on the sofa, Gurleen was repulsed by the sounds and realized that her son had blown away six hundred thousand dollars over a sex job.

~

Around noon, Gurleen got out of the apartment to clear her head. She was soon out on Champa Street, walking aimlessly. A few hundred paces later, she stopped, seeing a nice little signboard that read 'Little India' with an elegant little portrait of a village woman wearing a ghagra choli, resting near a well. The menu list included two of her favourites: mango lassi and lamb saag. It made Gurleen homesick. Tempted and famished, she stepped inside.

The interior was decorated tastefully, rich with framed pictures bearing vignettes of the Punjab, like the bhangra, the village women and a fort, among others. A nice silver statue of Krishna playing the flute adorned the most prominent corner. The place was empty, it seemed still early in the day for lunch. She sat at a quiet, corner table, close to the statue. Soon, a well-dressed elderly lady waddled past with an incense stick, placed it before the statue and offered a short prayer. When done, she looked at Gurleen with a charming smile.

'From India? Welcome to Little India!'

The affable lady turned out to be Mrs Malhotra, the matriarch of one of the two families that owned the restaurant. She had come to Denver thirty years ago, to begin a new life in a new country, like thousands of Indians. Little India had the most authentic Indian cuisine in all of Denver. So she said, and Gurleen agreed. It turned out that Mrs Malhotra also knew someone from the Rambals' extended family in Punjab.

By afternoon, Gurleen had told her just about everything about herself, including Veronique.

'I want to go back as soon as possible. I don't mind living in the rubbish even as they renovate the first floor!'

Bibi—that's what the staff addressed her—agreed. 'Respect is more important than comfort. Now tell your lawyer you're coming back.' She brought out her phone and pushed it towards Gurleen. 'Come on, do it now.'

Gurleen dialled Raina's number, not realizing that it was two in the morning in India. She heard him mumble amidst a yawn, '*Kaun hai*? Who the hell is it?'

'Sorry, Mr Raina, I didn't realize the time difference. But now that we're talking, I'd like you to know that I'm cutting short my trip. So, keep my ground floor as clean as possible. Hope I haven't upset your plans.'

'Mrs Rambal, you have already upset my plans,' she heard him say before disconnecting, and wondered how.

Bibi was smiling. 'Now you need a travel agent?'

It turned out Bibi's family ran a travel agency as well. She instructed her accountant to speak to them. While Gurleen sipped her delicious mango *lassi*, he arranged a reservation for the following Sunday. Only, it would cost twelve hundred dollars. That was because they had to buy a fresh, one-way ticket to India. Raina had bought a non-refundable low fare ticket with a fixed return date that was over three months away.

'I've got only seven hundred dollars on me,' Gurleen came clean. She didn't mention her international credit cards.

'*Ho jayega*, don't worry,' Bibi said.

'Can I get some part-time work for a few days?'

'You can't work without a proper work visa.'

'I understand. I just wanted to kill time.'

The lamb saag arrived and Gurleen kept looking at it. It looked, well, different.

'What can you do?' Bibi asked as Gurleen dug into the lamb. Her answer was ready. 'For a start, I could teach your boys how to make some great lamb saag.'

'What? You know that's our bestseller.'

'This lamb saag is pathetic. I can make your customers lick their fingers all the way home, if it's done my way.'

'Oh, really? Well then, let's find out!' Mrs Malhotra was piqued and summoned her star chef.

The portly Sri Lankan chef came over and stood brazenly before Gurleen. 'Tell us what's not working with the saag!' he thundered.

Gurleen was ready. 'I'll tell you everything, but first you tell me how you do it now.'

He rattled off a recipe she was sure had been mugged from a cookery book. 'Simple. Puree the garlic, ginger, chillies and onion, braise the lamb in olive oil, fry the spices in the same pan for a couple of minutes, add the onion purée and cook for two minutes. Add the lamb, tomatoes and spinach shreds. Cover and cook for forty-five minutes.'

She threw him off guard. 'That sounds like right out of a recipe book. Which one?'

'Jaffrey's!' His face reddened as he realized his faux pas.

Bibi was still unconvinced. The battle wasn't over yet. 'Let's hear how you do it, Leena.'

'Let me show, not tell.'

Over the next hour, Gurleen showed them some tricks. 'Never use frozen lamb, it's got to be fresh meat from the butchers.' She ordered half a kilo from a butcher close by. By the time it arrived, Gurleen had organized her ingredients.

'The lamb needs to be pierced with garlic pods to let the juice seep inside.' She put in a few cloves, slices of green chilli and crushed peppers, and mixed them well before tossing it into the frying pan. The spinach went in at the end.

'Hey, that's almost like what I said!' the chef protested, but stopped when he saw her reject the tomato. He was dazed when she asked him to bring her her secret ingredient: white rice wine, which would soak in all the juices and blend into the meat. After that, it was slow cooking.

Forty-five minutes later, when the lamb melted in the chef's mouth, he generously agreed that Gurleen had brought out a winner.

'Leena, you're our recipe advisor for one week, at fifty dollars an hour,' Mrs Malhotra announced, as she licked the saag off the plate.

'Thank you, Mrs Malhotra.'

'Call me Bibi. They all do.'

That afternoon, Little India's new lamb saag was served as a free sampler at every table. That evening, a new entry 'Leena's Lamb Saag' made it to the Little India's signature dish list. It was priced at fifty dollars. And Little India ran out of the dish in all four of its restaurants. Gurleen got a two-week consulting assignment with Bibi, to keep her busy until her return.

~

Gurleen walked back home around nine after a long Friday shift, thinking how soon two weeks had passed. She had not spoken to Aryan since the showdown. It was time to make up and move on. She consoled herself and readied for a truce. *You'll be leaving tomorrow night. Cheer up, Leena. Why not make them a nice hot Indian meal before they return? After all, you're a Little India signature dish creator now!*

Neither Aryan nor Veronique were in. The kitchen was a filthy mess and had a stink that almost made her puke. There was nothing fresh, only leftovers or frozen packages. Reluctantly, she took out the frozen chapatis and a can of pre-mixed chana daal. *Okay, let's do a nice, yummy daal tadka.*

She picked up a saucepan that still had dry grease and egg remains, cleaned it up, smelt it and cleaned it again. When it had dried over the flame, she put four spoons of corn oil and sprinkled chilli powder and cumin into it. The heady fumes rose, and the aroma filled the kitchen. Just as she was about to pour the daal into the pan, a loud alarm went off.

The sound was right out of a James Bond film. She froze with fear. Before she could even blink, the sprinklers turned on and the entire kitchen was wet and squelchy, with Gurleen right in the centre. Soon, water had filled the saucepan, the daal had splashed out, and the chapatis were soggy. Gurleen remained unmoved.

Within minutes the main door opened and Aryan raced into the kitchen.

'Imma, what are you doing in here?'

No comforting words. Instead he yells at me. 'I was just trying to cook something for you. How would I know chilli powder would set off a smoke alarm?'

Veronique came in, panting, and thrust a long mop and a bucket into Gurleen's hands. Her eyes spat fire. Seeing that Gurleen had dropped the mop, she boomed. 'Whatchawaiting for? Clean the fuckin' mess up!'

Gurleen dissolved into tears. 'I've had enough, Aryan. I'm going back to India!'

He watched her, reactionless, spineless.

After Gurleen had finished cleaning up the wet floor and the cupboards, she tossed the squishy chapatti into the dustbin, along with all her dreams of being happy with Aryan.

Back in her 'room', she realized what it meant to belong to a place, any place. She loved India, with all its dirt, dust, grime, noise, smells, caste, corruption, crime. It was the one place to which she would always belong.

She left at the crack of dawn and waited an hour for the roadside joint to open. When they were ready for business, she wolfed down a coffee and doughnut and turned up at Little India two hours early. Bibi was already in, dealing with a problem. She had taken on a special order to supply dough for a religious event and the cooking had to be done on site. The dough had to be fresh and supplied before noon. But the cook had fallen sick.

'Four kilos is a lot of dough to knead,' Bibi mumbled as she began kneading. Gurleen could see that she stopped every few seconds.

'Joint pains,' Bibi explained. 'I stopped kneading dough ages ago. I would have refused, but they are close friends, I couldn't say no.' With that she resumed her painful task.

'Let me help.' Gurleen rolled up her sleeves and got cracking.

Helping Bibi reminded her of her mother-in-law Lajjo, who had been like a mother to her. She pushed the thoughts away and soon, the two women were cracking dirty jokes as Gurleen worked the dough. When it was ready, Bibi pinched it. It squeezed through like toothpaste.

'*Vadiya!*' said Bibi breaking into the Punjabi equivalent of 'superb'. 'That's so soft, how'd you manage to do that, Leena?'

Gurleen laughed it off, saying that she prayed to Waheguru while kneading. She couldn't tell her the truth, that she imagined herself tearing into Veronique's face each time she pounded the white dough into soft pulp until there was no anger and hatred left. Only a pleasurable pain in the knuckles that brought peace into her heart. And perfect dough for fluffy naans that would surely become another signature dish at Little India.

When she had finished, Gurleen was tired and sleepy and wanted to leave early. 'Can I go, Bibi?'

'Of course. But before you leave, could you just take those and toss them into the incinerator outside?' Bibi pointed to two large bottles of pickle that stood abandoned on the sink counter.

'What's wrong with them?'

'Some exporter from India left these samples. Take a look. This could kill someone and lock my place forever.'

A thick mould had formed over the pickle inside the large glass jar.

Gurleen nodded. 'Where is the incinerator?'

'Back lane, on the left. And come back in the afternoon, I'll have all your accounts ready.'

'Yes, of course.'

Gurleen stood before the incinerator door, holding the two bottles in her hands. A thought crossed her mind, making her chuckle.

Gurleen returned in the afternoon, to end her 'consulting'

project at Little India. She protested on seeing Bibi take out a crisp, thick envelope. 'No, please don't do that, Bibi. You've done me enough good by funding my ticket. I'll never forget it.'

Bibi hugged her and thrust the packet into Gurleen's hands and said, 'I'm glad to help my folks from India. Everything will work out fine, Leena. Our Indian men always return one day. Let him fail first. Meanwhile, you take care of yourself. And I'm going to have my driver drop you off at the airport. Don't say no.'

~

After a tearful farewell, Gurleen arrived home one last time. Her flight was at midnight and Bibi's driver was expected at eight. There was just enough time for one last act of kindness.

She deactivated the smoke alarm and checked the fridge and found some potato, canned *chole*, and two chunks of frozen mutton. *Good enough to make alu fry, chana pindi and mutton tikka achari.* She put the mutton in the microwave to thaw and whipped the yolk of two eggs. When the microwave beeped, she took out the pickle jars she had brought from Little India and scooped out the entire fungal layer and spread it over the mutton chunks. Next, she added the yolk in, mixed it afresh and put it all into a saucepan.

In an hour, she had set the table and was ready to have a refreshing shower.

Exactly at eight, there was a knock on the door and Bibi's driver walked in to collect her baggage. She checked her passport and ticket and wrote out a note for Aryan.

My dearest Aryan beta,

I'm going back. Please don't feel sorry for me. Rather, I feel sorry for you. Hope you'll come out of all this stronger. But if you don't, know that you can always come back to me.

P.S: I know you hate mutton. I just wanted Veronique to have no hard feelings.
Rab raakhe.
Imma

As Bibi's driver zipped past the gate into the main road, Gurleen saw Veronique's dirty Chevy pulling in.

Three hours later, just before boarding, she had a wild urge to call Aryan and dialled from the free phone kiosk.

Aryan sounded genuinely upset. '...Imma? You left without even telling me.'

She fought back her tears. 'Don't bother. Take care of yourself. Have you eaten?'

'You know I can't stand mutton.'

'It's a pity there wasn't anything else in the freezer.'

'But Veronique loved it. She licked the saucepan clean! Said she wouldn't mind you staying longer if she'd known you cook this well—'

'—Aarrrgghhhaarrrr! Arrrgghnnnn!' Aryan's voice was drowned by loud groans. He spoke in a hurry. 'Imma, something's happening to Veronique! She's throwing up everywhere!'

Gurleen tried to sound apologetic. 'Alright son. Take care. Watch your money and your back. God bless you.' She was thankful Aryan couldn't see her giggling.

15

*g*urleen cried all through the flight and had just dozed off when the Airbus made a bumpy landing in the early hours of the morning. Jolted by the crude touchdown, she reached for the immigration form tucked in her seat pocket and began filling it up, even as fellow passengers clamoured to retrieve their overhead luggage. Reminded of her premature return, she hesitated over 'Purpose of Visit', which had options like business, conference and tourism, but nothing like separation or reunion.

An hour later, she was in a taxi, desperate to get home—Rambal Acres, designed by the famous Edward Lutyens for the Earl's cousin. Closing her eyes, she pictured orange bougainvillea vines caressing its huge gate, the terracotta brick tiles over the windows and the beautiful lawn on the left, running all the way to the servant outhouse and into the woods beyond, touching Humayun's tomb. And the huge central courtyard, where so many famous musicians and dancers had performed to distinguished audiences.

Even though life was under a dark cloud now, Rambal Acres evoked pleasant memories.

The taxi pulled up outside the imposing gate. To her shock, she found them secured by a crude length of chain held by a lock. Something was amiss, the gate was usually latched, never locked. She rang the bell. It was a while before a guard in a black uniform walked up lazily, a hosepipe in hand and his trousers wet at the ankles. She had never seen him before.

'Who are you?' he asked her.

She snapped at him. 'Who the hell are you? This is my house! I am the owner.'

The guard took out a key and hesitated. 'This is Advocate Raina's house.'

'He is my lawyer. Now open up.'

The perplexed guard trotted off the gravelled driveway, leaving Gurleen fuming, locked out of her own house. He returned with a tall, ill-dressed man, and opened the gate as the other man greeted Gurleen.

'Good afternoon, madam, how may I help you?'

'You must be my tenant on the first floor, right?'

'Yes. We couldn't meet earlier.'

'Do you know Raina, my lawyer?'

'He's my brother.'

'What? He never said he wanted the house for his family!'

Just then, Raina walked over to the gate. 'Hello, hello, Mrs Rambal, we weren't expecting you for three months!' He frowned, betraying the even tone of his voice.

'Raina, I don't understand any of this. I think you should leave.'

His voice rose. 'Leave? This place has been rented forever.'

Her legs slumped. *Rented forever! Is that what he just said? Did I hear right?* She now understood why her gut had squirmed when Raina had given her the 'good news'.

'I thought we had agreed on a short-term lease, renewable.'

'Relax, madam. I'll show you exactly what you've agreed to.'

She climbed the stairs and entered the living room, which was still unfurnished, except for three cane chairs and a cane table with a glass top. Raina brought out a wad of papers and turned to the second page and held it before her. Gurleen remembered how on Raina's advice she had left the lease period blank and initialled across. Only, someone had filled the word 'Perpetual' in the blank space, right before her initials.

'It's downright fraud!' Gurleen was breathless. 'You cheat! You swindled me! You told me you would negotiate with the client for an eleven-month lease. That's why we left it blank. Don't you have a conscience?' she shouted.

Raina's eyes darted away, and he stepped out of the living room with the papers, leaving her to come to terms with the truth.

She was still in a daze when Raina's cellphone vibrated on the table. On its large screen, she saw the caller's name: Arvind—Global Bank. Unable to hold herself any longer, she snatched it and yelled. 'Arvind, you schemed with Raina to cheat me out of my property!'

The call disconnected, and the screen went blank. Raina walked back into the room and saw his phone in Gurleen's hand. Her composure had returned. 'I want the keys to the ground floor.'

He hesitated then dropped another bombshell. 'I could give them to you, but it'd be of no use.'

'Why?'

'The bank has taken it over.'

'What? Why?'

'Last week someone from the bank sealed the main door and pasted a notice for repayment of loans.'

'Impossible! Aryan's bank was to send out monthly instalments. And Arvind could have phoned me! The least you could have done was tell me when I called you from Denver!' She was hysterical.

Not believing the man, Gurleen charged down the stairs to the ground floor and reached the main door. Tears streamed down her face on seeing the 'Defaulter' notice pasted on the painted glass face. Huge wax blobs had been melted into the doorframe to prevent it from being opened.

Turning to Raina, who had followed her, she broke down. 'Please don't do this to me, Raina. I'm a lonely woman with more problems than I can handle. I don't know how much more I can take. Please leave my house, leave me in peace!'

She hoped he would thaw; instead, his reply stunned her.

'Madam, peace comes only from being close to God. I have

a nice one-bedroom apartment in Hardwar, overlooking the holy Ganga. I can arrange for you to stay there until things get sorted out.'

With that he left her and trudged up the stairs.

The world whirled before her as she ambled out of the gate, to confront her future that now seemed like a black, bottomless pit.

~

An hour later, she was at the reception of the Imperial Hotel on Janpath, to spend a few days until she could get to the bottom of the goings-on. The owner, Lakhbeer Singh, who had known the Rambals for many years, spotted her. 'Gurleen ji, *Sat Sri Akaal*. What a surprise!'

She kept her calm with great effort. 'Lucky Singh! How've you been? The hotel looks magnificent after the renovation.'

'Are you giving us the honour of serving you?'

She invented on the fly about the house being done up and needing a room for a few days. Soon they were in his office. 'Imperial Suite for madam Rambal,' he instructed the reservations manager and asked Gurleen for her card.

Over her favourite, Cona coffee, she answered Lucky's uncomfortable questions about Vikrant's death. Minutes later, the reservations executive walked in looking a bit embarrassed. She returned Gurleen's Global Bank Platinum Card and said, 'Madam, do you have another card? This one is getting declined.'

Lucky brushed it off. 'It might be a server problem at the bank, you know. Just take some other card.'

Gurleen handed him her Amex and Diners cards this time and helped herself to another coffee. The girl was back soon, with both cards, worry creasing her brow. Not as diplomatic as the first time, she spoke to her superior instead. 'Sir, both cards have been declined.'

The coffee mug shook in Gurleen's hands. 'What are you saying? That is just not possible. There has to be some mistake!'

Lucky pacified her. 'Relax, Gurleen ji, it happens sometimes. You can arrange cash tomorrow. We'll check you in. How many nights?'

Her cheeks went pale. 'I'm not sure what's happening. Lucky, can I go home and check what's wrong with the cards?'

'Sure. I'll have you dropped in our limo. It's the least we can do.' He flashed a big smile, but as Gurleen looked into his cold, distant and somewhat disbelieving eyes, she felt ashamed. *I've fallen in his esteem.*

Lost in thought, she got off the limo at the wrong road, and started walking home, panic settling in over the recent events that had taken place in her life. Soon she was at the end of her street, in front of Brigadier Fauja Singh's house, a dilapidated ancestral property in dispute for as long as she had known. The brigadier and his wife Satpreet—Preeti to her—had held on to the house, hoping to win it from their cousins. Vikki had never invited them to his high life dos, but Leena had had Preeti over for tea on a few occasions. But all that was before Vikki's illness.

She was still wondering what to do, when the rusty gate opened noisily, and a servant walked out towing Frieda, their Labrador. She recognized Gurleen and was soon all over her. Gurleen looked up and caught Preeti peeping through the curtains. 'Preeti, it's me, Gurleen. I need to see you,' she called out.

Fauja Singh opened the door and took her into the living room, crammed with ancestral furniture in tatters. After she had told them about the bank and Raina, she wasn't sure how her hosts felt. She felt that the fleeting gleam in Preeti's eyes said, *Aha, the mighty Rambal has bitten the dust.* However, the brigadier seemed genuinely shocked. 'What do you plan to do now?'

'I need to find out why the payments haven't come into the account. Then, I need to find someplace to stay tonight, while I look for an alternative. Can't think of anything else for now.'

She caught the eye contact between husband and wife. She knew what they were saying.

Don't commit anything, Fauja.

Don't worry, dear, I won't.

'Preeti, can I leave my bags here while I check for some guest house?'

'Oh sure, why not. Think of this as your own place.'

Gurleen wasn't sure if Preeti meant it, as she called for a taxi.

Gurleen spotted Kartaar Singh and the blue Altis outside. She remembered she still owed him for her airport ride.

'*Kithe*, memsahib, where?' he asked her through the rear-view mirror.

'Take me to a property agent who can show me some places for rent. Know anyone?' She handed him a five hundred rupee note. 'Here's for the last time.'

'There's no hurry. I knew it was safe. Any problem with the bungalow?'

'It's just temporary.' She hoped he would pry no further.

Her five text messages to Denver had remained unanswered. *Maybe something serious had happened to Veronique.* Unable to wait any longer, she called Aryan and got disconnected twice before he answered.

'Imma! Veronique is in the hospital with salmonellosis. It's going to take her a while to recover.'

'Oh Oh! That's sad. But I'm upset about other things.'

'What other things?' he sounded irritated.

'The bank's sealed off our premises because it seems you haven't sent the payment. Is that possible?'

'Is that so? Let me check and get back.' He sounded defensive.

'Do that right away, because I have no place to stay until we sort this out.'

'But we have the first floor, don't we?'

Avik Davar

'Don't you remember I told you I had leased it out? It was the only way for us to service the loan!'

'No, you never told me—'

'So many things happened in Denver, it must have slipped my mind.'

'What are you going to do now?'

'I'll figure something out. Will you call me tomorrow to tell me when the payment was sent to the bank?'

'Ok, I'll see.'

'Bye, Aryan.'

She then called the banker several times, but Arvind's phone remained switched off.

She searched for places away from her neighbourhood. It turned out to be futile. No one wanted to deal with her—some thought she was an impostor, and others doubted she had lived at Rambal Acres in the first place.

When she returned, dejected, the brigadier and Preeti were not in; she learnt they were having dinner at the Defence Services Club. After a spartan meal of rotis, curd and her pills, Gurleen settled on the sofa in the front room and shuddered as her new reality sank in like slow poison.

She was alone, without a home, without money, with no one to help her—how long before Preeti and the brigadier showed their spots? She could not go back to the US, and had no idea how to get sanity back in her life. *Will things ever be normal again?*

The jetlag had begun to take its toll, and she dozed off.

Her best friends were with her. Sabrinder, Baani and her brother, the naughty Bitta. Always surprising her, holding her from behind tickling her waist. But never anything more than that. But suddenly he grabbed her, locked lips and was feeling her up. Indecent fellow. Why was he stinking of alcohol? Someone stop Bitta, please!

She was breathless and unable to scream. A giant hand had

muffled her throat, while another probed inside her. A beard stung her cheek and a hungry mouth reeking of whiskey and garlic slobbered her lips. She struggled in her impaled position, too scared to shout.

A door opened on the first floor and the stairway light came on. The hands backed off and slunk into the darkness. Preeti stood at the railing and returned to her room, satisfied that everything was fine.

It's just a dream, Leena. Aryan, please come back, please!

~

In the morning, Gurleen sneaked out to the taxi stand, and surprised Kartaar Singh who was chewing at his neem stick. While he got ready, she texted Justdial services and was soon calling brokers and jotting down addresses to visit, leaving Kartaar puzzled.

Around noon, she stopped by at the Global Bank ATM to withdraw cash. Though she knew the PIN, she had never been to an ATM before; the accountant had always brought cash home. She asked a teenager to help her. The card came out, and a message blinked on the screen.

Card invalid.

She tried three other cards and got the same message. *What's going on?* She called the relationship manager, who kept her on hold a long time and then asked Gurleen to drop by at the branch next morning. *How insolent! I'm still a Platinum customer, aren't I?*

She moved on to the more important task. By evening, she had checked out seven places. The best she could get was a women's hostel room in a few weeks, if she brought a recommendation letter from any parliamentarian.

A part of her knew that she could easily solve her problem by calling someone from the Page 3 list. They might even help, if not out of compassion, then at least lured by the fresh gossip they stood to bring to parties for a while before the Rambals became stale again.

Another part rebuked her for even thinking about it. The socialites were gone from her life forever, with Vikki. She had no love for them and she would certainly not give them the chance to pity her or gloat over her condition. No, if she had to seek refuge, it would rather be at the gurdwara than elsewhere.

Another part of her trashed the gurdwara option too, out of anger at God, who seemed to be taking a perverse pleasure in making her suffer. Her anger at God did not stop her from praying, though. *Help me find some place today, Rabba!* She wanted a clean break from everything. It was time to be orphaned once again in life.

Finally, someone gave her a lead about Shanti Nivas in Timarpur, near the northern border of Delhi. It was a shelter for the homeless, the destitute and the abandoned. Gurleen realized, with a cold sweat breaking on her forehead, that she met all three criteria.

After an hour, Gurleen arrived with Kartaar Singh before a rusted gate that had a board held by wire. 'Shanti Nivas.' She walked into the 'Office' furnished with a wrought iron table and two chairs with broken cane meshwork. A stern looking lady—the badge said 'Matron'—sat at the table, evaluating everything on Gurleen's body to assess her value before striking up a conversation. Finally, she spoke.

'Yes, how may I help you?'

'My name is Gurleen…I'm looking for…'

'Family name?'

She hesitated. 'Hmm…Rambal…'

'Let me show you around.'

It was a relief that the matron didn't react to the name.

The matron walked Gurleen through the West Wing of the campus. She saw two nice lawns. One had walking tracks, swings, rocking chairs, marble benches and a fountain. The other had a small temple. The loudspeaker was blaring out a devotional hymn and some twenty inmates were on the grass, gently swaying to its rhythm.

The matron detailed all the amenities—Bridge table, Internet with broadband, gymnasium with a masseuse and a library that doubled as a mini-theatre. There were twelve serviced apartments, equipped with Wi-Fi, TVs, room service, besides a hotline to a doctor and ambulance. At rupees seventy-five thousand a month, the West Wing had every comfort of an upper middle-class home, except the warmth of family.

The matron carried on. 'Five-star old-age homes are the new thing. For those who can afford them, they symbolize respectable arrangements for elderly care, or good riddance, depending on circumstances. Who's got time for old people anyway? But with places like these, there is no guilt or remorse. They're better off in these modern sanatoriums.'

'The East Wing?' asked Gurleen.

'Not for you. East Wing is free and for the poor and destitute. The East Wingers help around, mostly by serving the West Wingers. So, what do you think?' she asked as they walked back to the office.

Gurleen muttered, 'Am not sure yet.' She first had to find out why her cards weren't working. 'I'll tell you tomorrow.'

The matron then prodded Gurleen about her background and finally the key issue. Her financial assets. She was incredulous at once.

'You have a house in Nizamuddin? It must be worth many crores. Why are you here?'

Gurleen told her the bare essentials. 'There's a legal dispute. Can you assure me of a place in the West Wing?'

'Look Mrs Rambal, we need to do our own verification. Why don't you fill up the form now and meet me tomorrow afternoon? I am sure something will work out.'

Gurleen wanted to scream. *You don't understand! I can't go back to my neighbour's place.* Instead, all she said was, 'That's a huge relief, indeed.'

She filled in the form, ticking West Wing without hesitation.

Kartaar Singh dropped her outside Preeti's home after 9 p.m. She told him to be ready the next morning at six; she didn't want to stay for even one second after dawn. The door was opened by the brigadier; he was licking gravy off his fingers and was startled to see her.

'Oho, come in, come in. Where did you go away so early? We were worried.'

Preeti was her usual cold self, but when Gurleen announced that she had found a place, she insisted that Gurleen eat something and trudged upstairs. The brigadier had taken his plate to the living room to catch the breaking news of an army scam.

Gurleen ate in peace. The butter-oozing chapattis were divine, well earned after a long, hard day's work. The curd was laced with red chilli powder, which gave it a zing that was quelled by the butter. She asked the cook for more chilli powder. He brought a full bottle. Chilli. Much more than just a spice, she thought as she tapped the lid.

Aryan hadn't called back. She checked her phone for missed calls and messages. There was nothing other than a real estate offer and a horoscope reading. As she dialled Aryan, she couldn't help wondering *Why do I have to be the one to call every time*?

'Hello, Aryan. It's me. How's she?'

She heard '…Still in hospital. Doing better.'

'And what about the bank?'

He had forgotten. '…What bank?'

'The loan instalment, we talked about it yesterday. Don't take it lightly. It is very urgent.'

The reply shocked her. 'Imma, do you realize what happens to my visa if something happens to Veronique?'

'And what about me? I'm in this mess because of *you*!' She didn't realize she was screaming.

She heard him yell back. 'And I'm in this mess all because of you!'

'Okay then. Take care of her, I'll sort myself out,' she disconnected.

I'm less important than Veronique and a Canadian visa. Fine. So be it.

She distracted herself by focusing her thought on the other problem waiting for her. Fortunately, the solution was in sight.

She went to sleep thinking of Aryan.

Does he not care for me? How close we used to be! How he would snuggle next to me under the duvet and hug me tight. His feet could barely reach my knees... in his sleep, he'd put his legs over me... they were as light as a feather.

Oh, time has flown... He's grown up, his legs are so bloody heavy... I'm powerless... And he's prodding me with... behave yourself, son... he isn't giving up... the beard hurts... Aryan never had a beard before... He's gone mad... I need to stop him.

She reached under her pillow and uncapped the bottle and flung it at his face. Then again and again, on his hardness. Chilli dust got into her nostrils and she sneezed. Then the lights came on from the first floor. And shone on him. He was red all over and screaming.

Thankfully, it wasn't her son.

Thankfully, it wasn't blood either. Fauja Singh was feverishly brushing the chilli powder off his crotch, his eyes puckering in pain. He fumbled blindly to open the bathroom door. Not realizing that his undone pyjamas had fallen loose around his ankles, he toppled and fell on his face. The doorstopper slammed into his teeth. He yelped and crawled inside the bathroom and bolted the door. Gurleen saw a chipped tooth on the floor.

Preeti stomped down the stairs, crying. 'Leena please forgive me. That's why I wasn't keen on you staying here.'

The two women sat at the dining table and cried through the night.

After breakfast and a third glass of sugared tea, she was ready to leave. Preeti assured her of help, but with the disclaimer on her husband. As Gurleen reached the front door, she saw Fauja stagger out of the bathroom in a towel. His legs were wide apart, as if hit by a rash on the inner thighs.

~

Her first port of call was Global Bank. The Credit Cards section manager tapped some buttons, read off the screen and looked at Gurleen with a frown. He sent her downstairs to the Defaults section, where a long queue had formed. An hour later, Gurleen came to know why her cards hadn't worked.

'I can see you tried to use them thrice yesterday. It's just that there's no balance in the account.'

Gurleen almost fainted when she heard that, but she remained unconvinced. 'How can that be? There should be over fifteen lakh rupees in the loan account, deposited by Mr Raina. Check it again.'

'Madam, all we have here is a red alert to freeze your account. Anyway, let me check with my boss. Please wait a minute.'

She disappeared into a cabin and came back in a bit. 'Madam, your son has withdrawn the fixed deposit in Canada and revoked the automatic debit instructions. And there has been no deposit by any Mr Raina.'

She couldn't believe any of it. 'You're telling me I can't draw any money from my account?'

'There's nothing to draw from. Even your credit card limits will be released only after you settle the outstanding.'

'But how could the bank act without even checking with me?'

'Our records show that the collection centre called you for a week without an answer. Following which, the bank sent people twice to your residence, where no one was available. Only then did we freeze the account and seal off the property. A usual precaution in case a defaulter is absconding.'

'Absconding? Arvind knew that I was not in the country, he

could have reached me!'

'Loan recovery is a different department, madam.'

'How much do I owe the bank for now?'

'Let me check…. Yes, three crore fifty-five lakh, sixty thousand rupees.'

'Come on, that's even more than the entire loan!'

'They've added a penalty for default.'

Then Gurleen remembered the cash she had put away in the locker. 'Give me ten minutes. I'll be right back.'

Minutes later she was at the Christian Bank, in the adjacent building. She had closed the account there years ago, but had retained the locker. The manager was a friendly fellow who had always pestered her to reopen her account.

She looked around and found him talking to a staff member and waited for his attention. When he turned to her, the usual smile was missing; instead an incredulous frown came on his face.

'Who… hello, Mrs Rambal, where have you been all this while?'

'I was in the US for two weeks. What happened?'

He struggled for words. 'What can I say?'

'Anything wrong?'

He spoke with reluctance. 'Some people from the income tax department came here… We had to tell them about the locker becoming active after a long gap.'

He asked the peon next to him for the locker register. Gurleen's jaw dropped when she saw the instruction.

'LOCKER 19—Gurleen Rambal. SEALED by Income Tax Dept.'

Dark clouds formed before Gurleen. She broke down, sobbing. 'I want to die, Rabba. I just can't bear this anymore now.'

She wiped her tears and headed to the door.

As she staggered out, the manager smiled. 'Have a good day, madam.'

Gurleen was livid. She resisted the urge to slap him but let go with a sneer. 'Have a heart, you fellow, wishing me a good day after all this.'

As she staggered into Kartaar's taxi, it dawned on her that all the money she had in this world was four thousand three hundred rupees and change, besides the few items of jewellery on her body.

16

Fortunately, there was good news at Shanti Nivas. The verification had been positive, and Gurleen's case had been approved. Yes, they had found out about the loan. But the board had concluded that Gurleen was resourceful enough to cover her stay at Shanti Nivas for as long as she wanted.

Gurleen left the matron's office with a receipt for her earrings. They were good enough for up to six lakh rupees in expenses. Gurleen soon learnt that her earrings were not the only marketable commodities she had.

She was taken to the Medical Wing, which was just a small clinic with an X-ray room and an Operation Theatre. She saw a few nurses and a couple of doctors, all in smudged white dresses. There was dirt on the floor, and the linen on the test beds was soiled. Three people walked in carrying a stretcher, ice boxes and strange tools she had never seen before. She asked the nurse if anyone was unwell.

Her answer had a deathly chill. '301 died an hour ago. They've come for eyes and kidneys.'

Gurleen's mouth dried up when the nurse ordered, 'Let's take your abdomen X-ray.'

'For what?'

'To confirm the liver and kidneys.'

'Confirm, why in heaven?'

'To be pledged, if necessary.'

'*Hai Rabba*!'

By the time she was back at the matron's office, Gurleen had learnt that she could borrow one lakh by pledging one kidney, three lakh for her eyes, and up to five lakh each for her heart and liver.

With so much to leave behind, the East Wingers were worth more dead than alive.

~

Day One.

Gurleen was assigned the richest of the West Wing inmates, Mythili and Muthukrishnan, well-educated south Indians and strictly vegetarian. Krishnan was seventy-five, diabetic and suffering from Parkinson's. Mythili was seventy and had arthritis but her fingers were nimble enough to use her laptop all day.

Her duty was to sit next to Krishnan and keep him from falling over during Mythili's Skype sessions with her son Varun, a VP at Google.

It was their granddaughter's birthday and Mythili was desperate to wish her and had asked her son to take his laptop into her room. The screen showed a girl sleeping in shorts, and nothing else.

The teenager was rattled by the intrusion of her privacy. 'Dad, how dare you enter my room? And what is Patti doing out there on Skype?'

The man's sound erupted in short bursts. 'Wishing you happy birthday, Su! Say hi to grandma and grandpa!'

'Happy birthday, Sukanya!' Mythili's voice echoed from inside the screen. The teenager wrapped herself in a sheet and turned away without responding. The laptop bobbed up and down until Gurleen saw a fat lady walk past the screen. Like the teenager, she too had nothing on. Catching Mythili on the Skype window, she let out a shriek, which was followed by a monologue that sounded like a machine gun's report.

Mythili tapped her head with her hands, chanting, 'Shiva! Shiva!'

Soon, the fat lady was back on screen, dressed in a towel. Looking into the camera, she spoke more machine-gun language.

Gurleen needed no translation. *Listen you old cow, never ask*

Varun to show you inside my house. One more time, and I'll cut you off Skype permanently. Got it?

All the time her son stood in the corner of a screen in stony silence. When the woman had gone, Mythili asked him, 'Varun, is this how she walks around in the house? Shiva Shiva!'

'Amma, is everything okay at Shanti Nivas?'

'Do we have a choice? I wonder which sin of ours has brought this punishment upon us in old age. We never imagined living apart from our son, after all the sacrifices we made.'

'Amma, fortunately, we can afford good facilities. And, think about it, you'll be here next month.'

'This time I want to fly first class. Emirates A380 looks very nice.'

'No problem. Spend some days transiting in Dubai, if you wish.'

'Thank god for Google.'

'Yes, Amma. But don't tell Shailaja you are flying first class.'

'Why should you be secretive? After all, you are only doing it for your parents, no?'

'Please, Amma. Promise you won't breathe a word about first class. Deal?'

'Listen, I want to watch the birthday celebration. I'll Skype you at 8 a.m. tomorrow. '

'Okay, Amma.'

Gurleen's room in the East Wing was ten feet by ten, with a small wash and toilet. She had got a new mattress and bed linen, which would be adjusted against her deposit. After the long day with the old couple, she was tired and bored. She didn't get up to switch the fan on and even downed her Galvus 500 night pill without water. She was too afraid to sleep; she kept seeing hands in the darkness, hands that felt her everywhere. There was some comfort from the sporadic squeaking of crickets on the wall. They seemed to be saying 'Gurleen, it didn't happen. It was just a bad dream. Good night.'

Day Two.

Mythili looked as though she had aged ten years overnight. She was howling away in her incoherent Tamil, bleating something that sounded like 'saniyan…Shailaja…naasamaa podi…paavi… chandali…'

'What happened?' Gurleen asked her. Mythili did not acknowledge her.

Krishnan broke the news. 'Our daughter-in-law has deleted us from Skype.'

'Why?'

'Varun was showing Mythili the birthday party on Skype, from his camera phone. His wife did not know about it. When they cut the cake, Mythili couldn't control herself and shouted, "Happy Birthday!" Varun's wife saw her face on the phone and switched it off. Mythili hasn't been able to connect with them since. She has been deleted from their contact list.'

Gurleen consoled and force-fed Mythili a few spoons of porridge. Mythili spat it all out and pushed Gurleen hard, making her lose her balance and trip. Her ankle twisted a bit and she hobbled in pain. Ouch!

'Please forgive us! She has been uncontrollable,' Krishnan apologized, his head and hands shaking uncontrollably.

Soon, Gurleen had reported the matter and the paramedic had given Mythili a sedative. After Mythili had dozed off Gurleen tended to Krishnan who ate his food and medicine like a docile child.

When she rose to leave, he looked at the ceiling and remarked without feeling, 'Old age is a curse! I wish we could be put to sleep forever, instead of suffering like this.'

Gurleen woke up in the darkness. Something had hit her. She was too scared to even breathe. Summoning all her courage, she turned on the light. There was no one. Relieved, she pulled the pillows and placed them above her chest and slept. It was back.

Only this time it was pressing against her chest, crushing the ribs and pushing the air out of her lungs.

Is it Death? Aryan, where are you? Aryan! Can you hear me? Death spared her, but she couldn't sleep anymore.

Day Three.

Sundari Devi had lived at Shanti Nivas for two years. Gurleen had seen her at the evening prayer the day before. Sundari had sung the closing hymn. But she hadn't turned up for dinner and hadn't come out in the morning either.

The door was slightly open. Gurleen knocked, pushed it open and stood at the doorway. Sundari was sitting in her easy chair, with a clutch of old photographs in her hand. Several more were strewn on the floor. At a distance, beside the foot of the bed, lay a crumpled ball of paper.

Sundari looked at Gurleen, first with curiosity, then with caution.

'Hello, I am Gurleen. I live in the East Wing. May I come in?'

After a long silence, Sundari waved her in. Gurleen took her hand in hers, and said, 'I was passing by and just wanted to talk to you. You sing so well.'

She smiled. 'Yes, I like singing.'

'Do you want me to put these photos back someplace?' Gurleen had begun picking up the photos scattered on the ground.

Sundari snatched them and tossed them on the other side of the bed. 'Out of my life.'

'Whose photos are they?'

'My son's. I'm angry at him.'

'What's that?'

'His letter. He refuses to gift my daughter a washing machine on her wedding anniversary.'

'Is it a dowry demand? You know there's a strong law against it.'

'No, it's not dowry. I want to gift it for her wedding anniversary next month. Our prestige is at stake.'

'Why?'

'My daughter is married into a rich family. They have two cars and two houses. My son-in-law is in IT.'

'Computers?'

'Income tax.'

'And your son?'

'Municipal school principal. No side income. He's always short of money. Duffer.'

'Why aren't you staying with him?'

'I was until last year. But then his mother-in-law fell ill, and came to stay with us, bag and baggage.'

'What did she suffer from?'

'Nothing major. But she insists it is cancer. I told my son it had to be either her or me.'

'And he decided to keep her?'

'No, he wanted us both to stay. I couldn't. So, his wife works and pays for my stay here, so her mother can stay with them. Honestly, this place is better.'

'What if she stops working, will you return home?'

'If I have to return, her mother has to move out. Simple.'

Gurleen was shocked. She bent over and picked up the crumpled piece of paper. 'Can I read it?'

'Yes. See what he says!'

Dear Ma,
Pranaam.

As you know, I will be eligible for a new loan only next year. Can we wait six months to buy Shruti her washing machine?

Here, Indu's mother isn't going to last much longer. Indu has quit her job to take care of her. I cannot afford you staying at Shanti Nivas with one wage. Can you come back? You can have the big bedroom and the cable.

Please decide and please take my calls. I shall visit you as soon as I am back from election duty.

Vardhaman

Gurleen folded the letter properly and looked at the photos strewn on the bed. One of them was crumpled. In it, she saw a gaunt man, not in good financial health from the fit of his clothes. Beside him stood a little girl and a thin woman with bright purposeful eyes.

Anger rising in her, Gurleen left, worried that she might end up hitting Sundari if she stayed any longer.

Back in her room, she switched on her phone. There was no call or SMS from the US. She sent out an SMS to Aryan, like every night before. She forced herself to sleep, the pillows clutched in her hands and breathing in rhythm with the lulling sounds of the crickets on the wall.

Day Four.

Kaka was by far the sweetest person in the East Wing. He always smiled at people and cared enough to ask about the little things he noticed out of place.

'Leena ji, what happened to your foot?' He had asked noticing the slight limp in her gait.

Gurleen felt his friendliness was a cover. It seemed to her that he was afraid of something, and his banter was merely to distract himself from whatever bothered him deep inside. She knew a bit about his history from the gossip going around. A retired peon, Kaka had lost his wife and most of his property in a caste riot in UP. He had a son who was jobless and an alcoholic. Concerned for his daughter-in-law, he had got her a job and had moved into Shanti

Nivas upon learning that his status would get him free boarding and lodging as an East Winger.

Gurleen was scheming how to wriggle out of his banter, when the office peon came running.

'Kaka, there's a phone call for you.'

Kaka walked a few steps and then turned. He ran past her to his room at the other end. He returned with a crudely knotted plastic bag, which he hurriedly thrust into her hands.

'Leena ji, have this sent to my daughter-in-law, the address is in the bag. Don't let anyone know about it. Please.' He then rushed towards the office room.

It was bizarre.

She took the bag into her room and opened it to see what he had trusted her with. There were three wads of five hundred rupee notes, stapled in multiple places. A date—three months earlier—had been handwritten on top of the bundles. Rupees one lakh fifty thousand was a lot of money for someone like Kaka.

A few hours later, she remembered the phone call and started looking for Kaka. Not finding him anywhere, she sought out the peon, who was dozing off at the main gate.

'What happened to Kaka?'

'Someone took him in a jeep. His son has been admitted in hospital. Kidney failure.'

'When did he leave?

'In the morning.'

She was worried about the package. Why did Kaka give it to her? Wouldn't he have needed it at the hospital?

At five in the evening, a crowd of East Wingers had gathered near Kaka's room. Two policemen were packing his belongings. One of them pasted a paper on the door while the other was asking the matron some tough questions.

'How is it that you don't have the latest address of his family?

And how come you didn't verify the identities of the people who took him away?'

The matron cringed in humiliation before the residents. Then two lawyers walked in and handed the cops a sheaf of papers. One of them in a blue suit said to the matron, 'Don't worry, they can't touch you. It's not your fault.'

Gurleen muscled her way to Kaka's door. The notice read: 'Criminal evidence. Do not enter.'

A cold fear grabbed her stomach.

The crowd had dispersed. Gurleen sat in the lawn when the peon tiptoed and sat next to her. He was dying to talk to someone.

'He was found on the main road. Abandoned. Dead, badly stitched up.'

'Stitched up? What do you mean?' asked Gurleen.

'His stomach had been sewn up crudely, and his eyes had been taken out. The police found his body and saw the Shanti Nivas label stitched on the uniform and came here right away.'

'My god!' she trembled. 'But where did he go?'

'They had taken him to the Gandhi hospital, for a kidney transplant. Kaka was donating a kidney to save his son.'

'What went wrong then?'

'It turns out the paperwork was bogus. The police found out his son had died months ago.'

'But you said he was doing it for his son?'

'The whole thing was a cover up. With the law so strict nowadays, organ donation is restricted only to family members. And that too only in life-saving circumstances.'

'Why was the matron being questioned?'

'We come under flak every time someone dies here. The police love to harass us. But this one has really shaken up the matron.'

'How long had Kaka been here?'

'About three months. He was such a nice chap.'

Three months! Of course! Gurleen figured out Kaka had brought the money with him. He must have planned it all. He had sold his kidney in advance and was waiting here for the paperwork to be completed in the name of his 'dead' son. But surely Kaka couldn't have counted on dying. Something must have gone horribly wrong with the transplant.

It then struck her. *Waheguru! That money's still with me.*

She knew what had to be done.

An hour later, the police inspector took her statement and the money. He was very pleased with her. Someone even clicked her pictures.

Day Five.

Shanti Nivas made it to the City News page, with a half-page article about organ selling. But it was the story below it that shocked Gurleen: 'Rambal Lady in Exile!'

It was a full-blown article that covered the will, the loan default and Rambal Acres being sealed by the bank. The pictures were more devastating. They showed Gurleen tending to Mythili, having tea on the footsteps to the lawn, and the defaulter notice stuck on the front door of Rambal Acres.

Gurleen locked herself in her room all day.

It was past three in the morning in Denver. She didn't care and made the call anyway.

Answer the phone, Aryan. It's the last you'll ever hear of me! Pick it up, you insensitive, ungrateful boy! Are you dead?

The voice that answered drove her into a killing rage.

'Ye been feedin me poison meat, broad!'

Gurleen summoned all her calm. 'Please ask Aryan to come on the line!'

'...Your baby boy's busy suckling 'is big Momma right now. Whynt ya go find someone else ta give ya tit suckle!'

Gurleen was no longer listening. She looked for something, anything to put a stop to it all. She saw the can of olives Mythili had given her; it had an easy-open lid. She ran her thumb over it, and the thick drip told her it would do the job.

'*Waheguru!* Enough!' Gash!

'Aryan!' Gash! Gash! Gash! Gash! Gash!

There was collage of faces before her. She recognized Mythili, who was sobbing away. She recognized the quack doctor from the medical wing. He was bandaging her wrist.

Then she was brought into the matron's office.

'Sorry, you'll have to leave us, Mrs Rambal. We can't handle such a high-profile resident; surely not one under a controversy.'

Gurleen shocked herself by saying, 'You're right. I gave in too soon.'

Repacking her humble belongings, she felt disgusted at herself. *How could Gurleen Rambal give in so easily? Yes, some lawyer has cheated me. Yes, my son deserted me. Yes, my neighbour tried to molest me. Yes, my bank has locked me out of my home.*

But I can still survive and live on my own terms. I haven't lost hope. I'm going to win back my home, my money and if Rabba wants it, even my son. I just need a bit of time to pick up the threads and rebuild my life. And I swear I'm going to hurt that Raina real bad. Show him not to mess with me. I'm going to fix him. It's time to move beyond Shanti Nivas.

~

The next morning Kartaar Singh was waiting outside the gate of Shanti Nivas.

'Where to, madam?'

She had no answer yet.

'Nizamuddin?'

After some thought, she said, 'Yes'.

Kartaar pulled up outside Rambal Acres and was surprised that she told him to keep driving.

She seethed at the sight of the locked gate. The rose bushes were wild from neglect and her favourite jasmine creeper had wilted. As the taxi inched ahead, she looked at her home and resolved.

I'm going to win you back!

Kartaar was confused when she asked him to drive to his taxi stand a kilometre away, on the other side of Humayun's Tomb. When they had arrived, Gurleen remained seated in the Altis. After some hesitation, he asked her, 'Would you like to share with me what has happened?'

And she told him everything.

He listened dumbstruck. Tears dripped onto his beard as he asked the inevitable question. 'Where will you go now?'

It was Gurleen's turn to muster courage and ask him.

'Kartaar, can I live in your taxi?'

His offer turned out to be a tad better, for she got a cot at the taxi stand, and a curtain and clothes line to cordon her from the three male drivers who stayed there in the open yard. Kartaar also warned his brethren to take care of Gurleen as they would their own mothers.

She got up at three in the morning, her back stiff from the sagging ropes of her creaky charpoy. The toilet door was locked, and the men were snoring away. When necessity had overcome upbringing, she let herself douse the roadside, shocked and relieved at the same time. However, the spooks did not bother her that night as she slept under the open sky.

She woke up again, stung by an insect. Unable to sleep further, she checked her phone for messages. There were none from Denver; there had been none since her return. Gurleen knew just then that it was time to sever all connections and memories from the past and bury them away forever. She took out her SIM card and crushed it under the cot's leg and gave up only when the plastic had cracked and the circuit board, mangled beyond repair.

Goodbye, Aryan. Now, you've got to look for me.

Sleep returned to her.

In the morning, she got her key to the functional but sparse toilet. Kartaar brought *kullads* of steaming tea, and two packs of glucose biscuits, which carried enough calories for an adult's daily needs. She cut loose from another shred of upbringing by dipping the biscuits into her tea. As they were midway into the tea, she caught Kartaar looking at her chest.

Damn all men. Now this driver wants his pound of flesh!

His eyes shifted away. She looked at him with disdain and lashed out. 'Have you never seen a woman with breasts before?'

Kartaar slapped his cheeks and fell at her feet, protesting, '*Tauba, Tauba,* you are like my mother. I was only looking at your locket, madam.'

Gurleen felt ashamed of her outburst. *How cruel of me! After all, he's been there every day, doing my bidding, running my errands, without a frown. And he isn't anything like Fauja Singh. He's just curious about my locket.*

She apologized and held his hand. 'Forgive me, Kartaar, I've been unkind!'

'*Main twaddi vaddi respect kar da'aan,* Mataji!' He reiterated his maternal respect for her in Punjabi.

Eventually, she asked him. 'Kartaar, will you do me a favour? But I may never be able to repay it.'

'Just order me.'

'Can I get to drive a taxi?'

17

*g*urleen had been at the taxi stand three days now. Kartaar had to concede that she drove confidently and had a good sense of Delhi's main roads. To honour his end of the deal he had found a spare vehicle, which she could ply as long as she took care of the monthly instalments. She would get the car in a week. Finally, she would have an identity of her own. Gurleen Rambal, Taxi Driver.

Until then, she was content to be the handyman for Kartaar's Altis. As a mark of gratitude, she had given it a makeover: dry cleaning, shampooing and a bottle of Ambi Pur to freshen up the fart-laden interiors. She was sure Kartaar's new client would be impressed.

FM radio announced 7.30 a.m. Kartaar should have been at the stand by now. It was not a good sign to report late on a foreigner's duty, especially a Japanese.

Kartaar's mobile remained unanswered until the fifth try. Eventually, she heard his voice, coughing and faint.

'Hell… lo—cough, cough—Bibi ji!'

'Kartaar, you are late!'

He was running a temperature and hadn't slept all night. 'Can you ask someone at the stand to fill in for me, Bibiji?'

'There's no one here right now. Everyone's left already. What is the duty?'

His throat was hoarse and badly congested. 'Airport drop. The passenger has to—cough, cough—be picked up from Okhla. The address is—cough—on the duty sheet in the register.'

'Don't worry. You rest today. Drink lots of water and go see a doctor. Okay?' She hung up.

The Altis looked brilliant with its scrubbing from the previous day. The gleaming aquamarine blue exterior, the white upholstery and the fragrance of night jasmine were inviting. The key was in the ignition, waiting to be turned. *By whom?* She wondered. *Me? Why not?*

An Altis wasn't overwhelming after driving a Mercedes. She picked up the duty sheet from the stand window.

In under half an hour, she was outside a white building in Okhla, an industrial estate that housed several multinational companies. She saw the familiar logo: A sportsman holding a plastic bottle with a light green liquid inside it. The print on the bottle read: 'Tai-Yo!'

At the porch, a well-dressed Japanese in a black suit and white shirt (did they wear anything else?) walked across. Seeing a lady driver dressed in fawn slacks and a Dockers shirt, he bowed in the typical Japanese way, and asked, 'Singh Taxi?'

'Yes, sir. Good morning. Domestic airport?'

'Indigo. Terminal 1D. You ten minutes late.'

'Sorry, sir. We'll be on time!' She held the passenger door for him and set off, hoping to reach the airport within twenty minutes in the light morning traffic.

They were at the one-sided Savitri Cinema flyover when the traffic came to a halt. The Japanese woke up from his snooze and checked his watch. His face was drawn and red but his tone was composed.

'We reach airport on time?'

Can't he see we are stuck in a jam? So much for helping Kartaar and getting myself into trouble. She kept silent and ran the air-conditioner at full blast and directed all the louvers to the rear seat hoping to cool him down. Meanwhile, he had begun taking pictures of the jam. She thought he was either a pervert, or desperate for evidence to show why he had missed his flight.

Soon, she had a crazy idea.

They were almost at the end of the flyover, at the last concrete slab beyond which the overhead carriage merged with the traffic from below. A battered grey Mitsubishi Lancer was waiting ahead of her Altis. She considered the situation. *If only I can manage to get just a few feet of turning space, I can get out of this ruckus.*

And then as if God had heard her, the Lancer inched up three feet before stopping again. Normally she would have moved to close in. But she remained stationary. Soon loud horns blasted behind. The Lancer moved a little more, giving Gurleen just enough turning room. She stepped on the gas and swerved the car to the left, made a U-turn and drove back against the traffic coming into the lane below. She knew she had done something terribly wrong, but the bottom line was, the Altis was the only car that had moved out of the jam. The Japanese was still clicking photos.

Her dream run ended as a Honda City met them head on; the driver slammed his brakes and honked incessantly.

'Sorry brother!' Gurleen folded her hands apologetically as she shot past, avoiding him by inches. She could make from his lip movements that he was swearing at her mother.

Soon, there was a screech of tyres, and the loud sound of a collision behind them. She took the scene in from the rear-view mirror. The Honda City had collided with an Alto that had tried to imitate Gurleen's trick, although unsuccessfully. The Japanese, now balanced on his knees in his seat, was shooting the fistfight between the Honda and Alto drivers through the rear windscreen.

Gurleen kept her pace and turned into a side road that she knew would join the Ring Road further on, hopefully ahead of the jam. The digital clock on the dashboard showed 7.30 a.m. as she hit the outer Ring Road again at Panchsheel. Feeling a rush of adrenaline, she yelled, 'We'll make it on time, sir.' The Japanese was smiling.

They hit T1 at 7.47 a.m. The Japanese was struggling to take his wallet out. Gurleen rushed him. 'Please run. I will take the money later. And I will return in ten minutes; to take you back in case you miss the flight. Okay?'

He smiled wider, bowed and ran inside the terminal. When she returned, the Japanese was at the entry gate, waving his boarding card. He had made it! She wondered why he hadn't rushed in for security check, then she heard the announcement.

'Indigo regrets to announce a thirty-minute delay in the departure of its flight 6E 185 to Mumbai, due to air traffic. The inconvenience is regretted.'

No wonder he wasn't in a hurry.

She drove back to the stand, proud she had saved the day for the client. It was her best moment since her return from Denver. Desperate to break the news to Kartaar, she broke Delhi's strict rule against using mobile phones while driving. His phone was switched off.

Aryan would be happy to learn of her exploit, but it was midnight in the US and the black seal would choke him over a call at that hour. Then she remembered she had sworn never to call him again, ever! And now that she had a new number, there was no way he could reach her.

But it had been a wonderful morning. *Thank you, Rabba!*

Kartaar's phone remained switched off all day. She was restless. In the evening, she convinced Bihari, the senior-most driver at the stand, to check up on Kartaar and offered to pay his auto-rickshaw fare.

Bihari brought back news that Kartaar was in hospital.

She was shocked. 'Hospitalized for a cough and fever?'

He couldn't say what it was, except 'His stomach and legs were swollen, and he was in a lot of pain.'

'Can you take me there?'

'I am on duty tonight.' They agreed to go the next day.

The next day, there was a call from Tai-Yo to collect the payment. Gurleen still had her suitcase inside the Altis. She took out her favourite Cavalli trousers, put them back and settled for the faded

Escada jeans and old Gucci orange blouse. Both could be brushed off as fakes depending on who wore them. She had her five-minute shower in the makeshift bathroom, under a plastic showerhead that coughed and spat water, and pushed back all thoughts of the hour-long perfumed soaks in her onyx bathtub at Rambal Acres.

She changed inside the bathroom. Her jeans were wet at the ankles when she headed back to the Altis. Her comb and make up kit were in the glove compartment. Flipping the vanity mirror behind the sun visor, she brushed her hair and applied the mild Shiseido anti-ageing lotion. How long would it last, she wondered. Stepping out, she backed up until she could check herself full length in the side mirror before settling behind the steering wheel.

~

She was at the Tai-Yo office a second time in two days. Waiting in the reception area, she had her first taste of the green liquid that tasted like diluted pistachio *lassi*. Three young girls in light green uniforms walked up to the reception and picked up keys and some printed sheets from the counter. The sign atop read: Tai-Yo Ladies/Despatch.

Gurleen had finished another green bottle when the Japanese walked through the automatic door and bowed. She stood up and did the same. Her back was stiff from sleeping in the sagging *charpoy* at the stand, and she gave up midway, embarrassed. He said something like, 'Arigato' and switched to English. 'Thank you for taking me to airport on time. Vely impohtant meeting in Mumbai. Vely smaat. Thank you again.'

'No problem. You are welcome.'

He took out a sealed envelope; it looked much thicker than fifteen hundred rupees, unless he had stacked ten-rupee notes.

Handing it over, he introduced himself. 'I am Kino Tanaka, marketing director. Your name, madam?'

'Gurleen, sir.' She held back the family name.

'We like do business with your company. We sign monthly contract. Okay?'

'Thank you so much, Mr Tanaka. What will you need from us?'

'I ask manager to call you.'

'Okay, sir. I will inform the owner. Thanks again.'

'Arigato.' He bowed again and left.

Inside the taxi, she read the 'thank you' note and felt the neat single-stapled stack of brand-new fifty-rupee notes. *That's five thousand bucks! Kartaar, you lucky dog!* She thought. He would be delighted about the monthly contract. Did he even have a name for the stand? Kartaar Taxi Services? Yuck! They would need something better than that to deal with the Japanese.

At the stand, bad news awaited her. Kartaar had had a renal failure and had been taken to a government hospital in Chandigarh, where he had family. She put away thoughts of how she was going to get her new taxi without Kartaar around.

Three days later, Bihari brought worse news.

Kartaar had died.

Bihari was taking the evening train to Chandigarh and asked if she wanted to go. She couldn't come to terms that another good influence in her life had ended so abruptly. She declined and handed him two of her six thirty-gram gold bangles. It was her token of gratitude for Kartaar and her show of support to the widow. And she didn't need bangles on her hands; what she needed was a steering wheel.

Life was laughing at her and casting dark shadows around her again. In all of this, she saw one small ray of hope. It shone inside a little green bottle.

She had been waiting at the reception for more than an hour, during which she had gulped three 'Tai-Yo' when a lanky, bald man wearing rimless spectacles slid out of the glass door.

'Kartaar Taxi?'

'Yes, that's me.'

'Madam, what kind of company are you? We had a full month's duty waiting. I called thrice but no one answered the phone.'

'I'm sorry, the owner died in hospital. Please take down my number too.'

He was dismissive. 'But we've already contracted someone else.'

'I understand, sir, but is there no chance for me?'

'Maybe next time. But we need reliable people. At least someone to answer the phone.' He had a point.

Her ray of hope faded when he disappeared behind the opaque glass door. *What lies ahead?* Gurleen wondered, eyeing a group of young girls walk past, wearing stickers that said 'Tai-Yo Ladies'. A few others were filling out some forms.

'What is this Tai-Yo Ladies thing?' Gurleen asked one of them, who looked like a supervisor.

'Tai-Yo Ladies are door-to-door salesgirls.'

'How much do they earn?'

'Like, twenty thousand rupees, plus commissions.'

'How to know if there is a vacancy?'

'Just walk in, get tested and join. They need hundreds of salesgirls.'

'Can I try?'

'Can you drive a scooty?'

Gurleen laughed aloud, reminded of Tanaka's experience on the way to the airport.

The girl was apprehensive. 'Only you aren't as young as the others.'

'But I'm more desperate. Can you tell me where to go?'

'I'll ask the trainer to speak to you. I need to rush in now. Bye.' She ran inside the cubicle to join the others.

After a while, a woman walked towards Gurleen. She was barely five feet tall, waddled like a well-fed duck, wore outrageous canary yellow trousers and a melon-red shirt, and her clackety high-heeled footwear made her look even shorter.

'Please fill up this form and see me inside my cabin.' She handed a one-page form for Gurleen to fill up.

Gurleen checked what she had filled in.
Name: Gurleen.
Age: 45
Height: 5'6"
Weight: 63 kg
Education: BSc (Pass); Home Science (Nutrition)
Location: Delhi NCR
Why I want to be a Tai-Yo Lady (50 words max)

'The Tai-Yo Lady represents inner health, radiance and elegance with simplicity. It is also my vision of myself. I want to attain that in real life through self-respect and hard, sincere work, and putting honesty, sincerity, sociability, trust and leadership into my work at Tai-Yo'.

After reading it all, the trainer stated her decision. 'You've written a good essay. You have a good personality, but you are too old to be a Tai-Yo Lady.'

'Do I look old?'

'Tai-Yo Ladies are our models, our ambassadors. The company policy is to recruit ladies aged twenty-one to twenty-five, and not more than five kilos overweight.'

Gurleen was cheesed off. 'Did you fill up the form too, or did you join before they made the policy?'

She knew she had hit a raw nerve, for the trainer's cheeks went red. She looked at Gurleen with hatred and left without a word.

Heck with her. I'm no pushover. What do I have to lose now by pissing her off?

Gurleen got up to leave, when the glass door slid open again, and Tanaka came out.

'Hello Takusi san, who you drive today?'

Gurleen realized he was addressing her as 'Madame Taxi.'

'No one, sir. In fact, I've been driven away. From an interview.'

'What interview?'

'I want to become a Tai-Yo lady.'

He said something like 'Desune! But you aah very…very… very…senior. May be difficult.' She knew he wanted to say 'old'.

'Yes, I've learnt that now. I told you because you asked why I am here.'

She was about to leave when an Indian and a Japanese came rushing towards Tanaka san. They were talking about some problem with a tempo driver who had come in drunk.

Tanaka was disturbed. It showed in his red face and trembling lips. 'Cancel his contract.'

The Indian was concerned. 'Tanaka san, we have an urgent delivery to make.'

'If you want deliver on time, you drive van. Okay?'

'But Tanaka san, I am a sales manager. I can't drive a despatch van to deliver goods. We have to find someone else.'

Tanaka spoke in an even, deprecating tone. 'In Japan, company prestige more important than my prestige. If I have India driving licence, I drive now. You go or no go?' He thrust the keys into the Indian's hands.

The Indian didn't budge. Tanaka's jaw muscles were twitching, and he distracted himself away. His gaze fell on Gurleen, who had silently witnessed the tussle and now felt embarrassed. She had reached the main door and had pressed the exit button to step out, when she heard him call.

'Takusi san, wait!'

She spun around. Tanaka hurled the key bunch over. 'Take!'

She caught it deftly, extending her left hand.

'You drive Tai-Yo tempo from today.'

18

She drove the tempo to a warehouse on the eastern outskirts almost at the border of Delhi. The signboard read 'Jamaal & Co.' There was another board below that read 'Tai-Yo Depot'.

She was led inside a small foyer that had a huge glass wall. The area behind the glass looked a lot cleaner than most Indian hospitals: clean floors, freshly painted walls and a cold room at the end. Everyone inside was moving about in hospital-like uniforms. A forklift truck lugged several crates of little green bottles.

Soon, a prim lady—the badge said Prema Kumar—walked into the foyer and gave Gurleen two sheets.

'Please fill this so we can issue you a uniform. This other sheet has your schedule and the delivery addresses of our salesgirls. Feed all the mobile numbers into your cell phone. You must answer calls in no more than four rings. Understood?'

In an hour, she had a badge, a logbook, and the first roster to deliver Tai-Yo bottles to young Tai-Yo ladies who would deliver them in upmarket neighbourhoods across Delhi. After duty, she was to park the tempo in the office parking lot, hand over the keys to the security guard and get the logbook signed.

Her immediate worry was commuting to the office and back, without burning a hole in her pocket. Her mind went to Bihari's old TVS 50 moped, which was not being used now that he had bought Kartaar's Altis.

One afternoon, while doing her rounds, Gurleen saw a Tai-Yo lady at the Vasant Vihar crossing whom she did not recognize. She had driven out of the residential area and had pulled up on the other side of the road waiting for the traffic light to go green. Gurleen knew all the girls on her beat and was quite sure she wasn't on her list. She checked with Prema if there had been any addition to the sales force.

'No, we haven't appointed any new sales girl. Maybe you're mistaken, it must have been Selvi or Ameena who cover that beat.'

'Just wanted to be sure. Sorry.' Gurleen was still puzzled. *My eyesight is pretty good; I would have recognized Selvi and Ameena at that distance. The lady I saw wasn't either.*

A few days later she was on her way home, driving through bylanes to avoid the heavy traffic. She was forced to stop at a street where a crowd had gathered. She edged her way through. A brawl was in full swing. Two men were beating each other up, and the street was littered with thousands of crushed Tai-Yo bottles, she could make that out from the printed labels. Something bothered her; she couldn't put her finger on it. But her gut told her she was walking into trouble.

A whole month had passed, and it was payday. Gurleen got twenty thousand rupees, less four hundred for late arrivals for her first month as a tempo driver. She was happy, considering she had nothing just a month ago. But there was a small problem. The company wanted her bank account details to transfer the money. Her old account was useless, and she soon learnt she couldn't open a fresh bank account either. As soon as her name was entered, a red alert popped up from CIBIL, some bank warning system that turned up a list of all loan defaulters.

Eventually, she got Bihari to open and operate an account in the name of 'Taxi Leena'. Bihari deposited the cheque and cashed it for her, and slapped her with a five thousand rupee service charge. But then he wasn't Kartaar, and she wasn't paying rent for the stand either. It was fair.

Days later, she was waiting at the Munirka market for Selvi. Fearing a no-show after fifteen minutes, she issued a 'missed' call and got no reply. She was about to leave when she saw Selvi parked at the other end of the road, some two hundred feet away and shouted out. 'Selvi! Here!'

It shocked her that Selvi looked at her and quickly headed off the other way. Strange! *What's wrong with her? Why would she avoid me considering she's the one that's late!*

Gurleen was dialling the depot manager to report it when Selvi walked slowly towards her from a side street. Her cheeks were pale, and she smiled with strain.

'Hello, Leena, sorry I haven't kept well. I came here only to tell you not to wait.'

'What nonsense,' Gurleen burst out. 'That's a lie! I just saw you on your scooter a minute ago!'

'No, I didn't even go to the office today to pick my scooter.'

'You mean your scooter's still at the office parking lot? Well, let's find out.'

'You don't trust me, no! Let me call the office.' Selvi began dialling.

Gurleen stopped her. 'Relax. I'll dial.'

The despatch clerk confirmed Selvi's story. '...The scooter keys are here, and she hasn't signed in today.'

Gurleen was still unbelieving. 'Please check if the scooter is parked there, will you?'

She was put on hold and then told, 'Yes, her scooter is here. DL 1R A 4125.'

She turned to Selvi. 'What's your scooter number?'

'DL 1R A 4125.'

Gurleen was both relieved and ashamed.

'Selvi, I am sorry, but I saw another lady whiz past me just a minute before you came, and it isn't the first time. Is there another Tai-Yo lady on this beat?'

'I don't know! But my sales have dipped lately.'

'Something is not right. We must find out for both our sakes.

Let me drop you home. You stay closeby, right?'

'Yes, in Munirka village.'

'Hop on.'

Gurleen took Selvi to her small quarters close by. Selvi had passed her second test too. But Gurleen was convinced something much bigger was at hand. By the time she handed in the keys that evening, she had decided what she had to do.

Next day, she stopped at the usual meeting point at Munirka. She already knew from the despatch folks that Selvi hadn't called in. She reached half an hour early to make sure she didn't miss the mysterious salesgirl. Bihari's Altis was parked ahead as planned. She waited an hour and then gave up. Gurleen ran up a two hundred rupees penalty for late arrival.

Day two of surveillance.

No show again. Two hundred and fifty rupees penalty.

Day three.

Bingo! They hit pay dirt at Munirka. As soon as she spotted 'mystery girl', Gurleen repeated her instructions to Bihari, wished him luck and headed off on her beat.

In the evening, Bihari filled her in.

'I followed her for three hours and switched cars, to avoid suspicion.'

'How did you do that?'

'I called my brother and asked him to follow her midway in his taxi.'

'You fancy being a detective?'

'She made fourteen deliveries in Vasant Vihar. Then my brother followed her to Delhi border and took a photo where she stopped. Here, have a look.'

She peeped at his phone screen and recognized the board. 'Salaam Formulations P. Ltd.'

'Oh, that's so near the warehouse! I've been passing it everyday.'

Next day, Gurleen and Bihari reported the matter to General Pitambar, a retired army man, the head of administration. Tanaka san was away on vacation.

The general heard them out and interrupted with several questions before announcing his decision. 'Well done. I'll handle it from here. Obviously, an insider must be involved. But don't talk about this to anyone in the office or anywhere else. But you have done a wonderful job. Thank you!'

Days later, Gurleen got to hear the full story from the security officer.

'They copied the seals, filled coloured glucose in discarded bottles and repacked them. Who would have thought that a fake company would use fake salesgirls to deliver a fake product, right under our very noses!'

The incident had shocked everyone in the senior management. Soon, Gurleen noted that the managers kept away from the junior staff and heard more conversations in Japanese than before. She also noted that many people were being transferred to the new factory at Ballabgarh, sixty kilometres away from Delhi. It worried her. *Would I have to report at Ballabgarh?*

Her bigger worry was that Tanaka san hadn't called for her after his return from his vacation. Now that was quite strange! Unless he didn't know that she was the one that had busted the racket. As if her thoughts had reached him, she was summoned into his office right then!

Tanaka san was seated on the plush sofa and the general was by his side, holding a sealed envelope in his hands. Seeing her, Tanaka got up from the sofa, bowed and began.

'Leena san, the company thank you for your courage. We are very grateful. Arigato.' He took the envelope from the general. 'Small gift. Please take. Arigato.' He bowed again and sat back.

Gurleen thanked him and stepped out. She had been so wrong.

She tore off the tape and opened the envelope. Inside she found a cheque for one lakh rupees and a certificate of appreciation on the Tai-Yo letterhead.

Later that evening, she was back to hand in the tempo keys at the office. More than a hundred girls stood outside the building, the colour drained from their faces. Something was very wrong.

'What's the matter?' she asked the receptionist, who looked at her in anger.

'Thanks to you, they are closing down the office here and shifting to the factory.'

Gurleen was surprised that the secret had already spread. 'What? Who's going to deliver the stuff in Delhi?'

'They have appointed a Japanese agency to take over the depot and the fleet. No old staff will be retained.'

'Who told you that?'

'There's a circular on the notice board, signed by Tanaka.'

Book III

19

So that's how you became a taxi driver,' Chameli Singh deduced, as she rolled the empty Bacardi bottle on the floor.

'Yes. I was back, asking Bihari for a spare taxi. All he could find me was a night shift job at the railway station. The taxi owner works the day shift, and lends it to me for the night shift.'

'And then, I found you on the road.'

Weary from her story, Leena toyed with Chameli's Wills Femme pack. She had never smoked, except for a casual puff long ago at Vikrant's cigars, and had hated the acrid taste in her mouth. It was so long ago. She pulled out a stick and smelt it. *Maybe I won't gag now*, she thought as she flicked Chameli's purple Bic lighter knob.

She inhaled the burning nicotine deep into her lungs; it was still the same rotten taste and made her cough. She drew in again, slower, deeper and filled her lungs. She immediately knew from the rush of nicotine in the blood and the tingling in her nostrils that she would never be able to give it up.

The hearing was two days away. Chameli Singh brought in the forensic guys and took Gurleen's fingerprints for analysis. They also visited the spot where the incident had taken place. The wrench had already been analysed and was the key evidence against Gurleen.

On the morning of the trial, Gurleen was ready at nine, waiting for Chameli Singh to take her to the Tis Hazari Court. It worried her that she hadn't turned up even an hour later. Then a police jeep drew up outside the station to bring Gurleen to the court. On the way, the jeep driver dialled Chameli Singh and handed the phone to Gurleen.

Chameli spoke in a rush.

'Leena, listen very carefully. Just deny everything. Say nothing about the girl. Just tell them you heard a scream and slowed down, and someone attacked you in the dark. Don't say anything else. Okay? No girl. No fight. Got it? Completely deny attacking the guy. It's your only hope. And don't smile at me in court.'

Gurleen was bewildered. Before it all sank in, they were already at the court. She saw Chameli outside the courtroom, but she avoided her gaze, *deliberately*, Gurleen thought. She felt her heart race.

Inside the dirty room, five criminal cases were listed for hearings that day. 'State versus Gurleen Rambal' was the fifth one, announced at 1 p.m.

The inspector brought Gurleen before the bench.

'Counsel for the defence?' the bald judge asked, his pen playfully swiping the tufts of hair jutting out of his nostrils.

Before Gurleen could respond, a pleasant voice answered from behind. 'Your Honour. Advocate Ravi Dhar from Rustom Law Offices, advocate for the defence.' Gurleen turned and saw a tall, young man in a well-cut black suit and a dapper lawyer's gown.

Now who in heaven's name was this? She wondered, then remembered Chameli's instructions and fought the surprise off her face. After accepting the defence counsel's credentials, the judge asked the prosecutor to present the case. When the prosecution had finished, Gurleen's self-appointed lawyer approached the bench.

'Your Honour, my client pleads not guilty. She just happened to be at the scene of the crime. She heard a cry for help and slowed her taxi. Someone attacked her and she fell unconscious. The prosecution's statement confirms that she was still unconscious when picked up by the police, Your Honour.'

Next, the judge called Inspector Chameli Singh and waved a document at her. 'Is this the report filed by you at the station?'

'Yes, that is my FIR report, Huzoor,' Chameli confirmed.

The lawyer spoke. 'Your Honour, there is no mention in the FIR about the defendant hitting the van driver.'

Chameli Singh looked at Gurleen for a fleeting second, nodded faintly and looked away.

The prosecutor was insistent. 'Your Honour, a wrench was found lodged in the victim's skull. The forensic department has a fingerprint analysis report. With your permission.' He offered a sealed plastic envelope and a report.

The judge looked at the submission and ordered, 'Register it as an evidence exhibit.' He then called the defence counsel over and opened the report. After they had gone through it, the judge thundered.

'What kind of evidence is this? There are ten sets of fingerprints in there, but none matches those of the accused.' He then handed the report back to the prosecutor, who was scratching his head. The judge then turned to Gurleen and announced, 'Bail granted,' and admonished the prosecution. 'I'm giving a date two months from now, and the prosecution better present serious evidence, else the case will be dismissed.'

Gurleen hadn't the faintest idea what was happening but waited outside the courtroom for Chameli Singh to return with the lawyer. They came out half an hour later. The lawyer was smiling. He shook Gurleen's hand and said, 'Mrs Rambal, you are free to go home. Don't worry. We will win the case in the next hearing itself. They have no evidence.'

Gurleen was numb with disbelief. 'What makes you so sure?'

The lawyer interrupted. 'The wrench doesn't have your fingerprints. You didn't run away from the scene. You were found unconscious, hurt and bleeding. And there is no motive either.'

Gurleen sensed something was at play but couldn't fathom what. 'Who are you, Mr Dhar?'

He smiled. 'It's a long story. I'll tell you about it in our office, where I am going to take you now to finish some paperwork.'

Gurleen hugged Chameli Singh and didn't let go until the lawyer's gleaming blue SUV parked before them. 'Thank you, Chameli ji. I'll be back at the station when I'm through with this.'

'I'll be around.' Chameli Singh said, as she faded out of view from the BMW X3's rear screen.

They were outside the gate of Rustom Towers, a huge, sprawling office building inside Okhla in South Delhi. The BMW honked thrice, and the electric gate opened. Soon, she was at the top floor, seated in a huge room with a giant screen, savouring the finest coffee she had had in a long time. The lawyer had gone briefly to finish another small matter.

When Ravi Dhar walked in, she was impatient. 'Mr Dhar, I don't know you. And I can't afford any lawyer, let alone someone like you.' Her voice trailed off, and a tear inadvertently rolled out and fell on the shiny table surface.

He handed her a tissue and put his assuring arm over her shoulder. 'Don't worry, Mrs Rambal, you don't have to pay us. It is our privilege to serve a brave lady like you.'

She composed herself and took another swig at the coffee. 'Who hired you?'

'Her father.'

'Whose father?'

'The girl who was raped.'

'How would she know me?'

'We got a call from Tokyo. Her father's a valuable client of ours. My colleague reached the spot at two in the morning and took her away.'

'And left me there, bleeding! Of course, why would you wait for me?'

'Of course not, Mrs Rambal. My colleague had a doctor with him. They first put the girl into their van and then told me about two other bodies lying on the road. I dialled the Police Control Room.

My colleague left after seeing a police jeep turn into the lane. That was the best I could do. Hope you understand.'

'Who's the girl?'

'A very important person's daughter. And her father would like to thank you personally.'

'He's here?'

'Kind of,' he said, switching on the giant screen with the remote-control button. He punched some numbers, and Gurleen's face came up in a small window at a corner of the giant screen.

The big window came alive, showing a girl and a man. She was beautiful despite the gashes on her neck and forehead and bandages on both hands. Gurleen couldn't see below the hips, but knew there would be some torn muscle in there.

'What's her name?' she asked Ravi.

'Yumiko Takematsu. She's Japanese.'

The girl saw Gurleen and bowed her head again and again. Gurleen could understand only the *Arigato*, from Tanaka san's vocabulary. Then her father, dressed in a black suit, took over.

'Rambal san, I am very grateful to you for saving my daughter's life in India. I can never forget your kindness. We will remember you all our lives.'

After more than fifty *Arigatos*, the screen went blank. Gurleen was speechless, and not just because she couldn't speak the language. It was too overwhelming, and she asked to be directed to the toilet.

When she returned, Ravi had a few papers laid out on the table. After she had signed them, he asked, 'Is there an address I can reach you at?'

'DL 3T Q 26311,' she offered without hesitation. He didn't realize it until he had finished writing it down. 'That's a taxi number.' He raised his eyebrows.

'It's home for now,' she spoke without a trace of shame.

'Oh! But you must have a permanent address in Delhi, no?'

His eyes widened when she said, 'Rambal Acres, ZA3, East Nizamuddin.'

He was stunned. 'Gosh, you're that Rambal! I am sorry I didn't recognize you.'

'If life kicks you like I've been kicked, you'd look very different too. I've been kicked out of my house by that Raina...'

'You mean Rattan Lal Raina, the lawyer?'

'You know the swine?'

'We have sued him for fraud twice. Unfortunately, bad guys like Raina ruin the reputation of all lawyers.'

'You seem decent and honest.' She felt assured by the soft-spoken young man, a complete contrast to the shady Raina.

'It's not all black and white, unfortunately. But what's your problem with Raina?'

She ended up telling him everything.

An hour later, Ravi's secretary announced that the radio taxi had arrived. As Gurleen rose from the plush leather chair, she remembered what had bothered her in the courtroom.

'Mr Dhar, don't you believe I broke his skull?'

He smiled, and a mischievous glint came into his eyes. 'I know that from two independent sources. Yumiko and the policewoman.'

'The cops found a wrench on the man's body, right?'

'Yes, it was embedded in the skull.'

'Unless I am a fool, I'd be right in thinking that my fingerprints should've been on it. Right?'

'Right,' he was grinning.

'Then, how did my prints vanish from the wrench?'

He laughed aloud, sounding like a movie villain, and seemed to enjoy himself until he coughed. After collecting himself, he broke the suspense. 'You see, it wasn't the prints that disappeared. It was the wrench that disappeared.'

'What?'

'There was a wrench inside the van's tool kit. We switched them job. Only, the man's skull had to be broken a bit more to insert the new wrench, which was bigger than yours.'

'*Hai Rabba*! No wonder they let me go!' Gurleen stared at him in disbelief.

'Sometimes, truth can only be rescued by subterfuge. So we aren't that honest, you see! But as the principle of justice intends, a thousand guilty may be allowed to go free, but not even one innocent person must be punished wrongly.'

Ravi hugged her lightly and held the door open as she eased into the radio taxi.

It was dusk when she reached her destination, after a detour to the iconic Nathu Sweets. She arrived just in time to see Chameli Singh step out of the station.

Chameli, caught by surprise, hugged her. 'I didn't expect you to come back, honestly.' When she let go, Gurleen held out her hands, one holding a bottle of rum and the other, Chameli's favourite salted matar kachori, which she thought Nathu Sweets made better than the whole world.

'Where would I go, Chameli ji? After all that you've done for me at the court, I'm not letting you out of my sight, unless you want me to leave.'

Hours later, they were both satiated after gorging on Nathu Sweets' crackers and listening to Radio City. Only, this time, they hadn't misused the police station. But their venue was no less unique: DL 3TQ 26311.

When the bottle ran out, Chameli shook Gurleen with the words, 'Leena, move in with me.'

'Pitying me?' Gurleen's words came thick and slurred.

'Hell no, I told you I'm scared of the dark myself.'

Being with Chammo—Chameli insisted on being called that— had turned out rather easy. In a short time, Gurleen thought they had grown to be each other's anchors, filling up voids in each other's lives. Gurleen had learnt to look beyond the horrid scar, and saw Chammo was a beautiful person, with a mischievous twinkle in her eyes, a ready smile, a positive mind and a heart of gold. It must have taken a heartless one to splash acid on her face.

One Sunday morning, they were cleaning the little quarter, when Chameli stumbled across an album; it had fallen off while moving their clothes to dust the shelves. She flipped through it in front of Gurleen, who didn't seem to mind.

'That's you, Leena? You look great in this suit.' She held out a page showing a fit Gurleen in a Versace suit and mean Armani shades. The bungalow loomed large behind her as she stood in the gravelled driveway. To her left lay the outhouse. 'It's huge. Even your garage must be thrice the size of my quarter. Wow!'

Gurleen came over and stood next to Chammo. 'Our garage can accommodate an entire family. The outhouse, another. My driver and servant lived there with their families.'

They turned the pages at random until Chammo stopped at one taken at a swimming pool. An attractive woman, hour-glass shaped, stood in a micro bikini, next to two men, one very toned and good looking, and the other, average and somewhat portly. Gurleen sat away from them under a parasol.

Gurleen explained. 'That was on our yacht, in Cannes, France.'

'Who's the woman?'

'Shalini. Visham's wife.'

'Visham who?'

'Vikki's cousin.'

She pointed to the portly one and raised her eyebrows.

'Yes, that's Vikki.'

'See the way he's holding that woman so close to him. Strange, isn't it?'

'I was jealous of her.'

Chammo poured two tall glasses and looked expectantly at Gurleen.

'No wonder you sat at a distance. She's a real looker.'

And a real hooker, Gurleen thought.

~

1984. New Delhi.

'Live Life King Size!' was the heady advertising tagline for Kingfisher. The ad had been shot with bikini clad girls hanging on to a sailboat's pole and muscular men having beer, strumming guitars and cigarettes dangling from their mouths, with the sun setting beyond the sea. While millions of Indians vicariously experienced that heady high, it was a rare few who lived that king size lifestyle in real life. Fewer lived off it. Like Shalini Gupta.

A former Miss Delhi, Shalini had had a dream debut in Bollywood that ended rather soon. A string of flops later, she had returned to Delhi to find new hope in the city's party circuit. Her luck turned when, one day, following a business lead, she ran into Visham Rambal.

'Mr Rambal, aren't you?' Shalini sought out the stylishly dressed handsome man waiting for her at the private business chambers at the Oberoi Hotel.

'Call me Visham,' he said, offering to relieve her of the heavy sample book of imported leather swatches. Shalini found herself drawn to the dignified, unassuming man. He was irresistibly good looking, an inch or two over six, well-groomed hair, and those deep blue eyes, wow! While he was evaluating the samples, she was evaluating Visham Rambal as a million-dollar insurance policy. Taken out in her name.

Days later, they met again at a party, and soon they were dating. One day, he shared an important development.

'So, you're going off to England?' she rued as she took his palm into hers, at the poolside of Hotel Ashok, where she had landed a job at the front desk.

'I've always wanted to study law. And grow out of Vikki bhaiyya's shadow.'

'Where in England?'

'East Anglia University, Norfolk.'

'Must be expensive, living there.'

'Luckily, I won't have to wash dishes or work at petrol bunks part-time. Someone has arranged an apartment for me in Elveden Close.'

'Elveden? Never heard of it.'

'It has a historical connection to India.'

'What connection?'

'Duleep Singh, who was Maharaja Ranjit Singh's son and the last emperor of Punjab, lived there. At Elveden Hall.'

'I'm going to miss you, Visham. I worry that you'll find a white woman, or a maharani.'

'I've been thinking the same.'

'A white woman or maharani?'

'About you, Shalini. You need to know that I am a Rambal just in name. I don't own the business or for that matter anything in this house. And I will be walking out of it all now.'

'Why?'

'Vikki's always taunting me. Like, "these are my things you're enjoying, Visham, you hand-me-down Rambal".'

'Really? You own nothing?'

'Nothing.'

'Do you think your brother would approve…of me?'

'My gut feel is—yes. Maybe you can help him with the business while I'm in England.'

'How can I get to meet him?'

'Do you still want that deal for imported leather upholstery?'

As Shalini waited for Vikrant Rambal in the hall, her eyes took in the ornateness of Rambal Acres. The hundreds of photographs shown by the media didn't do justice to its real grandeur. Her eyes took in all the exquisite pieces of art, the stuffed tiger, a Hussain, a Lalique bust, the Earl's dinner jacket and other souvenirs gifted to Sir Lala Vijendra Rambal. She was engrossed in an intricate ivory carving when a loud 'Hullo lady!' shook her out of her reverie.

Wearing a non-descript navy blue safari suit, he was not in the same mould as the softer, irresistible Visham; and surely not one to make a memorable first impression. But Vikrant Rambal made up for his mediocre appearance and sartorial taste by his immeasurable wealth. She noted the Rolex solid gold watch, the huge diamond ring, the Bally shoes and Cartier satchel, calculating that the accessories on his body could buy an apartment in Delhi's upmarket Defence Colony. And there was something animal-like about him; he exuded a raw power that pulled at her.

As she withdrew her hand after a longish handshake, she knew that Vikrant was the key to her goal, of living at the Rambal house.

'Like the house, Miss Shalini?'

'Mr Rambal, I can't imagine I am here in this luxury.'

'We have been rather fortunate, thank you. And now it is in your hands to ensure that your work does justice to it.'

'I'll do my best, sir.'

'Call me Vikrant. After all I'm the same age as your friend Visham.' He unsettled her by asking, 'You both dating?'

She was quick to collect herself and retort. 'Visham is such an attractive young man to date.'

He ignored her remark and left her alone until a manager came to talk to her about the installation.

Bullseye Shalini! She complimented herself.

20

*Q*uite a colourful family, you Rambals!' Chameli said, rolling off the settee.

Gurleen was still looking at the photograph, at the big lawn at one end, occupying more than half the plot, and separated by a picket fence along the driveway. The main residence was a two storeyed bungalow, with a stairway inside that led to the first floor, now Raina's portion. Behind the bungalow, along the edge of the driveway was the outhouse and garage area. As she kept staring at the photograph, a brainwave hit Gurleen. *Oh god! How could I have overlooked it?* Soon, she was giggling uncontrollably, sobbing intermittently with relief.

Chammo was puzzled. 'What? What happened? Have you thought of a plan?'

Gurleen tossed the album on the settee and sprung into action. 'Just let me confirm everything once before I tell you.'

Soon she had frisked her suitcase, taken out the yellow folder with the unsigned 'rent agreement' and was reading it, engrossed.

Gurleen then called up Ravi Dhar and arranged to meet him in an hour. Chameli caught her muttering *'I have nothing more to lose. I can only win from here'* but thought better than to interrupt Gurleen's thoughts.

When Gurleen returned, her face was glowing. She hugged Chammo and twirled around holding her tight. 'Yaar Chammo, now, no one can stop me, sorry, us, from living in Rambal Acres. Not the bank. Not Mr Raina. Nobody.'

'What happened?'

'Lunch first. I'm famished.'

Over a quick lunch, Gurleen ended up telling her everything

she had discovered.

'See this agreement? The definition of the term "premises" leaves no doubt. I've read it so many times; I can even quote it with the two spelling mistakes. See, it reads:

"The premises being rented out consist of six bedrooms, one drawing room, two kitchens and five bathrooms along with veranda, all on the first floor. The lessee shall not be entitled to the use of any other part of the plot under this agreement."

'And this clause:

"The first party has the right to restrict entry of the first party through the front staircase on the ground floor."

'And last, this:

"The second party shall not carry out any, including minor repairs of any kind in the premises whatsoever without the written approval of the first party. No structural work, digging or breaking of walls will be permitted under any circumstances during the validity of this agreement."'

'So, what does it all mean, Leena?'

'It means that Raina can't set foot on the property from the front gate. How did I forget about it? The tenant was supposed to build an independent rear stairway for the first floor as part of his renovation. But my premature return must have upset his plans, for he hadn't even begun work on it. All this while, he has been using the front stairway from the ground floor. I'll stop him now. And, he can't even build anything anymore. He can't even fix a leaking tap without my written permission!'

She laughed as she capped the lid on her mineral water bottle and turned it upside down, the water settling at the lid but not flowing out.

'Leena, tell me you're going to seal his toilet pipe from below!'

'You bet! I'm going to put cement in the sewer pipes below. He can't touch anything.' She clapped her hands in childish glee. 'But I still have one big worry, Chammo.'

'What?'

'My entire plan is based on one big assumption—that Raina hasn't changed any other part of the agreement. I'm counting that he's just filled in the blank space with the word "perpetually". If that's all he has done, I'm ready. And I have to be sure Raina has registered the agreement.'

'How will you find out?'

'That's why I met Ravi. He can check at the registrar's office.' She leaned across and kissed Chammo's scarred cheek. 'I am going to hurt Raina real bad. Get ready, Chammo darling, there's lots of action ahead. I need your help.'

'You only have to tell me where to land my blows.'

'Oh, it feels great to return home.'

'Hold on! Not so fast. Don't forget the bank's sealed the ground floor.'

'Yes and no.'

'What do you mean?'

'My dear Chammo, it was you who showed me the way. Didn't you notice the garage and outhouse in the photographs?'

'What about them?'

'Well, the bank can't touch them.'

'I don't understand.'

'Rambal Acres is on two adjacent plots. The bungalow is on the left plot. The outhouse, garage and the clump of woods all the way to Humayun's Tomb, they're on the bigger plot on the right. That's where Vikki wanted to build a heritage hotel. That hasn't been pledged.'

'So, they can't stop you from staying in the outhouse?'

'Yes! That is right! Now, pack up.'

At the gates of Rambal Acres, the security guard hesitated before the two women who were bold from their new discovery and high from rum.

'This isn't your *baap* Raina's property. Open the gate, you bum!' Gurleen's lingo shocked him, and he could see she was tipsy. He pushed her as she wriggled through the partly open gate but was totally unprepared for Chammo's colourful police speak as she grabbed his collar. Embarrassed, he flung the gate open and watched in shock as the two women charged inside. Chammo spat on his shoes before treading on the gravel path leading to the locked outhouse.

Gurleen opened the latches on the creaky outer door and the inner mesh grille, both laced with cobwebs. A musty odour came through from inside and a spider lunged at Gurleen's face, unsettled over its web being torn. Gurleen brushed it off and stomped it under her feet in disgust as Chammo looked on and giggled.

By evening, they were done dusting and Gurleen was famished, her sugar levels down. Chammo set off to get hot sugared tea and Glucose biscuits, while Gurleen put on her thinking cap. She dug into her bag to find something to write with and settled on an old visiting card and an old ballpoint pen to list their survival needs.

She was at the end of the list when she considered her cash-in-hand, all of five thousand six hundred rupees, besides some forty-five thousand in the proxy bank account. Suddenly, it looked like a luxury list. After some strike offs, it got affordable: water filter, bucket, duster, Dettol, Harpic, towels, soap, shampoo, kettle, tea bags, sugar and three potted plants.

Three hours later, they inaugurated Outhouse@Rambal Acres, Nizamuddin.

'What next, Leena?' Chammo asked, sipping homemade tea in their new home.

'I've been thinking about Raina. Ready for a test run tomorrow?'

'What are you going to test him with?'

'Parking. He has no right to park inside the compound.'

Around 9 p.m., Raina's second-hand neptune blue BMW 323 pulled up close to the outhouse door. Its bright headlights seared through the grill door and stayed on longer than usual, as if to let Raina take in all the opulence of Gurleen's humble abode.

Eventually, Raina got out. Gurleen caught him looking at her and turned away. When he had gone, she realized he had parked the car so close to the door, it wouldn't open enough to let anyone through. She edged herself out with some struggle and inspected the clearance. It was apparent he had done it on purpose.

'Sorry, I upset your house warming!' She heard him call out from the stairs.

'Raina, you just wait until tomorrow!'

Soon, Raina's driver Raj Singh came out to pick up some packages from the car's boot. Gurleen reminded him. 'From tomorrow, park the car outside the compound.'

Next morning, Gurleen saw Raj Singh cleaning the BMW and reminded him again. His reply irked her.

'Mr Raina says, we'll see when you get your car.'

After an hour, Raina took his car out. It was the moment they had been waiting for. Chammo ran out and manoeuvred her jeep inside and parked it in the middle of the driveway. Gurleen parked her taxi behind Chammo's jeep. There was no space for a third car to enter inside.

Raina returned two hours later to find he couldn't bring his car inside the compound. His horn blared nonstop, and soon, a crowd of passers-by had gathered some out of curiosity and a saner few to put a stop to the unbearable noise.

Chammo walked out to the gate and asked Raina, 'What's this nonsense?'

Raina saw her, dressed in full uniform and turned away at the sight of her cheek, and cast a closer look at her, his eyebrows creased.

She looked at him, her gaze defiant. 'Look mister, if you honk again, I'll haul you to the police station. Understood?'

He stopped honking and stepped out. 'Let me park inside. Or I'll take you to court.'

Soon, a few neighbours, including Brigadier Fauja in walking gear, had joined in.

'What's this ruckus about?' Brigadier Fauja avoided looking at Gurleen and asked Chammo instead. Another neighbour whose name Gurleen couldn't remember—he too was a lawyer—walked across. 'Madam, what is the problem?'

'Sir, this fraud, he's tricked me and taken over my first floor, and now he insists on parking his car here. He has no rights to park, even in his forged agreement,' she burst out.

'Advocate Raina is that—' The man was cut off brusquely.

Raina fumed. 'Mind your business, sir. This woman is harassing me. I live on the first floor.'

Gurleen rushed inside and soon returned, waving the agreement before everyone. 'See in here, there's no mention of parking in the compound.'

'He is harassing her because she is alone,' Chammo chipped in.

The neighbour looked at it and admonished Raina. 'She's right. You have no right to park inside, Mr Raina.'

He warned them. 'Don't you people mess with me. I own the first floor.'

Hearing that, Gurleen went ballistic. 'You don't own an inch of anything, Raina! You cheated me. You know it and I know it. You scoundrel!'

Raina backed off, embarrassed, and walked off upstairs, leaving his car outside the gate. The way it was parked, Chammo couldn't take her jeep out. She barged up the stairs and rang his doorbell nonstop. No response. Even the driver was nowhere in sight. She stormed out of the gate, cursing.

In a while, she returned with a tow-truck with a motored winch.

They rang Raina's doorbell. Again. No response. Gurleen signed the complaint and the traffic cops took photos.

Raina's driver came out rushing with the keys, but it was too late. The tow truck had dragged the BMW away like a teacher dragging an errant schoolboy. They heard a loud crunch as the truck passed over a large speed-breaker and the BMW's rear bumper scraped the hump.

Raina came out, screaming at Gurleen. 'I'll make your life hell! I'll send you back to the streets.' He then looked at Chammo and warned her. 'And you, I'm going to make you lick my boots one day. Just watch it, you ugly bitch!' and spat on her uniform.

'You better remember this day,' said Chammo, ignoring the insult. There was a deathly coldness in her voice but Gurleen wondered why she didn't knock his teeth out.

Round One to Gurleen.

The rest of the day went by smoothly. The day shift driver had gone to his village, and Gurleen got to do the day shift. When she returned that evening, Raina's BMW was back in its initial place, parked so close to the outhouse door she could barely open it. The driver was nowhere to be seen. Nor was Raina.

An hour later Chammo came in and saw Gurleen sitting outside. There was no space to wedge between the car and the door. Working a rage, she scooted up the stairs and banged at Raina's door. 'Raina! *Baahar nikal*! Come out, you bastard!'

No one answered.

Both women stayed up all night, hungry and bitten by mosquitos.

Round Two to Raina.

Next morning, there was still no sign of Raina. Chammo, who hadn't brushed or showered, took off in her jeep. She returned with a man in overalls, his hands black with grease. He inspected the BMW and said, 'Thousand rupees.'

'Fine. I'll tell you when.' Chammo sent him away. When he had gone, she turned to Gurleen, with a wicked gleam in her eyes.

'What's up?' Gurleen couldn't hold back her curiosity.

'He's an expert locksmith. I caught him stealing cars. He works for the cops now.'

'Don't tell me you're going to steal Raina's car!'

Chammo chuckled, 'No, I'm going take it in safe custody.'

Gurleen didn't understand one bit.

Gurleen spent the weekend alone at Chammo's quarters. Chammo was busy with a new case and didn't come home. Monday morning, Gurleen went back to check if the BMW had cleared enough space for her to squeeze in.

She arrived to find a squad of police jeeps and a crowd outside the house. Nudging through, she saw the BMW's rear bonnet open. There were patches of dry blood all over. Following complaints of a foul stench, the police had come in and broken open the lock. A dead body had been found inside it.

Gurleen could see the media vans crowd at the gate. *Looks like Rambal Acres will be in the news again.* She ducked and hid from their view. Chammo was nowhere around, and her phone was switched off.

Soon, the body had been zipped and put inside a morgue van. The BMW was towed again, this time as evidence in a murder case. A notice was pasted on Raina's main door and a police constable took up post in the compound to book Raina as soon as he turned up.

Gurleen waited with rising anger to hear from Chammo and get a hang of whatever was going on in her house. It was almost ten in the night when Chammo walked in.

Gurleen was smouldering. 'Chammo, couldn't you call even once? Do you know there was a corpse in Raina's car?'

Her answer shocked Gurleen. 'It wasn't a corpse when he complained against a land mafia don at my station.'

'How did the body land up in Raina's car?'

'Raina happens to be the don's and his lover's lawyer. They were blackmailing the guy into selling his land cheap. I brought her in for questioning, but he went missing soon after. Yesterday, they found him dead, his body was dumped close to our station.'

'And then?'

'I found it convenient to tuck him nicely, inside Raina's car.' She held out a duplicate key for the bonnet. 'Remember the locksmith?'

Round Three to Chammo.

They didn't speak for a whole day. Gurleen feared the worst: *Is she involved in something sinister and doesn't want to tell me? Can I trust her? Hell, no, I'll confront her, I'll fight with her, but I'll trust her.*

Next evening, overcoming her demons, Gurleen made Chammo's favourite *kadi pakodi* and ordered *butter naan* from a nearby eatery. Chammo came in late and remained silent even while eating. After the meal, she asked, 'Did he turn up?'

'Won't you get to know first? You've posted a constable here!'

'Yes. I know. Serves him right.'

'Chammo, why are you after Raina?'

Chameli Singh took a deep breath. 'Sorry I didn't tell you this earlier, but I have my own score to settle with Raina!'

'I didn't know you would go that far to seek revenge if somebody spoilt your uniform!'

'No, but I would go a lot farther if somebody spoilt my face.'

'What?' Gurleen staggered in shock.

'Yes, he's not just your Raina, he's my Raina too!'

And Chammo came clean about everything.

'I knew this senior officer; he looked great and was smart. I fell madly in love. It was too late when I found out he was a real bad apple. One day, he asked me to tamper with evidence in a case. I walked out on him. They lost the case and he was suspended. The

Avik Davar

result: He turned me into Mona Lisa.' She rubbed her jagged cheek.

'Where's he now?'

'You know what happens when policemen get into bed with goons. They get bumped off one day.'

'But what's that got to do with Raina?'

'Raina was the slime who held me from behind as my lover performed this cosmetic surgery.'

'How do you know?'

'I'd recognize that raspy voice from hell. He was the one who yanked my hands behind, and kept saying, "Careful with the acid, okay? Make sure nothing spills on my hands. Or I won't be able to write." And then, I kicked wildly. The acid splashed on my lover's hands. He released me and ran to wash it off. Then Raina carved me up and poured acid into my wound.'

'How did you know it was him in the dark?'

'My boyfriend blurted out his name twice. Raina even cursed him for it.'

'Why didn't you identify him in court?'

'Everything happened in the dark. I couldn't identify him; I just heard his name. And he had a strong alibi.'

'Didn't he recognize you?'

'I was bandaged all the time during the hearings. When they took the bandage off, even I couldn't recognize myself. But how many policewomen in town have cheeks like mine?'

Chammo cried the whole night. But not before confessing something else. 'Leena, when I began my investigation about you, I soon found out about Raina and thought I could get to him through you. But I never thought we'd become friends. Sorry, I tried to use you.'

Gurleen looked away, her eyes clouded. 'It's okay, Chammo. I'd have done the same in your place.'

21

The Sub Rosa Club at Delhi's first seven-star hotel, the Constella, was the ultimate in discretion. It was a service accessible only to a select few members, and its latest testimony to secrecy was the ornate private conference rooms in the basement. Raina had wrangled a membership by pulling in favours for the owners.

It was Raina's favourite hangout, and he took full advantage of his membership to impress clients with this extreme attention to confidentiality and discretion, commensurate with the opacity of their transactions. Each visit to Sub Rosa carried a cover charge of fifty thousand rupees. It was another matter that the extravagance would be couched under 'out-of-pocket' expenses later.

However this time, Raina would pay for it from his own account. He was out on bail and wanted to sell the estate off somehow. For that he had to entice that obsequious dunce of a banker Arvind Nigam. Raina needed him to put his plan into motion. The Constella seemed the perfect setting to overawe the banker.

It was Arvind Nigam's first visit to the opulently shady lair in the centre of Delhi. He was stunned, as Raina had foreseen. 'What opulence, Raina! This place is mind blowing, I say!'

'I have all my important meetings here. I thought it would be good for you to know, so we can bring your clients here sometimes.'

'Yeah, that would be wonderful!'

After three large Red Labels and chilli chicken, Raina asked, 'What's happening with the loan?'

'Bad scene. The son is no good. And Mrs Rambal, as fine a woman as she may be, she can't raise that much money. Bad times have come on that family. I feel sad!'

'Sad, or horny? I've been eyeing her. She's over forty, but what an arse!'

'Come on, Raina, you lawyers are always thinking of screwing clients!'

'Literally, in this case! Jokes apart, what is the bank's hold on the property?'

'If payments remain overdue for three months, the bank can auction the property.'

'Arvind, haven't you noticed something strange? Don't you get the sense the man doubted her character?'

'Really? They were poles apart. But she doesn't seem loose.'

'I don't know, but it's the strangest will I've made in all my life.'

Arvind was nervous. 'Why? What's strange about it?'

'The will calls for a paternity test to confirm the boy's legitimacy. Or the woman's confession that he is a love child. And she has refused to give either. We are now close to the deadline.'

'Hell! What happens then?'

'Let me read out the clause.' Raina took out the copy of the will, and read aloud. 'In case of defaults in payment or upon expiry of the custodial period, the bank and my lawyer are empowered to initiate proceedings to recover the dues from Gurleen, including by auctioning the property on the market. Any surplus after settling bank dues shall be retained by the lawyer and disposed as deemed fit.'

Arvind was sweating. 'Let me see it. My neck will be on the block if this comes up at the bank. Why doesn't she agree to the test?'

'Perhaps she knows the boy will fail the DNA test.'

'But even if the boy were legitimate, how will they do a paternity test when Vikrant is dead?'

Raina leaned closer and spoke in a low voice. 'That's the point, Arvind. They can never prove the boy is the legal heir.'

'It's unfair. Isn't she being forced to admit the opposite just to settle the bank loan?'

'See how the man has screwed her! He wants her to lose either way, whether it shall be shamefully or honourably is the question. The honourable way is to raise the money to pay the bank and leave with her head held high. That's impossible. The shameful way is to confess to adultery, which will get her just enough money to settle the loan payment. She'll be left with nothing either way. Tough choice, no?'

'Honestly, I didn't know there was so much wrong between them. I thought she took real good care of him all these suffering years!'

'Let's not pity her. Maybe she was in sin. Maybe she was good to him because she wanted him to be generous to her in the will. Anyway, the deadline is close. That's why I called you here. What are you going to do now?'

'Now that I've come to know of this intricacy, my responsibility demands that I should inform my legal department immediately. With this strange will, the bank's risk has increased enormously. We might call off the loan or ask her for additional security!'

'Which she doesn't have…'

'Raina, can you give me a copy of the will? That way, I will be seen as acting proactively instead of the bank finding out later.'

'Here, take this copy right now.'

When Arvind had downed his fourth Red Label and headed to the washroom, a wicked smile crept onto Raina's face. His mission had been accomplished to perfection. Vikrant hadn't told Arvind about the final will or the PTI paternity test report. Wonderful. *You bitch, wait till I kick you out of the gate. So much for objecting to my BMW parked in the compound.*

One evening, Gurleen saw two men in black suits waiting for her when she entered the compound. One was the loans recovery manager, the other, a lawyer. They had come from the bank to get her signatures on an undertaking.

'This is an undertaking to arrange alternative security or pay up the outstanding within one month. Please sign here,' the manager said. The lawyer offered a typed stamp paper. All they needed was her signature and thumbprints.

Gurleen asked, 'What if I don't sign?'

'If you don't, we will immediately serve you a notice under Clause 41(a) of our loan agreement,' said the manager

'And what's Clause 41(a)?'

The lawyer lapsed into a lengthy, ominous monologue. 'If it comes to the notice of the bank that the properties against which the loan has been secured have come under dispute, or have been attached by a court order, we can ask for additional security, or push for cancellation of the loan and initiate action for recovery of the entire principal and other dues outstanding, along with penal interest.'

'And if I don't agree?'

The manager took over. 'Remember, you've signed those two blank undated cheques? We'll fill in the current date and present them for the entire value. One cheque for principal, the second for interest and penalty.'

'You can't be serious. If I had that much in the bank why would I need your loan?'

'I am serious. We know that the cheques will bounce. That will be a criminal offence. Section 138. Sentenced to jail.'

'You'll present the cheques knowing they're going to bounce?'

The manager licked his lips before replying. 'It is the final weapon in the bank's hands.'

'You rogues! What's your risk then?'

'When has a bank ever taken risks for its customers, madam?' he laughed.

'Good day,' the lawyer said, after she had signed the documents, without a clue how she was going to arrange the additional security in one month.

She hadn't noticed Raina hanging out at his—no, her—first floor verandah all this while. As they were leaving, he mocked, 'All okay?' and let out a wicked laugh.

The creep. Obviously, he knows. He must've told the banker, that's how they must have learnt of the will.

Round Four to Raina.

Ever since the visit from the bankers, Gurleen hadn't slept well. One evening, she fell asleep at the wheel while on duty. Fortunately, she was in a parking lot when it happened. The doctor wrote it off as stress build up and doubled the Telma and Galvus dosages and told her to stay off duty for a week. Chammo came early from the station and did all the cooking.

One evening, Chammo woke her, announcing a visitor. Gurleen got out of bed with some effort. She saw a man, turned away, engrossed in the sight outside. Hearing the door creak open, he turned to face her.

She had seen him before. It then struck her. *Oh No! Aryan! How could he have aged so soon!*

It hit her like a bolt when he spoke. 'Bhabhi!'

Vish! After more than twenty years!

They hugged and cried and caught up on the years since he had left her alone in Norfolk with Aryan and a parting note.

'Where did you go? You left me alone with the baby, Vish!'

He was embarrassed. 'I could never face Vikki after all that. I just left without knowing where to go. Eventually, I landed up in Pretoria, drove a delivery truck, studied law again and went to practice in Cape Town. Then came Independence and the Black Empowerment Act. Since then, I have been a partner in the firm with a native, and business has just been growing.'

'More lawyers are just what I need,' Gurleen said sarcastically. 'What do you specialize in?'

'Inheritance matters.'

She distrusted him at once. *Does he know about the will? Is that why he is here after so long?*

'You never felt like coming back, Vish?'

'No. I wanted to forget it all.'

'Then why now, after so long?'

'The urge to connect with the past never dies. I went to our ancestral village in Punjab. I had to pass by Delhi and couldn't resist checking up on you.'

'How long will you be here?'

'Leaving tomorrow.' He looked around and spoke with disbelief. 'So, you live here? Alone?'

'I live with Chammo, that's Inspector Chameli Singh, whom you saw earlier.' She beckoned Chammo over who acknowledged him formally this time. His face remained expressionless, wooden. 'Why do you live in the outhouse?'

Gurleen winced. 'Stay for dinner, and I'll tell you everything.'

Chammo did her best to lay a four-course spread and was gratified that Visham took second helpings of the fish curry and the poppy potato, her specialities. When they had eaten the sweet, juicy gulab jamuns brought in by the station guard, Vish was still full of questions.

'How did Vikki bhaiyya die?'

Chammo looked at Gurleen hesitate and drummed up an excuse. 'Leena, I've forgotten to file an FIR. I'll be back soon. You carry on.'

After she had gone, Gurleen answered, 'Cancer.' She couldn't tell him about the AIDS.

'And... and...?' Visham left the question incomplete but it was clear what he wanted.

'Aryan…. that's his name…'

'Is he here?'

'Denver. He's trying to settle down. But then, there's been all this distraction.'

'What happened out here?'

Gurleen let it all out in one torrent. A deep relief overcame her when she finished.

Vish had remained silent but his eyes were moist, his shoulder slouched forward, hands clasped under his chin and his eyes, distant, lost into the past.

'It's okay, Vish. I'm getting used to it now. Tell me about yourself.'

He spoke to her about his time in South Africa, Namibia, England and Netherlands, with modesty bordering on self-deprecation. *He still has his sense of humour. He's aged well, like old wine,* Gurleen thought.

Visham rose to leave around midnight.

She asked, 'At this hour?'

'I can find a hotel.'

'You can stay here.'

'Thanks, but don't bother, bhabhi.'

'Vish, it's okay. Whatever Vikki thought about us no longer matters.'

'Well, then. I'll sleep on the porch. I've got interesting stuff to read tonight.'

Next morning, it was already nine when Gurleen staggered out of bed. Chammo and Vish were having coffee.

'I'm sorry I overslept, Vish. Are you leaving already?'

'Yes. I was just waiting for you to get up. I need to go now.'

She hugged him and insisted on walking him to the gate. Before stepping into Chammo's jeep, he looked at the house and then into Gurleen's eyes and said, 'How could Vikki bhaiyya be so cruel? If I were living here, one of us would've killed the other.' He was gone before she could react.

Returning to the outhouse, Gurleen saw a book on the floor, face down. She flipped it over. Her heart stopped when she caught the title. 'Hindu Succession Act, 1956'.

22

hey had met a few times since their rendezvous at Sub Rosa, but Arvind noted that lately it had been less ornate settings like the nondescript Vikramjit Hotel or the affordable India International Centre. Therefore, he was pleased to be called to the Emperor's Lounge at the Taj Man Singh Hotel.

Raina had his reason for his renewed largesse. He had negotiated for the sale of Rambal Acres with a non-resident Indian, for twelve crore rupees. The buyer was confident of settling the taxman and had handed Raina an advance of fifty lakh. Raina had to deliver clean possession, which meant that the bank had to issue a no-objection clearance. The clock was ticking away but Arvind had shown no sense of urgency. He needed Arvind on his side more than ever.

'What's the hold up, Arvind? Where are we with the loan cancellation?' Not caring to ask for Arvind's preference, he accosted the waiter and ordered two beers with masala peanuts on the side.

'Raina, I've told you before; I've done my part, the file has gone to the legal department. The lady surprised us by signing the undertaking to repay, hence the grace period of another month. What's your hurry, I don't understand!'

'I've got a buyer who wants it right away. But he insists on a "no-legal-encumbrance" certificate. Understand my problem now?'

'But the bank isn't going to approve until the loan is paid off.'

'Arvind, the woman is broke; she's never going to be able to pay up. Meanwhile, I'm stuck. Tell me what to do!'

Arvind pondered a bit before speaking. 'Suppose I get you a deal, what's in it for me?'

Arvind's rating went up with that one sentence. Before he could continue, Raina stopped the waiter passing by and ordered, 'Two large Red Labels with soda and ice.' Turning to Arvind, he said, 'Depends on what you can get me, Arvind.'

'I can convince our recovery department that we have a deal at say two and a half crore rupees, with an advance of fifty lakh. The no-objection letter will be conditional on the bank getting paid in full before the title is transferred.'

'That's great. I can advance the fifty lakh right away. Let's do it.'

'Raina, if the bank agrees, you save one crore. What do I get?'

'Ten lakh.'

'Make that twenty-five. I've got to settle my legal guys too.'

Raina knew it was futile to dither. After paying off the bank and Arvind, he would still make some nine crore and change, in two months. *You won't get another chance like this. Think Raina, think.*

'It's a deal. Let's toast to it.'

'Not yet. It will be a deal when you give me ten lakh advance. By the way, I've outgrown cheap stuff. I'm on to smoked single malts these days. Henceforth, it's got to be at least a Laphroaig.' Arvind got up, threw three crisp thousand rupee notes on the table for his share of the whiskey and left without shaking hands.

Raina considered the changed stakes over another Red Label and the distraction of the lobby pianist's unbearable rendition.

~

Rustom Towers was adjacent to the BMW showroom, which at any time had over fifty cars on display. However, it paled before the grandeur of the Porsches, Rolls Royce and the occasional Bentley, Ferrari and Maybach parked at Rustom Towers. Opulent toys of the firm's high-profile clients. Amidst the powerful line up, Gurleen's new toy, a cute little canary yellow TVS scooty, jostled for its space between a Maybach and a Porsche, defiant, a pygmy posing among giants. Soon, a valet came out, recognized Gurleen and parked it inside.

After the customary coffee and cookies had been served, Ravi Dhar smiled at Gurleen and shook her hand. But he didn't acknowledge Raina, who had arrived earlier and had been waiting. It was a deliberate snub that wasn't lost on Raina, for they knew each other.

'Mr Dhar, I've waited a long time. Why have you called me and my client?'

Ravi brushed him off. 'Is she your client, Mr Raina?'

'Well, her late husband was.'

'That doesn't make Mrs Rambal your client. She shall speak for herself. Is that clear?' Ravi turned to her. 'We've been retained to challenge your husband's will. I'm sorry I'm on the other side this time.'

'That's okay, Ravi. I've gotten used to people crossing over to the other side. I don't know what this is all about but let me tell you I want nothing to do with my husband's will.' But she was curious to know what it was all about.

'What's the case, Mr Dhar?' Raina asked.

'The will of late Vikrant Singh Rambal, s/o late Lala Vijendra Singh Rambal. It is being challenged as invalid, for violation of Section 2 of Hindu Widows' Remarriage Act, 1856 and Section 14 of Hindu Succession Act, 1956.'

Ravi handed Raina a copy of the case filed before the Delhi High Court. 'Mr Raina, I thought we might share this advance copy. The court summons may take time.'

Raina cursed, 'Damn!' as he thumbed through the texts.

Gurleen was flummoxed as well. 'Ravi, what's this nonsense with a Widows' Remarriage Act? I am not marrying anyone.'

'I can explain everything, but first Mr Raina has to leave.' He turned to Raina. 'Is there anything else I can give you, Mr Raina?'

'No, thanks.' Raina got up and left in a huff.

Ravi re-ordered Gurleen's favourite coffee and pressed a remote console to bring up the projection screen. A slide beamed the contents in slow motion as he explained the Act.

'Section 2 deals with the rights of a widow on remarriage. The Act says that all rights and interests that a widow may have in her deceased husband's property by way of maintenance or by inheritance to her husband or to his lineal successors—'

She interrupted him. 'Stop, Ravi! English, please!'

He laughed. 'Put simply, a widow loses her rights in her dead husband's property when she remarries, unless the husband has given her permission to remarry after his death.'

'You mean it should be written in the will that she has a right even after she remarries? Which husband would write that, for God's sake? And which wife would even tell him she might remarry?'

'You have a point. But that's how the Act was made back then.'

'Well, Ravi, I am not planning to get married. What's the issue?'

'The problem isn't in your husband's will. The problem is that your husband's father, Lala Vijendra Singh Rambal, died intestate.'

'What is intestate?' she interrupted.

'Sorry again. "Intestate" means dying without leaving a will.'

'What's the connection?'

'His wife Lajwanti Devi remarried in 1955, and thus lost claim to his estate. Therefore, your husband's ownership is null and void in the first place.'

'Who is the heir, then?'

'Lala's blood brother, Chattar Singh, who was his next of kin, became the rightful heir to the estate. That is why this litigation.'

He took out an age-worn photograph showing a young man tying a mangalsutra around a woman's neck, the undeniable proof of Hindu marriage. On a large calendar in the background, the date was visible.

14 December 1954.

Ravi turned the photograph over to show Gurleen a handwritten sentence, signed by Chattar Singh, Lala's brother.

Jivan Singh ties mangalsutra on Lajjo bhabi in my presence, on Lala's instruction.

There was also a rubber stamp that read 'Das Studios. Dec. 1954'.

Gurleen sighed. 'Who filed the case, Ravi?' Her voice was almost a whisper, low and expectant.

Ravi Dhar was restless to break the big piece. 'Chattar Singh's heir. Visham Singh.'

'Oh!' her hands began to tremble.

After a long silence to assimilate it all, she spoke up. 'Hang on Ravi, something doesn't add up here. When Lala ji died, his wife was pregnant. Wouldn't his own son Vikrant have as much right as his brother's son? And, as far as I know, Vikki was born some weeks before Vish.'

'You are rather sharp, Mrs Rambal. You've hit the crux of the issue. But I didn't want to talk about it.'

'Why? What holds you back?'

He tapped at a folder. 'It's all in here. Please read it. It's for your eyes only.'

Gurleen opened it and saw photocopies of a handwritten diary's pages, written by Chattar Singh, Visham's father. It was dated some weeks before the photograph.

Nov 16, 1954

I had fallen into bad times since eviction from the estate. And Lala's condition had worsened beyond hope and he was nearing his end. He wished to reconcile with me. My wife Nidhi and I were called back into the estate. Soon, the women were quarrelling. Lajjo felt insecure that Nidhi would dominate her and worse, even conspire to evict her from the estate. And she even blamed Lala for destroying her life, by marrying her forcibly.

Lala came up with the best arrangement to protect Lajjo's security and his own reputation. He was as surprised as relieved that Lajjo accepted his outrageous suggestion; less surprised that I consented.

When it was settled, Lala told me, 'You have witnessed my last wish, Chattar. You are now the head of the family. May the children grow and prosper together under your leadership.'

One day, Lajjo's ex fiancé Jivan Singh was brought to the estate. Lala apologized for forcibly snatching Lajjo from him, and, as atonement, placed her hand into his. He made them promise to marry after his death, no matter what the conservative society said. To consecrate their union, he even made Jivan Singh tie the mangalsutra around Lajwanti's neck.

I witnessed and photographed the moment and kept it in my custody, as mutual indemnity, as agreed with Lala.

It was a special day. It was the day when it was confirmed that Lajjo had conceived and held my seed, at Lala's bidding.

Utterly unpardonable by society, it was a practical deal that secured every one's interests. It was the only way Lala could avoid posthumous ridicule for being an empty vessel; it was Lala's only assurance that I would take care of Lajjo, and it was the only way Lajjo could lead her life with Jivan Singh.

Lala passed away soon, without an heir. However, at the ceremony, grief was momentarily replaced by cheer when the family priest announced that Lala would not be missed for too long, that he would soon return; for Lajwanti Devi had been blessed by Heaven with long-awaited motherhood.

As promised, Lajjo and Jivan Singh got married at the estate, under my blessings. Jivan was given a respectable position in the business but all powers effectively remained with me.

On the first death anniversary of Lala, the first spoon of ghee on the sacred fire was poured by the ordained heir to the estate Vikrant. My son. The second spoonful was poured by Visham. Also my son.

As the flames soared, it drizzled for a few minutes, and I knew Lala was blessing us all from heaven for keeping our word and his honour. Late that night, tragedy struck again. Jivan Singh died of a snake bite. Lajjo was widowed again.

She pushed the folder and sighed. Her eyes were clouded in disbelief. 'So Vikki was Chattar Singh's son and Vish's half-brother! No wonder Vish wants to have his revenge, he was treated as a hand-me-down lackey all his life. And no wonder Lajjo wanted to offer Visham half the estate, it was his right anyway! What a lady!'

'A most colourful family, I must say!' Ravi was euphemistic.

'Do you know even Vish is a lawyer, Ravi?'

'Yes, he's rather well known in Cape Town.'

'I feel sad, though. Vish could have told me about this. I was very fond of him, but now I feel cheated. Why are the people closest to you the ones that hurt you most, Ravi?'

Ravi was silent. As she sat there some more, she came to a decision. 'Ravi, I am not interested in fighting this case.'

'What? Are you sure?'

'Yes, I can't bear the thought.'

'Fine. It will be Mr Raina versus our client.'

'Give him hell. I know you will win.'

Coming out of the imposing building, Gurleen drove mindlessly over the Ashram flyover, jumping traffic lights thrice. She slowed only when she sighted the beautiful bougainvillea at Rambal Acres. A stab of pain hit her as she wondered about its unfortunate destiny.

Just as she turned towards the outhouse, Raina stepped out and accosted her. 'What did he tell you?'

Seething at his sight, she struck out. 'He told me that your dreams are going up in smoke. You're going to grow apple-sized fissures on your asshole trying to save your forged title.'

'How?'

'They're going to ram Vikki's will up your anus. He was never the heir. I've seen the proof with my own eyes.' She rubbed the last bit in for effect.

'What proof?' The look on his face showed he was zapped by her sudden confidence.

Striking a Wills Femme with her new Zippo lighter, Gurleen smiled and lifted her middle finger twisted it in the air. 'Get lost, you slime.'

Since the legal notice, Raina could proceed neither with the will's execution nor with the sale of the estate. Meanwhile, the buyer's phone calls were getting more frequent and imposing. Finally, there was an ultimatum. The buyer's lawyer, Jiten Jakhad had said, 'Mr Raina, just return our money.'

'Sir, I had no idea someone would challenge the will. Please understand.'

'It's your problem, not ours. We want a definite date for the refund of our advance.'

'I need time, Mr Jakhad.'

'You have three weeks. After that, we'll go to court to recover the advance and also lodge a complaint to the bar association about your misconduct.'

'Misconduct?'

'Yes, conflict of interest. You tried to outgrow your boots from being a lawyer to become a real estate dealer. Now, accept the consequences.'

Arvind was in a meeting, staring at the stay order invoked by Rustom Law. His head was clouded with fear. His boss listened in rapt attention as the bank's chief legal officer said, 'The bank cannot attach Rambal estate as it doesn't belong to Vikrant Rambal.'

'We are not attaching it, we are only releasing our charge against payment of our dues. Is that a problem?'

'Sir, we should watch our backs. The audit team will surely take this deal up for scrutiny if things go wrong, like now.'

Arvind had the most to fear from a scrutiny. He was the one who had disbursed the loan, and he was the one who had brought Raina's deal. Worse, he had made that side deal with Raina and even worse, he had put it all on the stock market, which was spiralling down. It was time to dump Raina like a fast-rotting apple.

'So, what is the decision?' The legal head asked.

The boss had made up his mind. 'Let's issue a notice to Mrs Rambal and call in the loan immediately. Then, let's cash in the blank cheque for the full value of ₹3.5 crores.'

'Sir, shouldn't we return Raina's advance?' Arvind reminded his superiors and covered his back.

The answer knocked the wind out of him. 'Should we? Is he asking?'

The two men in black were back, this time along with a policeman. Gurleen was irritated. 'What do you want me to sign today, gentlemen? And why have you got the police with you?'

'Madam, he's come to arrest you. Your cheque has bounced. It's a criminal charge, Section 138, Negotiable Instruments Act.'

'What cheque?' The ground sank below her. '*Hai Rabba*, those blank cheques Arvind made me sign, did you use them, you thugs?'

The suited thugs remained silent but menacing. There was only one person in the world she could call.

Chammo was shocked. 'They can't arrest you, the case must be heard first. I know that for sure. Put me on to the bloody banker.'

The banker explained it all. 'Of course. But we filed a case in Assam, where the bank has its headquarters. The judge decided it ex parte as she never came for the hearings.'

Gurleen's heart sank. There had been no summons, or some postman had become richer for forging a delivery receipt. Or, Raina had received and trashed them. She looked at the white-collar thugs in disbelief. 'You'll never be happy in life for this, bastards, all of you!'

Chammo then asked to be connected to the policeman. After the policeman had heard her out, he passed the phone back to Gurleen.

Chammo comforted her. 'I've asked him to detain you at Naba Karim. Go with him, and I'll see you in an hour.'

She was back in the same cell. Somehow, she didn't panic this time. *It's only the first time that things scare you, Leena, even jails. It'll blow over, Waheguru di fateh.* All she felt was that she was in a dream, waiting to break out. The dream ended when Chammo came in with the daily rum and snacks. 'Leena, have a swig, you'll feel better,' she consoled Gurleen.

Three pegs later, they had loosened up.

'What an incredible family I have! A psycho husband who sets me on a challenge to reclaim my home, a brother-in-law who's taking me to court, and a son who is the reason all this is happening to me. Add a lawyer and a banker for thrill and comedy.'

'Don't pity yourself, Leena. What's the use?'

'Where am I going to get ₹3.5 crores, Chammo? A year ago, I would've dusted it off my wardrobe.'

'Three lakhs or three crores, it will be the same sentence in jail. Then you'll have your life back.'

'And what about my name, my honour, my reputation?'

'Leena, the world's not worth worrying over.'

'Maybe you're right. There isn't anyone to worry about me anyway.'

'Let's drink to that. Cheers!'

The deathly fear overcame her at last. 'Chammo, will I survive in jail? Promise you'll visit me daily. Promise.'

Next morning, she was brought to Central Jail No. 6, Tihar Jail, entitled to Class B facilities, based on her upper middle-class status. She was passed first through a big body scanner to make sure she had nothing hidden on her. The second step was somewhat cruder. She wore a gown and was made to lie down on a metal table as three thick latexed fingers probed her interiors long enough to make her want to puke. Eventually, she was given her uniform, a white sari with a navy-blue border, and her identity.

Gurleen was #321, one among 153 convicts serving sentence in Jail No. 6. Along with some twenty others, she was assigned duty at Tihar Baking School, Jail No. 2, to make bread, biscuits and other bakes for the city market. Her monthly wage was ₹400. About the price of a Domino's pizza.

After two weeks, Gurleen had accepted prison life. She was allowed up to three visitors per week, one visit per person. That made it just one visit in her case, for she didn't have any visitors except Chammo. Her situation was better than several others who were still under trial—some for more than four years—but hadn't yet been convicted.

Like poor Salma, a widow from Bihar.

Salma had been in Tihar for three years, and was still under trial, for murdering her father-in-law who tried to rape her one night. Her two sons, aged five and seven, had been abandoned by her husband's family and sent to an orphanage. Salma didn't have money for a lawyer, so the state had appointed one, for free. In three years, he had visited her only twice; once to introduce himself and the second time to tell her that he would work on her case only if she paid him rupees fifty thousand. Gurleen was baffled when Salma told her, 'He didn't turn up despite getting the money. No one cares that I have two children. I don't know whether they are even alive....'

Next time Chammo visited Tihar, she also saw Salma at Gurleen's insistence. Two weeks later, Chammo dropped in with two packages. She asked Salma to open the thinner one. Salma squealed on seeing the clutch of photos of her children playing with others their age. A lady constable in Patna known to Chammo had traced the boys. They were safe in an orphanage.

Salma clapped her hands in joy, kissed Chammo's cheeks and

lifted Gurleen high in the air in joy. It was Gurleen's best moment in Tihar, a moment to feel good and worthwhile.

Chammo then opened the second package and pulled out a carton of cigarettes and a two-litre Coke bottle. The plastic cap seal had been broken. The three women swigged in turns, though Gurleen took most of it. Chammo left when the bottle was polished, leaving Gurleen to her cigarettes. They would last a week, going by her burn rate of three packs a day.

Salma's story made Gurleen stop complaining about anything. She just wanted to go through her sentence and move on with life. Time would pass somehow, as long as Chammo was around. Which was not to be the case.

Chammo didn't visit the jail for three weeks. When she turned up the week after, Gurleen was both angry and upset.

'You know what a long wait every weekend is, Chammo. I have no one else to look forward to.'

Chammo was withdrawn, not her usual positive self.

'What?' Gurleen asked. 'I'm sorry if I hurt you.'

'What would you do if I can't see you every week?'

Gurleen brushed it off. 'Let's not talk about things that aren't real.'

Chammo looked her in the eye. '*Yaar*, this is real.' With that she pushed an opened envelope across.

Gurleen took out the letter and read through.

The world came crashing down. It was a transfer order, to goddamn Gorakhpur. In goddamn Uttar Pradesh.

Gurleen walked back to her cell without a word, and didn't turn even once, until she could no longer hear Chameli calling her.

Over the next weeks, Chammo visited the jail daily, but Gurleen refused to meet her, even on the day Chammo was leaving town.

Gurleen lost ten kilos within a month since Chammo's last visit and had to be hospitalized. She returned stronger, resolving to learn to live alone and not be hurt by anyone. She would never get attached to anyone again. And she never wanted to leave Tihar Jail.

One afternoon, she was called to the gate to meet a new visitor. It was the last person she expected to see. Her feelings had dried like branches without water under the scorching sun. Her impulse was to walk back but she remained still, her eyes livid. But her tears flowed when she heard 'Imma!' *Oh God, how much I've missed that word!*

'So you found out I'm alive? See what a great frigging gift you've given me?'

'What's happened to your language?'

'Damn you, I don't need a character certificate from a horny little beak! Who told you I am in jail?'

'Mr Raina, our tenant.'

'Slime bag! He's the reason I'm here.'

They were silent for a while, then Gurleen flared again. 'What're you going to jolt me with this time?'

'I'm the one that's had a jolt; and it's all because of what you've done!'

It is still all about him! 'Because of what I've done? I didn't bow down before your perverted father's will. I didn't sign a statement that you are illegitimate. Instead, I put my neck on the block to get you the money to live your dream. And I'm the one behind bars. Because of you!'

The guard rushed in. 'No shouting, 321! Is this man troubling you?'

'Sorry. I'll be fine.' She placated the guard with two cigarettes and lit one herself.

'You've been smoking, Imma?'

'It's merely a cigarette I suck at. Not like your broad. OK, Mr Rambal, why are you here at all?'

'I couldn't get through to your number.'

'Oh, you couldn't? That whore wouldn't even let me talk to you.

What brings you now?'

His answer razed her last hopes to the ground. 'I've come back for good.'

'You mean you killed the bitch and fled?'

'I've been deported. Remember, I was a co-borrower for the loan? After you were jailed, the bank sent me a legal notice through the Indian Embassy, and Canadian Immigration cancelled my visa. I can't even re-apply until we are both cleared.'

'Serves you right for tricking me!' She glowered at him.

'How you hate me, Imma!'

'No, I don't hate you; you just don't matter to me anymore. Where's the money?'

He lowered his head. She feared the worst. 'If you've been deported, you don't need the money! Come on, where's my damn money?'

His furtive eyes said it all.

She thundered. 'Blown away! Right! At three crores, Veronique must be the most expensive whore in the world.'

It must have hit a raw nerve. 'Don't you talk about whores, you are no different.'

She was shocked he had said that. 'How dare you compare me with that sleaze!'

'Come on! Your husband never trusted you. He even had my DNA tested. You know what, he died right after seeing the result!'

She held on to the grill to steady herself. *What is he saying?*

He took out and handed her a folded note, smudged with dirt, its folds coming apart. She read Vikki's letter, with rising horror and disgust.

'Is that why you've been talking to me like that?'

Aryan snatched it away. 'Now don't you flaunt your *faithful widow* image! Just admit that I am Visham Singh's illegitimate son, so that we can move on. I want to hear it from you, that's all!'

'You bastard, I've sacrificed everything for you. Get lost.'

'I'll get the truth out of your lover. He's got some nerve, first screwing you and now claiming all the inheritance for himself!'

'Stop it, Aryan! I'd have strangled you with my bare hands if it wasn't for these damn bars between us.'

'Bye.' Aryan walked out.

She kept shouting, 'Son! Listen, sorry, please come back. Don't leave me like this. Trust me, please! Aryan!'

I've lost him once again, this time forever. Gurleen bumped her forehead against the grille until she sank to the floor of the meeting cell, bleeding.

~

Raina had come to hate the number that flashed on his Blackberry daily these days. He could not ignore Jiten Jakhad. After a minute-long battle of will, he picked up the phone and spoke even before hearing the voice at the other end.

'Have patience, Mr Jakhad. Please give me some time.'

'...You've been saying that for a long time. Maybe we should find some other way,'

Jakhad's softening stand intrigued Raina as much as it reassured him. 'What other way?'

'This vendetta you have with the Rambal widow, maybe we can work something out if we knew what's going on. After all, this whole issue is about the will, isn't it?'

'Seems you know everything, Mr Jakhad.' Raina remained dodgy.

It seemed Jakhad had already worked things out and was merely informing Raina. 'If you can't prove that the dead man was the boy's father without a DNA test, can't you just hand over the estate and wash your hands off the whole thing?'

And what do I gain, you fool? Raina almost said it aloud as he heard the unsolicited advice. 'Well, let me share a secret, Mr Jakhad. I do have a DNA test report in my possession; it was done days before Mr Rambal died.'

'Why haven't you declared it?'

'I was following my client's wish to the letter. The will doesn't ask me to disclose his DNA test. It only asks the other party to prove their bonafide. How do I know what my client had in mind? Anyway, how does it help you?'

'Mr Raina, give us the test report. We'll take it over from there with the bank.'

Raina couldn't believe what he had heard. He decided to play on to know what was behind it all. 'Sure, it's your call. But I've also committed the banker a private bonus of twenty-five lakhs.' *Would Jakhad bite?* 'And what do I get for all this effort?'

There was a silence. *Have I pushed him too far?* Raina worried as the line crackled again.

'The fifty lakhs we've advanced, keep it for yourself and your associates at the bank. We will settle the bank separately. That should please everyone.'

Raina was puzzled by Jakhad's recklessness. *This is getting too easy. Should I have pushed him more? After all, I would have made a nine-crore profit just weeks ago.* Another part of him cautioned though. *Raina don't get too greedy. Count your blessings and quit, you fool.*

'That should be fine,' he accepted. 'Let's all sit together next week and sort it all out.'

Raina hung up still in disbelief over the favourable turn of fortune. *It takes all kinds to make this world.*

The following week, Raina and Arvind were at the bank with Jiten Jakhad. When they had completed all the paperwork and the bank's legal head had checked every document, Jakhad turned to Arvind.

'I take it Mr Raina has given you fifty lakhs already. We'll pay the remaining three crores when we get the letter releasing your claim on Rambal Acres.' Jakhad then looked at Raina. 'And then you will hand us the test report. Right?'

Raina nodded. 'Sure. And my fifty lakhs, remember—'

'Yes, I'll bring that too, in our next meeting. When do we meet?' asked Jakhad.

'Next Monday. Right here at the bank,' Arvind's boss said.

Aryan was unprepared for the call from Rustom Law offices. It had come on his US cell number, which they seemed to have got from Global Bank. The lady had said, 'Our chairman would like to meet you as soon as possible.'

He turned up an hour late. The receptionist complained, 'Mr Aryan Rambal, the chairman's been expecting you for an hour now. Please go to Megasthenes Room, it's the last one on the left.'

When Aryan walked in, the chairman rose, patted him on the shoulder and left the room. There was another man, who remained seated. He was an exact of replica of Aryan, except that he appeared older. Visham Rambal, the root cause of all the drama, all the mess in his life.

'Come here son, it's been ages,' faltered the well-dressed, handsome man as he rose to receive Aryan. Aryan remained where he was and stiffened as Visham Rambal shuffled across and hugged him. 'I know it's been tough on you, son. But I assure you we'll get it all sorted out soon.'

Aryan stared at his look-alike and spoke in an icy voice. 'I don't trust you, sorry.'

The following Monday, Raina, Arvind and Jiten Jakhad were seated in the main Board Room, which had been in use since the 1880s. It still had a traditional fireplace, which was activated during Delhi's cold winters. However, modern technology had replaced ancient ingredients. Wood logs and charcoal had given way to smokeless, briquetted coke chips without taking away the pleasant crackle and the radiant warmth of the fire.

True to his nature, Raina had moved himself to the chair closest to the hearth to get close to the radiating warmth.

Jakhad began. 'All set, gentlemen?'

Raina tapped the triple-folded single sheet that lay before him, secured by his pen clip.

Arvind offered the bank's release documents for Jakhad's signature. Jakhad signed and retained one set, and passed the rest to Raina and asked him, 'Your resignation as custodian of the will?'

Raina handed the folded sheet over to Arvind. Jakhad handed Arvind a demand draft for rupees three crores. A peon served them green tea, collected the draft and returned with a note. Arvind read aloud, 'The money has been credited,' and handed over the bank's release letter along with Raina's resignation as custodian for the will to Jakhad.

'Step one is completed.' Jakhad announced and took out the second bank draft of rupees fifty lakhs. Placing it before Raina, he asked, 'The DNA report?'

Raina opened his briefcase and took out an envelope with a blue 'PTI' logo embossed on it. He took the demand draft, and extended his right hand for Jakhad to reach across, when the intercom rang.

Jakhad, who was closest to the device, pushed it towards Arvind, accidentally pressing the speaker button. Everyone froze as the secretary's voice announced, 'Arvind, just heard Mrs Rambal has been released.'

Raina's mouth opened in shock.

Jakhad lunged to snatch the test report, which was still in Raina's hand. But he was a second late. Raina had already wrenched it off, tearing off over four-fifths of the envelope from Jakhad's fingers. Before anybody could react, he had tossed it into the hearth behind. It was all smoke and char by the time Jakhad reached the fireplace.

Raina's wicked laughter rang in the room for a long time. Then he rose, patted Arvind on the shoulder and cursed, 'Double-crosser!'

Pausing again at the door, Raina looked at his 'buyer'. 'Well tried, Mr Jakhad. But tell your client Visham Rambal that what I just consigned to the flames was Vikrant's only DNA test report.' He slammed the door hard and stormed out.

Later, driving his new second-hand Honda Civic, he smiled at the way he had handled himself. He had made fifty lakhs and was off the hook. Only, his dreams of settling down in Thailand would have to wait longer. Soon another Rambal would turn up in his life. They always did.

Gurleen couldn't believe the bank had dropped its case. *What had happened?* It felt strange, being asked to leave when she had just begun to feel at home in jail. Thoughts swam in her head as she completed her forms. *Wonder who can tell me what's been happening. Ravi, would he know about it? The bank, should I even bother calling them? Chammo's left town, where do I stay? Waheguru, am I supposed to thank you for this, I don't know what awaits me next!*

No one stopped her at the gates of Rambal Acres this time. On reaching the porch, she noted that the seal had been removed, and the notice, torn down. Stepping inside, she saw Vish seated at the dining table. The last man she had trusted. And he too had let her down.

She charged at him. 'Vish, you came back after twenty bloody years, only to file a case against me? I can understand you're angry at Vikki, but why would you want to take the estate away from Aryan?'

Vish remained silent.

'Tell me, why did you have to sue me, Vish? I'd have given it to you. You owe me an answer, come on!'

Finally, Vish spoke, in his usual soft, self-assured tone. 'Don't you see that I did it for your good? I wanted to stall that slime lawyer from selling it off.'

'And don't you understand it only adds to Aryan's suspicion?'

'I'll reason with him when the time comes.'

'Forget it, Vish. Nothing will clear his doubt about you. If I were him, I too would have trusted Vikrant's letter.'

He looked at her and spoke with firmness, 'I don't worry about Aryan. It's you that I care about.'

'You are—' her words froze as she caught Aryan standing at the doorway, looking at them. From the rage in his eyes, she guessed he had heard everything.

Aryan locked eyes with Visham and mocked him. 'So, this is a grand family reunion, heh? What do I call you, uncle or dad?'

'Watch your words, Aryan,' Vish spoke in a tone that chilled Gurleen.

Aryan was not one to give up. 'Look, do you think I'm a fool? I took a DNA test with dad, sorry, her dead husband! He cried until he was dead. So, let's cut the bullshit.'

'You're beyond convincing.' Vish shook his head in despair.

Aryan was uncontrollable. 'Where were you all these years after banging my mother and leaving us in the care of a loveless man? And now, you are so overcome with guilt that you want to help us protect our property. And how? By filing a case against us! Great parents I have, a spineless father, and slut of a mother!'

Whack!

Aryan didn't see Vish's hand coming. It left four welts on his right cheek but did not stop him from aiming at Gurleen instead.

'If it's not him, whom else have you been sleeping with?'

Vish slapped him again. Thrice. 'Treat her with mercy if not with respect, Aryan. You must learn to make peace with her; otherwise you won't be able to face yourself.'

'Defending your old flame, ha!' Aryan said.

Gurleen couldn't handle it anymore. 'Stop it, you wretch!'

The air was thick with gloom, hurt and embarrassment. No one spoke, and everyone was dazed with questions for which no one had answers.

Then Aryan remembered something. 'Wait! Dr Koeli…He ran the test for dad. He would know. I'll believe whatever he says.'

He dashed to the drawer and fished out the phone book and dialled Inder's number before anyone could figure what was happening.

'Hello, Dr Koeli's clinic? It's important that I speak with him please!'

There was a long silence. Aryan disconnected and looked at Vish, his eyes blank. 'He immigrated to Australia last year.'

Vish was curious. 'So what? Take his number and call him there.'

The answer shocked Gurleen.

'No use. He died last Sunday.'

23

*R*ambal Acres had lost its meaning. Gurleen yearned for a clean break from the painful memories that it evoked. Aryan no longer trusted her and constantly snapped at her. *Well, at least he can direct his anger at me…Where do I give vent to mine?* The least she could do was to resettle him in Canada, as he'd wanted before. The more she thought the more she was convinced. Yes, she would sell the estate and get Aryan his investor visa once again. This time around, she had Vish to protect her against any fraud.

Vish was his silent, stoic self. Composed on the outside, nurturing a volcano within, she knew he was as tormented as Aryan. He felt it was best they moved to Cape Town; it would help them pick up the threads and patch up their lives. She had agreed. Aryan too, although reluctantly.

In two weeks, they had packed almost everything and had called in the ragpickers to remove all the discarded things. Old cartons filled with souvenirs, relics, and piles of books and photos, some dating back a hundred years, had all been taken off the lofts and unloaded on the floor, to sort through one last time.

Gurleen had managed to trash a lot. Having sorted her empty jewellery boxes, the bullion coin cases, albums of the PIL, and other such articles. At last she looked at the plastic folder that contained the old will and all the medical reports. Pain shot through her chest as she held it in her hands. She looked at it one last time and tossed it into the trash pile. It was all over. *The past is gone. Can the past go away so easily?*

Vish stood watching as the ragpickers threw themselves over the richest pickings they'd ever laid hands on. They pummelled through the spoils. Metal stuff, books, photographs, clothes, sports goods, shoes, and all kinds of other souvenirs. His gaze fell on an old leather diary peeping out of a bundle of dust-laden photo albums. Curious, he picked it up and wiped the dust off the cover. He could now see the richness of its crocodile leather cover and the gold-engraved lettering: Lala Sir Vijendra Singh Rambal. He took the diary to his room, leaving the ragpickers to fight over their booty.

Loud noises were coming from the hall. Aryan rushed out of his room to see what was up. Several pieces of paper lay strewn on the floor. He saw two ragpickers fighting over a plastic folder with a label: Norwich. One of them was bleeding. He shooed them away and took the folder, curious. He had never heard of Norwich before.

As Vish flipped through the diary, he noted entries dating back as far as 1926. Most of them were small entries, often a sentence or two, a page at most. However, there was one long entry.

April 13, 1939.

Amritsar.

It was Baisakhi and my first time to the Golden Temple. An amazing incident took place.

As I stepped into the cold water, I saw a lady, a foreigner with flawless white skin. However, she wore a salwar and chunri and spoke Punjabi words. She was waist deep into the water, chanting 'Waheguruji da khalsa, Waheguru di fateh'. After three dips, she took a shining object off her neck. It had a huge pink stone set in its centre. She dipped it repeatedly in the holy waters, saying aloud: 'I beg forgiveness, for my father who forsook the faith of his ancestors and sought refuge in a foreign land. He wanted to return, but that was not to be. Please forgive him; for he did re-convert, he did take the Khande de Phaul in Aden.'

Finishing her conversation with the Holiness, she waded back to the bank and swung the locket hard against the marble steps. The stone flew off and fell into the sarovar. As she held the chain up, the locket had split open, like a book's cover. There was something inside, which she took out, held in her fingers briefly and released into the sarovar. She then washed the open locket, set it on the water and pushed it away. Seeing it float, she climbed up the steps and continued on her parikrama.

Aryan opened the folder. On top was a document titled *Laissez-Passer*. He understood it was a travel document for a child who had yet to get a permanent identity document. He saw the signatures and stamps across the names Gurleen and Vikrant Rambal and an unnamed male infant. It was easy to understand that the unnamed infant was Aryan himself.

What unsettled him was the handwritten note attached behind it.

Forgive me for being a coward.

Do what you consider right: Bring him up or give him away. I will understand your decision as I hope you will mine.

Don't forget your promise. Whatever happens, it must never come out, or it will shame the whole family.

God take care of you both.

Vish

Vish's breath shortened and his heart raced as he continued reading.

The object bobbed and floated towards me. I reached over and took it in my hands and held it up against the golden sun. She was still within earshot; I called aloud to get her attention.

'Lady, your necklace.'

She turned back and said, 'It's no longer mine. I've released it to where it must go.'

'It's come into my hands.'

'It is yours then.'

'What did you take out and rinse in the water?'

'Hair locks of my father, the last emperor.'

'Who are you?'

'Maharani Bamba.'

'Maharani of which kingdom?'

'Punjab, of course,' she laughed and moved on.

When I returned to Delhi, I saw the beautiful locket had one ugly spot, the cavity from which the stone had fallen off. I decided to have another stone set in its place. And as I write, I resolve to continue the ritual.

My first son's hair shall be placed inside it, along with the new stone. When his first son is born, my son shall come here, take a dip and surrender his hair locks and release the stone in this sarovar. On returning, he shall put his son's hair inside and seal it with a new stone. The tradition shall continue for every first born in every Rambal generation.

Blood rushing to his face, Vish put the diary down and ran inside. Rummaging through the suitcase he had brought back from his father's ancestral house in Punjab, he found what he was looking for. It was an old photograph of his father Chattar Singh and two ladies, each holding a baby boy. One was his mother Nidhi. The other was Aunt Lajjo holding a baby boy with a locket hung around his neck, reaching all the way to the navel. The cavity wasn't empty; there was a blue stone in it. *Maybe... maybe... there is still a chance.* His pulse raced.

Aryan put all the bits together in the form of a bullet list.

I was born in England.

Vish disappeared in England.

Vikrant suspected Imma with Vish.

I look exactly like Vish.

Vikrant wanted Imma to prove or confess. Imma did neither.

Vish comes out of the blue and claims the estate.

Vish confesses everything in this note, written when I was born.

Damn Imma, pretending innocence and hiding her dark past!

Vish was down to the last entry in the diary.

Sept 17, 1954.

I wonder if I will be able to fulfill my pledge of going back to the Golden Temple. It seems I am not to be blessed with the joy of my progeny. Unthinkable as it may seem, there is only one way to perpetuate the clan. I hope Chattar will keep his word, and fulfill my pledge.

He put the diary down and ran towards Gurleen who was cleaning up the last shelves in the other room. She was surprised at the urgency and the excitement on Vish's face.

'Bhabhi, how attached are you to your heirlooms?'

'Why do you ask?'

'I can't be sure, but there may still be a chance to find out.'

'What do you want, Vish?'

'Your locket.'

Her hand instinctively went over her bosom to protect it. 'I've never taken it off.'

His intent firm, Vish reached across and tugged at the chain. 'Take it off. For everyone's sake. Please, Gurleen.'

There was an authority in his voice that she could not defy. It was the first time he had called her by her name.

Aryan had overheard the conversation and rushed in.

Everyone's curiosity mounted as Gurleen took the locket off and handed it to Vish, who placed it on a tablecloth. He looked at it minutely and examined both sides to detect a gap or a nick. There was nothing. It seemed just a solid piece of gold with a big stone in its centre.

Vish was almost ready to give up when he remembered the texts in the older entry of 1939.

She sat on the steps and swung the locket hard against the marble. As it hit the marble the third time, the pink stone came off and fell into the sarovar.

He swung the locket in vertical circles, and when enough

momentum had been built, brought it crashing face down on the table. A loud sound issued from the diamond's impact on the marble surface, followed by the snap of a lid being opened. The impact had pushed the stone inside, and the backside of the locket had opened a crack, like a partially open book. Inside the back face, there was a thin circular cavity.

Vish found what he had hoped for. 'Switch off the fan, Aryan, quick!' he shouted, cupping the locket to protect it from the blast of the ceiling fan. When the fan blades had come to rest, he opened his palms and held it out to everyone's view.

'What's that?' It didn't make sense to Aryan.

'May be the answer to every question,' Vish replied, his hands cupped over the locket.

Turning to Gurleen, he said with urgency, 'Can you ask Ravi Dhar over?'

In the evening, Ravi brought along a technician wearing blue overalls with a logo 'PTI' inscribed on the pockets. Using gloves with 'PTI' stamped all over them, the technician picked up the hair strands from the locket's compartment and put them inside a sterile plastic packet. He then clipped a few strands from Aryan's hair, which he placed inside another sterile packet. Both packets were sealed inside a big 'PTI' envelope on which he wrote, 'DNA sample—Vikrant Rambal.'

Aryan was clueless. 'DNA sample? I don't get it!'

Visham explained it with the precision of the lawyer in him.

'Son, after cheek cells, hair specimens provide the most reliable results for DNA testing. During the riots, I've had people courier their hair from Durban to Johannesburg, because they were in jail or couldn't travel for a test. It struck me when I saw this note by your grandfather. He kept a diary. Like my father.'

The technician left after collecting 'Express Charges' and promised to deliver the results within one week.

Avik Davar

'One week?' Aryan was impatient.

'Yes, sir. It takes that long.'

A week later, Gurleen and Vish were at the dining table when the doorbell rang at 6 p.m. sharp. Aryan was in the washroom. Vish opened the door, recognized the PTI logo on the package and snatched it even before signing for it. He took the package straight into the guest bedroom and locked the door from inside. Gurleen was perplexed with Visham's behaviour.

'Where's he?' Aryan asked when he walked back in.

'In his room.'

'Who was it at the door?' Aryan kept his tone polite, even as rage built up inside him.

Gurleen didn't acknowledge the question.

Not getting any reaction, he keyed in 'PTI' on his mobile search bar and dialled out the common number displayed in most of the search results. Soon, he was connected to the reception. '…You've delivered the report… signed by Visham Rambal… Sure…Thanks.' He hung up and faced Gurleen. 'Why didn't you tell me the report has arrived?'

'Vish took it with him.' It was all she knew.

Vish tore the envelope and opened the typed sheets filled with rows and columns of strange numbers. However, the last paragraph containing the conclusion was easy to understand.

He then took out an old envelope from his briefcase. It had the markings 'Sir Alec Centre, Leicestershire' and had yellowed with age. He spread out its contents on the table. It had gibberish similar to the PTI report. His eyes flitted from one to the other, comparing their contents.

Soon, he had the answer that had eluded him for more than twenty years.

Aryan had worked up enough rage to rap nonstop at the guest room door. Eventually, it opened and Visham walked out with a folder in his hands. It had the logo of Rustom Law Offices.

Aryan thundered. 'Would you mind explaining your strange actions? Don't test my patience, please.'

'What do you want to know, Aryan?'

'You bloody well know. What's in that goddamn report?'

Visham's voice was cold as steel. 'Aryan, do you want to lose all your rights to Rambal Acres and the chance to settle down in Canada?'

'What do you mean?'

'Here in my hands is your ticket to freedom: A fool proof investor visa for Canada, and a complete transfer of Rambal Acres to you. All I ask in return is: Forget the test report.'

Aryan looked at Gurleen. Her puzzled look convinced him that she didn't know what was happening.

'Take a look.' Vish thrust the folder in Aryan's hands.

On top was a sealed legal parchment inside a plastic folder. Aryan removed the lac seal with the paper knife and read the one-page deposition.

Undertaking

I, Visham Singh Rambal, son of late Shri Chattar Singh Rambal, resident at Cape Town, South Africa, declare as follows:

That I have filed a petition at the Saket Court, Delhi, contesting the Will of late Shri Vikrant Singh Rambal, s/o late Shri Vijendra Singh Rambal, r/o Rambal Acres, New Delhi, my cousin.

I hereby transfer all my rights and interests in the estate of late Lala Vijendra Singh Rambal, exclusively to Aryan Rambal, s/o late Vikrant Rambal, and appoint him my sole heir, with immediate effect, to all the assets including 'The Rambal Acres' with the sole exception of the rear plot and the outhouse, garage and the servants' block, which I transfer hereby to Gurleen Rambal, w/o late Shri Vikrant Rambal.

I further undertake to settle on demand, all outstanding loans drawn by Mrs Gurleen Rambal and Mr Aryan Rambal.

I hereby issue an irrevocable power of attorney to Mr Ravi Dhar to give effect to this declaration and communicate the contents to the beneficiaries.

This transfer is irrevocable.
Deponent
Visham Singh Rambal
In presence of:
Ravi Dhar

Aryan tossed the sheet on the table and opened the second envelope. It had a letter from Glenborough & Partners, Attorneys at Law, Toronto, Canada.

To whom it may concern
We hereby certify based on an inspection of the official records that:

The entire ownership of Rambal Lodges Canada consisting of 1000 shares representing 100% of the shareholding, allotted against an investment of one million Canadian dollars, is vested in the name of Mr Visham Rambal, endorsable to Mr Aryan Rambal.

Rambal Lodges Canada has also resolved to appoint Mr Aryan Rambal resident director and undertakes to procure his investor visa in keeping with his rights as an investor.

Richard Glenborough
Principal Partner

Aryan replaced the contents inside the envelope, raging inside, reactionless outside.

Vish complimented him. 'You should be happy. You are the legitimate heir to all this wealth, either way.'

'Legitimate? Legitimate?' Aryan's face was red and his hands were trembling with rage.

Looking at Gurleen, he said, 'You must have convinced him to hide it from me. I hate you both!' and stormed out.

Gurleen was bewildered. 'What's all this, Vish? You get Aryan's DNA tested, and then hide the report. Now you shower all these goodies on Aryan. What's your game?'

Vish didn't answer. Instead, he went inside and brought out the reports and laid them out on the table. He then took out a red pen and, riffling through both reports, he took down a whole bunch of entries from the new PTI report and entered them in various places in the old Leicestershire report.

He looked at both reports once more, crest-fallen. His eyes said it all even before he spoke. 'Bhabhi, see for yourself. There is a match in every location. She cheated me all the while. She even swore on my baby.'

Gurleen leaned over and picked up the old report from England that Vish had crossed out with red ink. The entries from the PTI report on Vikrant's hair samples matched the child's samples tested in Leicestershire, cell for cell.

'You never trusted Vikki all these years!' She gasped.

24

1986. Norfolk, England.

The man at the wheel drove in a frenzy. Passing the imposing statue of the Black Prince of Perthshire, he turned into London Road A11 and kept on until he heard the screams in the rear seat. 'Faster, Vish!'

They had gone strictly by the book and had waited at home for the 4-1-1 symptom—contractions at intervals of four minutes, lasting one minute each, repeating for over an hour—before getting to the hospital. Only, nature had hurried.

'We're almost there!' he said as he sighted the intersection New Market Road/ A 11. He took the second exit at the roundabout into Newfound House Way, and then half a mile later, the first exit into Colney Lane. As he approached the roundabout, the huge neon signs of the Norfolk and Norwich University Hospital appeared on the right, two hundred metres away. The car swerved into the kerb and came to a screaming halt, hitting the granite edge. They had made it in thirty-seven minutes from their apartment in Elveden, Suffolk, to the Norfolk and Norwich University Hospital.

The man rushed out, opened the rear door wide, and ran inside the hospital, shouting 'Emergency! Stretcher please!' A pair of legs flexed and shot out of the rear door, wriggling in pain. A woman got off from the other door and wobbled towards the legs, which were spread-eagled and flapped in discomfort as the other woman kept screaming. The head was already visible.

Soon, the man was back, with attendants who helped the woman onto a stretcher and rushed inside. Relieved, the man spoke to the other woman.

'I'm going inside to do the paperwork. Who would've expected it to happen so fast?'

She said, 'Run along, Vish. I'll park the car and be there soon. I may be a tad slow because of my condition. Hope you understand.'

'Take your time. Even you've got a baby coming pretty soon. I can't wait to hold them both in my hands.'

'Well, run along. Hurry, Vish.'

The man broke into a run to make up for the lost minute, eager to settle his wife into the deluxe wing, where her ward had been booked in advance.

When the stretcher arrived into the theatre, the obstetrician and the anaesthetist were already waiting in the ward. Easing the panting woman on the bed, the obstetrician peered through the gown and said, 'Oh, wow! It seems we are already there. The dilation is complete. She's ready to deliver in two or three minutes at most.'

It was all over the instant they had tied the Electro Foetal Monitoring belt over her waist and set up the drip. Within minutes of being brought in, Shalini, wife of Visham Singh Rambal, gave birth to a healthy six-pound boy. A tight whack smacked the butt and the much-expected cry of life permeated the ward. It was a perfect, natural delivery, without undue stress or abnormal pain to the mother.

The two-day old showed healthy signs. However, Dr Connolly was worried. The high blood pressure and the swelling of the mother's feet weren't good signs. Her fears mounted when the urine test results showed an abnormal build-up of protein. She sought a clarification before coming to her conclusion. 'Mr Rambal, did your wife take any medication in India?'

'Doctor, she's been on high blood pressure medication for some months now.'

'You should have told us right away!'

'Sorry, you never asked, and we had no time. She was already in labour.'

'Let's hope it's not as bad as I think it is.'

'What are you worried about, Doctor?'

'Eclampsia.'

Vish was too worried to even ask what 'Eclampsia' meant as long as they could cure it. Within an hour, Shalini went into a seizure and remained in coma for a full day. She died the next day.

The cause: Death due to deep vein thrombal clot in the brain, caused by Eclampsia followed by a mild stroke.

It was evening before Vish could complete the formalities at the crematorium. He then began his one-hundred-and-seventy-kilometre drive from Norfolk to Leicestershire; to deliver a small package as asked by the person he was about to meet at Sir Alec Centre, a lab tucked away in a quiet corner of the sprawling campus of the Glen Hospital. Except that it wasn't just another lab. It was the world's first lab for DNA testing, a process patented by Sir Alec.

Dr John Patterson was waiting for his old collegemate and county cricket opponent from Norwich. Visham's call and the urgency to visit by had surprised John.

'Vish, it's been ages. Don't see you at the counties these days.'

'I'm doing okay, John. Cricket's taken a backseat for now. I'm into inheritance and estate matters.'

'Well, that's all good for our work. As you might have heard lately.'

'It's why I am here. Here, the morgue handed it to me this afternoon. Tell me John, can paternity be proved at any age?'

'One hundred per cent. The results will be the same even after a thousand years, because a person's DNA never changes. It is the unique print of a being's entity.'

'Thanks, that's rather comforting. Err, is it possible to test a dead body?'

'When you called from the hospital, I made arrangements to have the blood sample collected and frozen right away.'

'Alec, what if you couldn't use the blood sample?'

'We do have back up methods. Like the package you've brought.' Dr Patterson opened the package and took out a sealed plastic pouch, which seemed to contain nothing. But whatever was inside seemed enough for Dr Patterson nodded his approval. 'Vish, I can work with this.'

'Thanks, John. When do I come back?'

'Four days. Say, Friday?'

'And this is just between us, right!'

'Boy Scout's Honour.'

The following Friday, Vish drove down for the second time to Leicestershire to Sir Alec Centre. This time he was to see Dr Jim Barnett, John's deputy, who was filling in for his busy senior. British efficiency reinforced itself as the door opened at 4.15 p.m. and a man dressed in smart tweeds greeted him.

'I'm Jim Barnett. Do come in.'

'Is it ready?'

'Would you like to see it here or in the privacy of your home?'

'Let's hear it out, doctor. I wouldn't understand all this medical stuff.'

Jim picked up the folder. 'Before I go over the results, let me tell you how we do it, okay?'

Visham nodded with anxiety as the doctor spread the report on the desk. It was a table with a string of numbers in every cell.

'You can see sixteen rows and two columns here. Each row is a locus—a location on the gene—and has two numbers; we call them "alleles". At each locus, one allele must match the mother's, the other must match the father's. Common sense, right? We only need to check whether there is an identical match at every location.

'For example, if the child's locus has the values of 16 and 14, and if the mother has values 12.1 and 16, we can conclude the child inherited the 16 from the mother. By the same logic, the other number 14 must come from the biological father—it's called the obligate paternal allele. If the father does not have the matching 14 at that locus, then he cannot be the biological father.'

'Can you be absolutely certain?'

'The uniqueness of the DNA test is that it always shows a 0 or 1 result for each of the fifteen loci. Even if there is a mismatch at one location, that's a 0, and the Combined Paternity Index or CPI, which is the product of all the fifteen indices, will be 0. The result will be 0 for everyone, except the biological father, who will get a result of 99.99 per cent, technically 100 per cent. That is why it's the definitive paternity test.'

'Can it be certified?'

'Of course, it is even admissible as evidence in court.'

'What are the results here, Jim?' Visham pointed to the blue folder.

'The CPI is 0. The sample does not belong to the biological father.'

'Are you sure?'

'Absolutely. The alleles don't match. See for yourself.'

'Do you know it's my child we're talking about, Doc?'

John spoke with characteristic British euphemism. 'I'm afraid that statement is biologically incorrect, Mr Rambal!'

25

It was past midnight. Using his key, Aryan slid the door open and crept into the house. He was drunk but still in control. He tiptoed past the master bedroom and stopped on hearing a rustle in the guest room. He hid in the shadows. The door opened, and Vish stepped out and headed towards the kitchen further down.

Aryan was in luck. He stepped into the guest room. He scanned the room and saw what he was looking for, inside the half-open cupboard. He heaved the briefcase and ran out, focusing as much as he could in his tipsy state.

He alighted at the porch of the Taj Man Singh hotel, where he had booked himself earlier that evening. When he stepped into his room, he could no longer stand straight. He collapsed on the bed, his face pressed against the briefcase.

The next morning, Visham was shaken out of his wits to find the briefcase missing.

'Gurleen, where's Aryan?' Vish came running into her room.

'Didn't see him. I don't think he turned up last night.'

'I hope you're right.'

'Why?'

'My briefcase is missing. It's got both the reports.'

'Oh God!' She frantically dialled Aryan's mobile number.

The Taj concierge was willing to solve his premier guest's problem. It was unusual but not improbable for a guest to forget a combination number. It took over two hours to manually unravel the eight-cylinder combination, with its ten million permutations.

Damn! Aryan cursed when he saw the cracked code.

6-8-9-1-8-0-1-2.

It was his date of birth. Reversed.

When the concierge saw the relief in his guest's smile, he reverted to his professional instinct. He opened the case and turned it towards himself such that its contents remained hidden from Aryan's view.

'Sir, what contents inside would identify you as the owner of this briefcase? Just joking.'

Aryan played up to the ruse. 'Sure. You will find conclusive proof of my identity in there.'

'An I-card?'

'No, a DNA test,' Aryan said.

Shifting his eyes, the concierge turned the briefcase towards Aryan. On top was the Paternity Test Institute report heading 'DNA Test; Vikrant Rambal'.

Back in his deluxe room overlooking the Lodi Gardens, Aryan pored through the senseless rows and columns of numbers in the PTI report. The only thing he understood easily was the conclusion.

Based on the DNA analysis, Vikrant Rambal, cannot be excluded as the biological Father, because they share the same genetic markers.

Dr Ritwik Ghosh

The shock drained the colour from Aryan's face. 'God, what have I done?' he mumbled as his phone rang. Seeing the number, he broke down. 'Imma, please forgive me,' he sobbed.

It was the first time he had cried over Vikrant's death.

Disconnecting the call, he returned to the senseless maze of numbers. In the PTI report, the column for 'Father' had typed entries. However, the 'Mother' had been filled in with hand-written numbers in red ink. It puzzled him, for Imma hadn't given her samples at all.

Then he noted the red ink. *Visham had a red pen.* His curiosity matched by his rage, Aryan set out for home.

Paternity Testing Institute
DNA ANALYSIS with PowerPlex® 16 system Gene Mapper®
Date: 3 July 2007

STRLOCUS	FATHER Vikrant Rambal		CHILD Aryan Rambal		MOTHER not tested		INDEX
AMEL	XV		X V				
D3S1358	14	17	16	14	16	15	1.036
Th01	6	9	8	9.3	8	6	1.132
D21 S11	28	30		28	23	28	2.867
D 18 S 51		12	12	18	18	16	4.000
Penta E	10	19	17	19	17	14	5.375
D5S 818		11	12	13	15	13	1.362
D 13 S 317		11	11	13	13	11	1.385
D 7s 820	8	11	10	11	10	9	3.432
D 16S 539	12	13	13	132	12	11	0.692
CSF 1RP	9	10	10	12	8	12	0.824
Pent D	8	10	7	10	7	8	1.667
V W A		17	17	20	17	20	1.900
D8S 1173	14	15	12	14	12	14	1.344
TPOX	8	9	9	8	8	7	0.983
FGA	20	22	22	25	25	16	1.365

Combined Direct Index: 17,446; Probability Percentage: 99.442%
Based on the DNA Analysis, the alleged Father, Vikrant Rambal, cannot be
excluded as the biological Father, because they share the same genetic markets.
Dr Ritwik Ghosh

Gurleen and Visham were in the living room. A pregnant silence
loomed in the air. Then Aryan breezed in, holding Vish's briefcase.

'Why did you hide my father's DNA report?' he charged at
Visham.

There was no reaction. Not even from Gurleen.

'Imma, this man's been playing games. The DNA test was positive. Dad was my father all along!'

She remained phlegmatic.

Aryan was confused. 'Imma, aren't you happy? See what this means? You know what I've been through.'

Gurleen looked up and repeated, 'Do *you* know what *I've* been through?'

Aryan kept looking at Vish while opening the lock. 'You even used my birth date for the combination lock!'

He took out the PTI report to show it to a still-disinterested Gurleen. As he was closing the briefcase, his eyes fell on a second report, from a Sir Alec Centre, Leicestershire. It had a similar gibberish of numbers, but all the columns had been typed in, unlike the PTI report. However, in the 'Father' column, over-written above the printed numbers was a second set of numbers.

Hand written. In red ink.

Aryan gasped. 'Hey, what's this old report from England?'

Again, there was no answer.

He studied the Leicestershire report line by line, his head in a maze on seeing the report's date and the names on it. 'This test in England was done days after I was born. The mother's name says Shalini, and the father's name, Visham Singh. Is it your child's test report, Vish uncle?'

The continued silence irritated him no end.

'Damn it, what's all this drama?' Aryan raised his tone in renewed anger. 'Will someone tell me what this means?'

The moment that Gurleen had feared all her life had come to pass.

Vish held her hand, and summoned all his strength to lay the truth. 'Aryan, it means that Vikki was the father of my wife's child.'

Sir Alec DNA Centre Leicestershire, ENGLAND				Record DX24AJC	
Date: 23 Aug 1986	Requested by: Visham Rambal, Elveden Close			Signed by Jim Barnett	
STRLOCUS	Mother Shalini		Child Male		Father VISHAM SINGH Vik B	
D3S1358	16	15	15	~~14~~	16~~14~~	1717
Th01	8	6	8	~~9.3~~	–6	7~~9~~
D21 S11	23	28		~~28~~	29~~28~~	31.230
D18 S51	18	16	~~12~~	18	15 –	16~~12~~
Penta E	17	14	17	~~19~~	710	13~~19~~
D5S 818	15	13	~~12~~	13	12 –	13~~12~~
D 13 S 317	13	11	~~11~~	13	0–	12~~11~~
D 7s 820	10	9	10	~~11~~	08	10~~11~~
D 16S 539	12	11	~~13~~	12	912	11~~13~~
CSF 1RP	8	12	~~10~~	12	09	10~~10~~
Pent D	7	8	7	~~10~~	08	5~~10~~
V W A	17	20	~~17~~	20	15–	17~~17~~
D8S 1173	12	14	12	~~14~~	1214	15~~15~~
TPOX	8	7	~~9~~	8	98	119
FGA	25	16	~~22~~	25	2120	43.2~~22~~
Maternity: **Inclusive** CPI:3874 Probability: 99.8765%				Paternity: **Exclusive** CPI: 0; Probability: 0.0%	

26

1984, Delhi.

One day, Vikrant overheard a phone conversation between Visham and Shalini. Visham was apologizing. '... I'm sorry about the passes for the James Bond film premiere. I know I did promise. But bhaiyya has already committed his quota to others. Sorry!'

Vish was midway up the stairs when Vikrant rested his Bristol cigar in the holder and surprised him. 'Vish, I'll see if I can get two passes somehow.'

'Really? You're great!'

'Let you know by noon.'

By noon, Shalini had called thrice and had hung up in anger. 'I didn't know your Rambal influence couldn't even get me a pass.'

Vish was still reeling when there was another call, very brief. Excited, Visham dialled Shalini. 'You are in luck. Be ready at five. Happy?'

They were escorted to the President's Box, an ornate mini enclosure with two plush reclining seats, and a personal butler on call.

'Wow!' Shalini gasped as she sat down in one of the seats and took in the richness of her ambience.

Vikrant took out the plain envelope and handed it to Visham. 'Hey, these are your seats in the front. J 10-11. Enjoy.'

Shalini heard the 'J 10-11' and realized her error of assumption. 'Oh, aren't we sitting here, Visham?' she said, still clinging to her red seat.

'I'm afraid not. These are only by invitation,' Vikrant sounded apologetic.

Vish was cool. 'That's fine, bhaiyya. We'll be fine down there.

Where's bhabhi?'

'She's come down with a migraine.'

'Oh, that's awful. These VIP box seats are fantastic!' Shalini whined.

'Maybe one of you could…' Vikki let it hang. *Test time, Shalini.*

'Let's go, Shalini.' Vish started moving. But she hadn't budged.

'What a waste! Visham, do you mind if I…'

Test passed, Vikrant thought.

Ten minutes later, as the credits rolled, Visham sat in J-10, cracking his popcorn. In the packed hall, only the seat next to his was vacant.

In the President's Box, the liveried butler placed morel mushrooms dipped in sauce on the side table and poured champagne into Shalini and Vikrant's flutes. Vikrant toasted, 'To the gorgeous lady on this side of the screen.'

She pecked him on the cheek.

'Are you really serious about Visham?' he asked, now that the gloves were off.

She took his Cohiba cigar, inhaled deeply and blew the smoke laced with her mint freshener, into his face. 'You know my answer, don't you?'

'I'd still like to hear it to be sure. You fancy Visham or…' he let the question hang.

She took a deep puff and came clean. 'I fancy the money. Filthy loads of it. What about yourself?' Her hand had cupped the back of his palm.

Vikrant levelled his eyes at her cleavage and paced his words. 'I want to see what money can buy that I don't already have.'

A month later Vikrant brought it up at the dining table.

'Vish, I can see that you and Shalini are serious. Why not make things official? It would also make things easier for me when you study law in England. That is if she's willing to take over your position here.'

'Are you sure, bhaiyya?' Vish couldn't believe his ears.

'Of course. I've been rude at times, but that's because I was always a bit jealous of your looks, those blue eyes, and even about Shalini. But then, I reasoned, it's all in the family.'

Visham and Shalini got engaged a week before he left for England to study at East Anglia University Law School, where he got a part scholarship, the rest of his fee funded by Rambal Holdings. Shalini helped Vikrant with the business and mixed it with huge doses of pleasure.

Two years later, the entire family attended Vish's graduation in England and spent a month touring Europe, ending it with a quiet, no-frills wedding in Cannes, France.

A month later, amidst an afternoon escape in the presidential suite at the Oberoi, Delhi, Shalini broke the news that she had skipped her cycle.

Vikrant was ambivalent. 'Do you know whose—?'

She interrupted him, 'Jealous, my little koel?'

'Koel? What's the connection?'

'The beautiful koel bird always lays her egg in the ugly crow's nest. When the eggs hatch and the young koel comes out, the poor crow dotes more on the beautiful one that isn't her own. Eventually, the koel leaves and joins its real mother.'

The answer delighted him. She had acknowledged Vikrant Rambal as lord and master of everything on the Rambal estate, including Visham, Shalini and even her child.

'I'll give him all rights, just as my legitimate son,' Vikrant muttered as he set about celebrating the latest addition to the Rambal family.

As Vikki helped himself to her, Shalini's thoughts drifted to the Vanderbilt heirloom she'd seen at Tiffanys. Bearing Vikrant Rambal's seed was a guarantee one day she would own it, and several more.

Life was good, if one learnt to look out for oneself.

27

Vish was crying uncontrollably. It was a huge release. The release of his worst fear, which had just come true.

Gurleen held Vish close to her bosom and consoled him. 'If it brings you any consolation, Vish, just know that you aren't the only one that's been cheated. In all this humiliation, let us be grateful it all remained within the family.'

Aryan was shocked. Another child, shit!

'No wonder he was guilty. Her ghost must have haunted him in the end. Tit for tat. That poor little bastard! He paid the price for his father's–'

Gurleen's thundering outburst cut him down. 'Stop it right there. Not one more word against that child!'

He couldn't believe her reaction. 'Whoa, what's up, Imma? You're defending your husband's little bastard against your own child?'

Her face was white with disgust. 'Yes. All my life, I have been defending my husband's little bastard against my own child. Except that the bastard is you, Aryan!'

Even death would have feared to invade the silence that fell on the room.

'It was my innocent little baby that died. So that a bastard— you—could live and enjoy all the comforts of life. You are the bastard here,' Gurleen broke down, and swooned.

Vish rushed to arrest her fall and eased her into the sofa. Aryan rushed into the kitchen and brought out a moist towel that he patted on her forehead. The two men brought her back to consciousness.

After Gurleen had come to, Aryan was plaintive. 'Vish uncle, I just don't get it.'

Vish explained it with a resigned calm in his voice.

'Aryan, I knew from the Alec Centre that I was not your father. But I could only speculate about Vikki bhaiyya. I suffered in silence all these years.'

Aryan was still unsettled. 'But what's all this about her child?'

Vish and Gurleen looked at each other.

Finally, heaving a deep breath, drawing on all her reserves, Gurleen let out the secret, forced by the one person for whose sake it had been kept a secret all these tormenting years.

28

1986. Norfolk.

The engine was still purring. Gurleen struggled to slip under the steering wheel, her stomach bulging with a twenty-eight-week pregnancy. Her discomfort increased, and she became breathless and felt giddy at the wheel. There was no strength in her hands. The hundred metres to the parking lot seemed endless, and she almost fainted at the wheel after parking awkwardly.

Suddenly, she felt a stab of pain, and the warm gush of something on her thighs. She wriggled out of the car and steadied herself by hanging on to the door. A brief touch on her pelvic area confirmed her fear: She was bleeding profusely. The blood started flowing down her legs and began splattering on the clean paved street. Steadying herself with more resolve than stamina, she traced the endless steps back to the porch and shouted 'Help!' as loud as she could but was barely audible.

Why is she taking so long? Visham wondered, after consulting his Longines Flagship. It was almost forty-five minutes since they had entered the hospital. His baby had already been cleaned up. But there was still no sign of Gurleen. He set out for the reception on the ground floor to check where she was stuck. He saw his car through the giant glass doors, parked outside, straddling two slots—uncharacteristic of Gurleen, who was a stickler for symmetry. Where could she have gone?

Soon the concierge came, with his obsequious smile and fondling a key chain in his hand.

'How can I help you, sir?'

Recognizing the keys, Visham said, 'Those are my keys. My sister-in-law had them.'

'Sir, would she be the one in an orange pullover?' The concierge seemed to have seen her.

'That's her. Do you know where she went?'

'She fainted right here. She was taken to the General Emergency section out there on the left. Right next to the Boots drugstore.'

'How do you know all this?'

'I took her there myself along with a couple others, sir.'

Vish found Gurleen asleep. Close by, a nurse was taking notes dictated by a tall and majestic lady whose badge read: Dr Ruth Jameson.

'Hello doctor. I'm Visham Singh. That is Gurleen, my sister-in-law. What happened? She was quite all right an hour ago.'

'We're afraid she's had profuse bleeding in the uterus. We're still investigating. She is under sedation for now.'

'May I request you to shift her to the deluxe wing? I'll pay anything you ask.'

'After we take her in for a caesarean,' Dr. Ruth Jameson reassured him.

'What? She isn't due for weeks, Doctor!'

'Well, she is, now,' Dr Jameson said as they rolled Gurleen inside.

Three hours later, Gurleen had been moved to a private ward in the deluxe wing, to the room adjacent to Shalini's suite. The cradle was empty, though.

'Placental abruption,' Dr Ruth Jameson stated her conclusion without emotion.

Vish looked dazed. Not seeing any reaction, Dr Jameson realized the need for demystifying the jargon. 'The placenta, which connects the foetus to the uterus wall, had come off. The blood flow to the foetus was severely affected. Heavy bleeding had begun in the uterus. Meanwhile, the contractions kept coming nonstop, but without any strength. The result was as feared.'

Stillborn. Cause: Lack of blood supply through the placenta.

Hours later, her bleeding hadn't stopped. The extreme pre-partum haemorrhage had caused severe maternal shock.

After monitoring her for a day, Dr Jameson performed a second inevitable procedure. Hysterectomy, removal of the uterus.

Gurleen Rambal would never become a mother again.

29

*A*ryan was crestfallen. 'I've re-claimed my father today, only to lose my mother.'

Gurleen was back to her protective self. All wounds had healed with the admission of the truth. 'You've had all my love as a mother, Aryan, right from the first feed off my bosom. But, you hurt me a lot!'

'Imma, I will never hurt you again. Swear!' Aryan reached over and hugged her with an intensity she had never felt before. She pulled Vish in and they all huddled and sobbed. The broken pieces of a portrait, some pieces missing, lost forever.

When they had composed themselves, some questions still remained unanswered.

Aryan asked, 'Why didn't you tell dad right at the beginning?'

Gurleen shook her head. 'With Shalini dead and Visham gone after leaving that note, and my loss of motherhood forever, I was all messed up. I needed time to settle things. And then, Vikki came in suddenly that night. I was too scared to say anything. I needed time.'

30

1986, Elveden, Suffolk.

She could see the agony throbbing behind Vish's creased brow. The agony of being cheated and betrayed by his spouse. Vish had serious doubts over Shalini's loyalty—she had made many friends while he was in England. However, she avoided talking about them. He had hinted about it to Gurleen at times, but she had brushed it off.

But getting a DNA test done for their child after Shalini was gone, she found that disgusting. She couldn't believe Vish distrusted his wife that much. But then, she hadn't expected the test result to show negative, either. It shocked her that Shalini was carrying someone else's baby. She felt somewhat responsible, because Shalini was under their care in Delhi while Vish was studying law in England. *It must be someone very special. Someone very secret.* She pushed away the few possibilities that crept into her mind.

They spoke about it at dinner.

Vish was practical. 'It will shame the whole family. Will you promise never to tell anyone?'

Gurleen nodded. 'Yes, I promise.'

She got up to warm the morning's *rajma* rice for Vish, who hadn't eaten a crumb since morning. From the kitchen she heard the main door open and Vish called out, 'I'll be back in a while. Don't wait for me, have your dinner.' The door slammed shut.

She wasn't up to eating either, and tucked the casseroles into the fridge. She stepped into the study to turn off the light and found a handwritten note under the paperweight, next to it the report from Dr Alec Centre. She read it again, clipped it on the inside flap of the report folder and, remembering her promise, locked it inside her suitcase.

The feeble cry from the bed brought her attention back to the grave responsibility at hand. She rushed to find the makeshift diaper wet. As she changed it with a warm, dry replacement, the crying stopped. The lips moved, seeking to be fed. The unsaid demand made her cry inside. Shattered by her own loss, Gurleen realized that only love could erase pain.

As she tussled between the bottle and her wetting breast, she knew that the choice was entirely hers. A gentle tug of the inch-wide palm stuck at her pullover settled it for her. She pushed the bottle away for the time being. And joy soothed sorrow as suckle soothed hunger.

She stirred. The baby was crying, woken by the church clock striking midnight. She put him to her breast and dozed off again. She was woken again by the church clock striking repeatedly. *Why is it striking so many times?*

It was the doorbell. *It must be Vish; he must have had a change of heart. Good!* Half sleepy, she opened the door, and taunted, 'Desperate to see your son!'

She froze at Vikki's sight.

'Why didn't you tell me? When? Where's he?'

Everything was happening so fast, she could not think what to say, what to withhold. Before she could compose herself, he had already entered the bedroom and picked up the baby. 'My baby! Why didn't anyone inform me? I thought you were due two weeks later.'

'I couldn't…there was no…' She struggled with the words, and was relieved that the baby had begun crying again.

As she comforted the baby, Vikki reasoned with himself. 'But then how would you have reached me? It isn't easy to reach anyone in Africa's copper mines. But I'm so happy! Our baby!'

She was desperate to give him the other news. 'You need to know… there's been a big problem. Vish left…there's been—'

Vikki cut her off. 'Don't worry, I know all about it.'

The blood drained from her face. 'What…what…do you know?'

'I know Vish has a client who threatened him over a lost case. Vish must have left town to let it blow over.'

She had regained some nerve by now. 'There's worse news. Shalini…'

'What about her?' He sounded very edgy at once.

'She…she died in the hospital.'

'Oh! That's…that's really sad,' he said, rocking the cradle, the baby bundled and secure. Gurleen could not help noting how easily he was taking it. *Why is he so casual? He doesn't seem upset at all. Wasn't he very fond of Shalini?*

Two weeks later, she was strong enough to take the strain of travel. It was time to move on and accept life. Vikki had applied for the baby's travel documents and learnt that the Indian Embassy would verify the hospital record independently. Gurleen was relieved; it made her task easy. The hospital record would confirm that the baby was Shalini and Vish's. And then she would have to tell Vikki about their baby, and the worse news that she would never be able to conceive again. How would he react to that? It was a relief that he was becoming so fond of the baby. *Thank you, Rabba.*

They were on their way to Heathrow airport, and Gurleen's worries had turned into fear. She panicked all the way about Vikki's reaction at the airport immigration. What would he do? Cancel the tickets and go back looking for Vish? What if Vish didn't return? Would Vikki vent all his anger at the baby? Would he put him in an orphanage? All she hoped was that they would board the flight. She would pacify him during the twelve-hour long flight with its halts at Beirut and Dubai. He would understand. He loved the baby and had even thought of a name. Aryan. Yes, Vikki would be upset with the truth, but would eventually get over it and accept Vish's baby.

The immigration desk at Heathrow had the travel documents

ready. Vikki checked and signed them and handed them over to Gurleen. He looked very calm.

She glanced through it, read it slowly, almost aloud and gasped.

Infant Name:	Unnamed
Date of Birth:	21 August 1986
Gender:	Male
Mother:	Gurleen Rambal
Father:	Vikrant Singh Rambal

31

'*H*ow did that happen?' Vish and Aryan asked in unison.

'That question has tormented me all these years. It's a question to which I have no answer,' Gurleen said.

Aryan was irritated. 'You never found out?'

Gurleen looked at him in the eye. 'No, I didn't want to.'

'And you never wanted to tell dad the truth?'

'Not until Vish returned. But Vish never came back.' She looked at Vish, who lowered his eyes.

'Bhabhi, I was bitter. I felt it was bhayya's responsibility to own the child. I never thought it would heap such suffering on you.'

'I hated you for leaving, Vish. I had no idea how Vikki would react to your baby. It was sheer luck whatever happened with the documents. Even later, I often cursed you, Vish. Vikki insulted and humiliated me so much in his last few months; he called me immoral, he suspected me with you, and still I kept my word. The only way I could deal with your absence was by consoling myself you might be dead. And yet, when you came back, you sued me.'

'Bhabhi, I always kept track. Everything seemed to be going well with the three of you. I didn't want to mess things up. Yes, I didn't come for the funeral, you can understand why. But I came back as soon as your troubles began. As for the lawsuit, it was the only way I could save the estate from Raina. Vikki bhaiyya had made a huge blunder giving him the powers.'

Aryan was irritated; his head was a maelstrom of doubt.

'But Imma, you could have told dad later, no? You had all the time in the world.'

'But I didn't have the heart. And it wasn't because I couldn't bear him children. It was because he was so proud of you. Your blue eyes. They meant everything to him.'

'In what way?'

'They were proof to the world that he was a genuine Rambal.'

'Gosh, that's why you said no to the DNA test? You'd figured from my blue eyes that my father was a Rambal.'

Gurleen wrung her hands. 'In the beginning they were "cat's eye" grey, but as you grew older, they got the trademark blue, with a small ring of grey. Vikki was overjoyed. And I was shattered.'

'And she knew from the DNA test in England that I wasn't the father,' Vish filled in.

Aryan was broken-hearted. 'We'll never get to know what happened with the birth certificate.'

'You've got to live with that, Aryan.'

Aryan remained pensive for a while. Eventually, he looked at his stepparents and smiled. 'If you both could live with it for twenty years, I suppose I'll learn to live with it too.'

They huddled again. Faith and affection would reinforce their fragile bonds with the passage of time.

It was just well that Aryan had put his trust in his stepparents. But even if he had remained in doubt and chosen to visit the Norwich Hospital archives, he would never have got to know the truth. For fate had played its hand through Nassim Abdullah, an Arab clerk at the record room.

32

1986, Norfolk.

Vish was waiting in the lounge inside the Infant Registry Centre of the hospital, which was an outlet of the Royal Registrar of Births and Deaths. Official birth—and in the rare cases, death—certificates were issued at the hospital at the time of discharge. Some certificates featured the newborn's name, while others were issued 'Unnamed'.

To enter the details in the registry, one had to fill in details on cyclostyled forms at the counter. They were still waiting for computers; until then, it would remain a painful drudgery for the clerks, who had to read hundreds of forms, interpret the handwriting, re-enter the texts manually on the register and prepare the temporary certificates.

An obese, garrulous woman, Nassim hated her task no end, and distracted herself by making full use of the free phone extension provided by the hospital. No one questioned her, for she was not hospital staff; she reported to the registrar's office in Town Hall.

Seeing Vish, she had called him over to the counter and shown him the stack of blank forms. 'Please print the spellings in the boxes, leave a space between first, middle and last names.' She hastened back to her banter in Arabic.

Vish took two forms and began filling them up, the first one for the one that was alive, and the second for the one that never came into life. When he had finished, still ruing the mixed fortune that had come into their lives, he bunched them together. He put the second form on top, to allow the ink to dry and pushed the forms over to the disinterested clerk who was still yapping away on the free hospital phone.

Seeing his rising impatience, she placed the receiver down once again, without disconnecting. With a fake smile, she took the two forms, held one in each hand and checked the contents. It was normal that she did not understand Asian names.

'You Indians have long and difficult names.'

'Yes, it is like that in our culture.'

'You can collect the certificates in two days.' She was still on the phone, as she began entering the details into the official register of the town records. Vish had just moved three strides when she called back.

'Excuse me, sir. Are these both birth certificates?'

Vish shook his head in irritation. 'No, no, no. The first one is birth, the second one is death,' remembering the order in which he had filled them.

'Okay, *Khalaas*, it will be done,' she said and returned to the still-connected phone call.

Mechanically, she ticked 'Birth' on the form on top, and 'Death' on the other, following the order as she had heard. 'The first one is birth, the second one is death.' Only, she ended up doing just the opposite, for Visham had put the second form on top for the ink to dry.

The Royal Registrar's records would continue to feature Nassim's inadvertent error. An error that would be disputed by neither Visham nor Vikrant Rambal.

One had no desire. The other, no excuse.

33

*G*urleen wanted Vish to stay longer. They all needed to heal, and she knew they could only heal together, by healing one another. She could see Vish was still struggling to forgive Vikki and Shalini, even though he tried hard to keep it deep inside. He was keen to return to Cape Town. Failing to reason with him using emotion, she reminded him of her financial obligation.

'Vish. Please stay here at least until I repay your debt.'

He was surprised. 'What debt?'

'I have to pay you the three and a half crores.'

He didn't seem to understand. 'What are you talking about, bhabhi?'

'You think I can't figure out who paid off the bank? I came to know that Mr Jakhad even paid Raina fifty lakhs. '

'Bhabhi, I don't know what you're talking about. I don't know any Jakhad!'

Aryan was perplexed too. 'Even I thought all along that you were behind it, uncle! If it wasn't you, then who?'

'Ravi would know, surely,' Gurleen said, more to herself than the others.

The next morning, she was called over to Ravi's office for some residual paperwork on the murder case, which was getting formally closed. They were having the usual coffee.

'How is the young lawyer doing?'

'Getting along Mrs Rambal, as long as there are big clients like you.'

'Clients like me can close up your shop, Ravi.'

He laughed. 'I have some papers for you to sign and two things for you to collect. It will take no more than five minutes.'

Surprised what the two 'things' were, she said, 'I can't wait to see them.'

He made her write her full name and address and sign on four pages, which had columns she didn't know much about. When she had filled them in, Ravi filled up some numbers, and then handed Gurleen a gold-plated certificate the size of a wedding invitation.

It read:

Nippon Rambal Limousine Company
Folio No. 1
Certificate No.: 01-4999
Shareholder: Gurleen Rambal
Holding: 4999 shares of equity value Rs 10/- each.

Then, he handed her a Bank of Tokyo Mitsubishi draft for a crore and a half drawn in her name.

She was dumbfounded. 'What's all this Ravi? I don't get it.'

'Welcome, Mrs Rambal, you are now 49.9 per cent shareholder in the Indian venture of Japan's number 1 Limousine Company— Nippon Limousine.'

'What? Are you crazy?'

'Not me, but it's Mr Takematsu who is crazy about you. He wants you to run India's first all-woman limousine service, one that can be trusted by every foreigner without fear of life and honour.'

It took her a while to register everything he had said. But the surprise didn't end there. Ravi took her to the giant glass window and pointed below.

She first saw the Baha'i temple in front of her. Then, guided by his hand, she looked at the road below. Outside Rustom Towers, a line of twenty white Toyota Camrys were lined up, with 'Nippon Rambal Limousine' painted on their sides.

Ravi then brought out a box filled with brand new car keys, and said, 'Mr Takematsu wants hundred such cars in every city where any Japanese will set foot upon in our country.'

She didn't know what to say. Finally, she knew. 'Ravi, I want to add a partner.'

'Aryan?'

'Chameli Singh.'

She rose, clutching two certificates and twenty keys and smiled at him. 'Ravi. You know, after Raina, I had lost faith in lawyers.'

Ravi brushed it off. 'It is unfortunate there are black sheep in black coats too. Don't worry about anything now. It has been my pleasure to work for you. And you are my Gold Class client now.'

After Gurleen left, Ravi called the owner of Nippon Limousine and Japanese Member of Parliament Mr Harunori Takematsu and reported completion of the task. He had distributed one million dollars—rupees six crores—as desired by the client. Three and a half crores for the bank loan, fifty lakhs for Raina, and one crore fifty lakhs to Gurleen Rambal, besides the shares in Nippon Rambal Limousine.

34

*R*aina realized that he had goofed up the biggest opportunity of his life. Despite all his cleverness, everything had worked against him.

Gurleen sued him for false declaration that he had deposited the rent deposit with the bank. The evidence was provided by Arvind, who exposed Raina by declaring the pay-in slip as an ingenious fake.

Aryan sued him for breach of fiduciary duty and conspiracy to deny him his due inheritance by concealing and destroying material evidence. It needed no proof beyond Raina's act at the bank—the entire meeting had been caught on video camera.

Jiten Jakhad wrote to the Bar Association about Raina's unprofessional and unethical act and issued a full-page ad warning the business community to beware of Raina. Ravi Dhar, the new president of the Bar Association, expelled him and recommended exemplary punishment—a ten-year ban from practising law in India.

However, Raina's biggest blow was his conviction for the murder of a businessman whose body had been discovered in his car. Raina was proven to be an accomplice in the case and was sentenced to jail.

The last that was heard about him was that he died in jail, under rather mysterious circumstances. The post-mortem stated the cause of death as immersion in a strong industrial cleaning solution that could eat human bone and tissue. When the body was discovered, there was no face or skin, only a white fluffy powdery lump above his neck.

The FIR had been signed by the new senior inspector at Gorakhpur Jail. Miss Chameli Singh.

35

*A*ryan got an investor visa for the province of Saskatchewan, as the owner of 'Rambal Lodges', a chain of motels set up along the Trans-Canada Highway. Unfortunately, he had to cancel his farewell party. Gurleen was adamant that they visit Amritsar instead.

~

The morning sun shone bright on the gold canopy of the temple, and reflected on the shimmering surface of the sarovar. As they dipped in the holy waters, Aryan removed the scotch tape off the locket—the stone hadn't been reset and hung loose in its crevice—and opened the rear cavity. As Vikrant's remnant hair strands fell into the water, Lala's wish came to be fulfilled. But the tradition would not continue. After kissing it one last time, Gurleen released the locket into the waters. As it sank out of sight, she felt an inexplicable lightness in her chest.

It seemed like the release from the spell of an ancient curse.

Waheguru di Fateh.

36

I was born with a curse.

The line of whoever touches me would vanish from the light. Many a king has suffered its wrath through the centuries.

My curse was contained by the Tenth Sikh Guru Gobind Singh, who neutralized its power with a strand of his hair placed inside me. Upon his orders, I, along with many others, were buried below his haloed resting place, with a warning: *The line of whoever touches it would vanish from the light.*

The prophecy went unheeded. I was unearthed and added to the royal jewels. I remained dormant in the tosha khana until 186 years ago, when I was reincarnated, my body recast by the royal joaillier into a resplendent locket with a hidden compartment in its rear part. It could only be opened by beating the precious stone set in the centre hard enough to break or unseat it.

I would have remained powerless, had the joaillier not burnt away the strands of the Guru's hair that remained in the hidden crevice. My powers returned in full force when the illustrious Maharaja Ranjit Singh held my reincarnated body but same cursed soul, and set me fondly on the chest of his youngest son, Prince Duleep Singh.

True to the legend, the royal line fell one by one. None of the Maharaja's children survived, except Duleep Singh, who was taken to England at thirteen, his mother exiled in the kingdom of Nepal.

Duleep Singh suffered much in his life, separated from his mother, his kingdom and his faith. All of his eight children: Prince Victor, Prince Frederick, Prince Albert Edward, Princess Bamba, Princess Catherine, Princess Sophie from his first wife Bamba; and Princess Pauline Alexandra and Princess Ada Irene Beryl from his second wife Ada Douglas Wetherill, died without bearing any offspring.

Faithful to my destiny and to the Guru's prophecy, I remained with Maharaja Duleep Singh for fifty-eight eventful years, mostly at Elveden Estate, before he gave me away to his eldest daughter Princess Bamba. She was different from the other seven, a lot more curious, fascinated by the tales of her ancestors in the Punjab, and intrigued by its painful history.

She spent long hours listening to her father, as he spoke about the legends of her grandfather, the Maharaja Ranjit Singh. She was the only one among his children who wanted to return and live in the Punjab. Her wish almost came true, when, in April 1886, my master, his wife Maharani Bamba and their six children—three sons: Victor Albert Jay, twenty; Frederick Victor, eighteen; Albert Edward, seven; and three daughters: Bamba Sophia Jindan, seventeen; Catherine Hilda, fifteen; and Sophia Alexandria, ten, set sail aboard SS Verona to Bombay.

Maharaja Duleep Singh had planned to be reconverted into Sikhism, and an elaborate ceremony had been lined up in Punjab. Unfortunately, when the ship arrived at Aden, they were stopped under orders from Lord Dufferin, governor general of India. After fruitless negotiations, the Maharaja sent his family back to England. And, banished from the empire, he went on to Marseille, France, instead.

As the family readied to set sail for England sans its patriarch, Bamba asked her father, 'When will I see you again, father?'

He said, 'We shall all reunite in our ancestors' land in Punjab, after overthrowing the British. Promise to keep your fire burning, my fiery one.'

'I will, father,' she assured him.

'Bamba, if something were to happen to me, will you promise to return to the Punjab and fulfil my last wish?'

'I promise. Order me.' Her eyes shone with truth.

That day, aboard SS Verona, Maharaja Duleep Singh took me off his neck and placed me on a hard surface. He hit at my heart with the butt of his kirpan and pushed the secret latch beneath. I split in the middle, the rear crevice inside revealing a small lock of his hair. It had been collected and preserved when his hair was shorn on the day of his baptism into Christianity, in the hope that it would be consecrated in the Punjab one day.

'Bamba, one day, you must surrender these locks of hair in the sarovar at the Golden Temple. And be sure to release this ancient heirloom in the holy water.'

'Why, father?'

'To release its ancient curse. Will you do it?'

'What curse, father?'

'Whoever holds this antique heirloom would either have a childless family or face enormous suffering with/because of their children. The curse was unleashed when the grand Maharaja Ranjit Singh, your grandfather dug out a box that had been buried.'

'By whom?'

'None other than our Tenth Guru, Guru Gobind Singh. Legend has it that he had put a strand of his own hair inside to restrain its ill effect. When I was born, the royal joaillier was unaware of its significance and melted the holy hair with the metal. As appeasement, he installed an engraved image of the Guru in its cavity.'

'Who told you all this, father?'

'My mother. She always said that the misfortunes in our family began with this heirloom coming into our lives. She even asked me to take it off when I last met her. I didn't believe her then. But now I do.'

'I will fulfil your wish, father,' said the seventeen-year old Bamba, with a resolve of a much older mind.

'From today, proclaim to everyone that you are the queen of Punjab.'

With those words, my master Duleep Singh placed me into his daughter's hands. I felt insecure and lost, a mind wrested from its body, a sail wandering aimlessly without anchor.

Princess Bamba took her father's wish and anointment seriously and believed herself to be the queen of Punjab. She kept me safe inside her collection box, which she carried to Lahore on her first visit, in 1924. However, my master's wishes would only be fulfilled fifteen years later, during her first visit to Amritsar, one year after the death of her husband Lt Col David Sutherland.

A strong supporter and patron of the Khalsa, Princess Bamba was surprised to be invited by the Khalsa College to commemorate the tenth Guru Gobind Singh's birth anniversary. Reading the invitation and the name of the tenth Guru, she remembered her father's wish and her promise.

We were received at the Amritsar station and driven to the prestigious university, which had received a generous trust fund and large tracts of land as an endowment from Maharaja Ranjit Singh. After the ceremony, Bamba requested an escort to take her to Harminder Sahib, the Golden Temple.

We reached there in the afternoon, Bamba looking every bit the native Punjabi in her *salwar kurti chunri*. The canopy of gold atop the beautiful marble palace on water was grander than a maharaja's palace. After all, it was the abode of the Rab, king of the whole universe.

Stepping inside, Bamba touched the marble steps and then her forehead, and moved clockwise, as instructed by the girl guide. More than two hundred steps later, we stood before a large peepul tree. On the left were the gates to the *langar*, the holy meal offering. On the right were steps leading to the bathing area, where devotees had dared to test the icy waters of the sarovar, the holy lake.

Chanting 'Waheguruji da khalsa, Waheguru di fateh' she stepped into the freezing waters and walked down the steps until she was waist deep in water. After praying for peace upon her family and her Punjab, she took me off her neck and dipped me thrice in the holy waters.

'I beg forgiveness of you, Khalsaji, for my father having forsaken the faith of my ancestors for a foreign religion. It was his desire to take the Pahul again on reaching India, but that was not to be. Please forgive him, for he did re-convert; he took the Khande di Pahul in Aden.'

Then she walked back to the bank and sat at the steps.

My time had come. She swung me and hit me hard against the marble. Thrice. The force loosened the pink diamond embedded in my heart. It flew off and fell into the sarovar. The force had opened my secret compartment.

She released Duleep Singh's lock of hair into the sarovar and dipped me once again to let loose any hair strands still stuck inside. Then she set me upon the water and bade me farewell.

My curse would have been released, had I been left to drown in the holy waters. However, I was to inflict and witness another round of suffering.

She had walked a few steps when I was picked up by a tall, handsome man, no less than a royal in looks, who held me up and shouted for Princess Bamba's attention.

'Lady, your locket.'

Turning back, she said, 'It's no longer mine. I've released it to where it must go.'

'It's come into my hands.'

'It is yours then.'

'What did you take out from the locket?'

'My father's lock of hair.'

'Who are you?'

'Maharani Bamba.'

'Maharani of which kingdom?'

'Punjab, of course,' she laughed and moved on.

My new inheritor Lala Vijendra Rambal suffered my curse when he chose to take me home. It passed on, when Chattar Singh honoured his brother's wish by storing Vikrant Rambal's lock of hair inside my secret compartment and sealing my cavity with a blue sapphire. Twenty-three years later, it unleashed its miseries on Gurleen, a wonderful gritty woman who bore all my ills with dignity and loyalty. And paid a huge price.

Today, the curse has been released forever. At the bottom of these waters I shall finally rest, my dark soul purified by the hymns of the *raagis* and the oration of the sacred texts of the holy Guru Granth Sahib.

Author's note

This story could have ended without the need for the locket to have its own history. However, there are two reasons for my giving it an elevated identity.

The first is gratitude for the serendipity when I first saw it. I had contemplated the extraction of Vikrant's hair strands from his old clothes, say a suit or a pullover, or from the bed linen. Entirely logical but not quite plausible, and rather staid. First, the bed linen of a dead person is invariably thrown away, especially if the person has been ill. And, in many communities, a dead person's used clothing is disposed off, with the exception of a few items that are kept as souvenirs.

As I was struggling with the ending, I chanced upon an article titled *The Maharajah's Box*, an intriguing account by a British journalist, of an unclaimed chest of treasures lying in a bank vault in Switzerland. It is said to contain the belongings of Maharaja Duleep Singh, the last emperor of Punjab and son of Maharaja Ranjit Singh. Delving further, I chanced upon several entries—including on Wikipedia (to which I promise to contribute from the proceeds of this book) on Maharaja Duleep Singh, including a portrait with a pendant adorning his chest. I got my answer in a flash and felt that it would be a good twist to include for the story's end.

However, I continued to be fascinated by Maharaja Duleep Singh's tragic story, and the myth about the Sikh Guru's warning that went unheeded by Maharaja Ranjit Singh. The sad end of the emperor's dynasty bore out that the curse had indeed played out. I felt it important to mention this poignant piece of history, without having to defend or justify any points of view or confirm or refute historic fact.

Everything mentioned about Duleep Singh's exile, his family, and the curse of the tenth guru is drawn from public domain.

The story of the locket itself is pure fiction, particularly that:

The locket was among the objects buried by Guru Gobind Singh, with his hair placed inside to neutralize its spell.

The royal joaillier recast the locket and inserted the Tenth Guru's image, having lost the hair strands.

The locket was placed on Duleep Singh's chest when he was born.

When Duleep Singh was baptized, the priest preserved the hair lock to be immersed one day in the sarovar.

Duleep Singh's mother told him to remove the locket for it was cursed.

Duleep Singh handed over the locket to Princess Bamba aboard SS Verona at Aden.

Princess Bamba visited the Golden Temple and released the locket into the sarovar.

Lala Vijendra Singh Rambal—an imaginary character in my story—met Princess Bamba and took over the locket.

However, there was a locket on Duleep Singh's chest. Whatever happened to it is not publicly known. What is known is that he ended in near penury and had sold off many of his precious possessions.

Who knows where his locket is, and what was inside it?

Time line

Fact	
1837	Maharaja Duleep Singh is born
1869	Princess Bamba is born
1886	The Maharaja is arrested aboard SS *Verona*
1893	Maharaja Duleep Singh dies

1924	Princess Bamba visits Lahore
1957	Princess Bamba dies
Fiction	
1918	Lala Vijendra Rambal is born
1939	Lala Vijendra Rambal visits Golden Temple
1955	Lala dies
1956	Vikrant and Visham are born
1965	Gurleen is born
1986	Aryan is born
2007	Vikrant dies